JB SCHROEDER

starting over together

Love That Lasts

BOOK 4

Two Feet
Press

11923 NE Sumner St., Ste 843916
Portland, Oregon 97220

Cover art credits go to dan.grytsku.gmail.com and NazArtVector via depositphotos

Print Edition 1.0
ISBN-13: 978-1-943561-22-3

❀ Created with Vellum

To Uncle John and Aunt Jill
Hey Baby ~ Always

1

"You are going to True Springs for me, Caroline Murphy, and you are not to come back home until you've taken a thousand—no, two thousand—photographs!" Neve held up two fingers right in front of Caroline's face.

Caroline lifted her palms up in supplication. An immediate queasiness gripped her gut, but no words would form.

Her best friend wasn't waiting for an answer anyway. Neve Hoffman had already begun tearing through Caroline's closet, her Lycra-covered rear wiggling in the doorway.

Just before this outburst, Neve had asked—insisted, really—that Caroline drive from Miami to Pennsylvania to deliver an engagement ring to Neve's ex-husband's family for her. Apparently dear Grandpa was old school and didn't trust a tracking number from the United States Post Office, UPS, or even FedEx. Not with this ring, anyway.

And Neve had a jammed schedule and a full life, while Caroline had, well, nothing.

Caroline shook her head and forced her jaw to move. "How did we get from personalized ring delivery to filling some scenic scrapbook?"

No response. Instead, her determined friend wrestled some luggage out of the closet and threw all of it onto the unmade bed. Two large duffel bags and Caroline's biggest suitcase. Not a weekend jaunt. Where in the world was this True Springs, and just how long did Neve expect her to stay?

As her friend fished for the zipper on the oversized roller board, Caroline turned away. She crossed to the high his-and-hers dresser, resting her chin on her hands before a framed photograph of her husband. Kevin looked handsome, proud, and a little uptight, buttoned to his chin in his starched police officer's uniform. Caroline traced a finger over his face. Her own reflection hovered on the dusty glass.

Zip, zip, zip. The suitcase had been opened. Caroline registered the noise, but she didn't turn to watch. Here on the dresser, with a trick of the light, she could see herself with Kevin again. She pretended that they were about to enter their fourth year of marriage, content and happy, and were ready to start a family. Perhaps their first baby would arrive near her own thirtieth birthday.

"Caroline, I need to get into those drawers." Neve pulled at her waist, shattering Caroline's optical illusion and impossible fantasy. She slid her hands from the dresser, sighed, and straightened.

Neve wagged her finger again.

"I get why you *need* me to be your errand girl," Caroline said. Neve's days were booked solid as a working, single mom, her daughter Bella was in school, and Caroline was doing nothing—not working, not socializing, not exercising, not shopping or cleaning, or taking care of herself very well. "But can't we just pay someone? There are people who deliver cars. Surely there are people who deliver rings."

"It has to be you."

"I don't want to leave." She'd barely left home in two years, and she certainly wasn't going to start now, just because Neve said so.

"Oh, I know. But you have to get out of this—this *shrine*." Neve's face twisted with disgust. "You need to connect with people again."

"I do. I—"

Neve planted her hands on her hips and pursed her lips. "Other than me, Bella, and Noreen."

Bella was Neve's seven-year-old daughter, and one of the only bright spots in Caroline's lame existence. Noreen was Neve's mother and— Caroline shuddered.

Neve rubbed Caroline's upper arms over her grungy, shapeless t-shirt. "Honey, you aren't grieving for Kevin anymore. You've just given up on you. It's been nearly two years."

Caroline felt nearly mesmerized by Neve's soothing voice and the friction of her hands.

"Instead of moving forward, you're falling apart." Neve stopped rubbing, and her focus shifted to Caroline's face. "Enormous dark circles have nearly swallowed up your gorgeous eyes. Your cheeks are hollow—I can practically see your bones."

"The Grief Diet," Caroline said. "Works wonders. Wouldn't recommend it to just anyone, though."

Neve shook her head and cupped her hands around Caroline's face. "I'm certain it's against Florida law for a person to parade around this pale."

"You sure know how to make a girl feel good," Caroline said without any heat.

"I'm trying to make you see what I see."

Caroline wrenched her chin away. "You think I don't know?" She rubbed her forehead with her fingers. "I just…"

She shrugged, giving up on words, but her heart whispered, *I just…can't… I'm lost… I'm scared…*

Damn. Here was her best friend, trying to help, no matter how misguided. "You're a good mom, Neve. I mean, not just to Bella, but to me, too."

"I'd rather just be your friend, but you need more than that now." Neve wrapped her in a fierce hug, then stepped away and looked her in the eye. "You need someone who's willing to push. I never should have waited this long to do it."

"I don't want to leave. Kevin's here, in our home." Tears welled in Caroline's eyes. "I miss him so much."

"Oh, sweetie. You'll miss him forever." Neve smoothed Caroline's lank hair away from her face. "But you can't stop living to keep his memory alive. You have to start shooting pictures—"

Caroline shook her head.

"You don't have to go back to the *Herald*. But you always found joy in using your camera."

Neve's tone had been gentle, but Caroline's reaction was vehement. "Not anymore. I'm not touching the thing."

"I can't see what photography has to do with Kevin's death. You were on vacation."

"Best friend or no, this topic is none of your business." Caroline's tone was harsh. She'd told Neve this over and over.

Neve pressed her lips together. "That hurts."

"Yeah, well, if you keep pressing me, you're gonna hurt a whole lot worse." Caroline avoided Neve's direct gaze and moved to sit on her unmade bed. The only reason the sheets were clean was because Neve's mother, Noreen, invaded every Tuesday like clockwork. All day long. Cleaning and washing and talking. And talking and talking. Loudly. Incessantly. And worst of all, she insisted on answers. Noreen thought conversation was "healthy" for Caroline and was determined to fit a week's worth into every visit. She wouldn't stop coming, no matter what Caroline said or did. Tuesdays equaled torture.

Neve raised her chin. "You leave me no choice. Hardball it is."

"You can't make me."

"Oh, but I can." Neve's eyes held a wicked glint, her smile a smug twist. "Noreen's waiting for my call. She's prepared to move in at a moment's notice."

Caroline gasped. "You wouldn't dare."

"I would, and so would she. In fact, Noreen has grown tired of seeing you waste your life." Neve tilted her head and admired her manicure. "And what's more, she believes you'll never get back on your feet if you don't gain fifteen pounds, have live-in companionship, involve yourself with a worthwhile charity—to remind you that you are not alone in sorrow—and"—Neve paused to look her in the eye—"discard ninety percent of Kevin's possessions."

Caroline's hands flew to her mouth. "She said that?"

"Word for word. Remember when she ransacked my place?" Neve grimaced. "Rand had to buy out Goodwill to get his things back, right down to his hair gel. And then she browbeat my attorney until he waived all his fees—a bribe to call her off."

Caroline had rather thought Neve's ex deserved all that and more, but… "I'm not her daughter."

"Ever since your mom died, she's considered you her daughter, too." Neve's mouth set in a grim line.

Caroline stared in horror. "You're dead set on this, aren't you?"

"One ring. Two thousand photographs." Neve didn't even crack a smile. "Are you packing, or am I?"

Triage nurse turned physical therapist—Neve Hoffman was skilled at bulldozing any patient who told her no. Her mother Noreen, on the other hand, operated more like King Kong: terrifying and destructive despite essential goodness underneath.

Caroline knew better than to stand in the duo's path while in a weakened condition. She flopped back onto the bed and pulled a pillow over her face. "You pack."

"I was hoping you'd say that," Neve said.

Caroline heard a drawer slide out as her friend murmured to herself, "Early September in True Springs. Should still be warm. Shorts. Tanks. Cropped leggings. Push-up bras are a must. Thongs definitely…"

2

Caroline arrived in True Springs, Pennsylvania, late afternoon four days after she'd started. The drive from Florida had gone slowly. She'd wasted hours every morning talking herself around to getting in the car.

She wasn't exactly scared of being on the highway or even losing her own life, but driving made it harder to block out her memories.

She drove slowly, marveling at the utterly charming downtown, decorated in red, white, and blue for the upcoming Labor Day weekend. Lush flowering plants hung in baskets from lampposts and the porches of Victorians, though there were clapboard and brick buildings, too. There was a lovely green space fronted by an old town clock and an eye-catching fountain. A couple seemed to dance—no, embrace—above the water. But True Springs proved a very small town, because in minutes, she was past it, heading northeast. The two-lane road curved through a forest of green, until she branched off onto a dirt road. Neve's ex's family had lived for generations on what they referred to as the Old Hoffman Farm. The property had a large garden and several small outbuildings, but it didn't appear to be a working farm. She pulled up in front of a white house with green shutters and a wide front porch that looked like it had weathered many years with painstaking care.

A tall, fit older man burst out the front door and leapt off the low porch.

Caroline envied his easy gait as she pried herself stiffly out of the driver's seat. She waved.

"Caroline." He'd crossed the yard and headed right for her.

She froze like a rabbit caught in a trap. Was it appropriate to hug him? Shake hands? She'd hidden out in her apartment—sleeping mostly, sitting and staring often, binge-watching stupid series when sleep eluded her. She'd forgotten how to interact with people in the real world.

"Hello, Mr. Hoffman." Too formal—she knew it.

He took her hands in his. "Call me Bert. So good to see you again." He squeezed gently, then let go. He wasn't a stranger. They'd met at Neve's wedding many years ago. And although Neve had divorced their jerk of a son Rand, she liked her in-laws and kept up with them for Bella's sake.

"Come on in and freshen up. I've got some iced tea— or something stronger." He winked.

Neve had warned Caroline that she'd probably spend at least a couple of hours visiting on the farm. And sure enough, after he expressed his condolences about her loss and lamented that his wife was away visiting family, she began fielding questions about Bella and Neve.

She handed over a card Bella had made for her grandparents, along with a birdhouse she'd painted all by herself in bright colors. There was an H over the little entry hole. He grinned. "She's talented."

"And precocious."

"Like both her mother and father," he said warmly.

Caroline dug into the zippered pocket of her purse and pulled out a little velvet bag encasing a ring box—the reason she was here.

Bert opened it and held it up to the light. "Ah, this ring. So much history here."

"Neve said it's more than just a ring. An extra-important family heirloom?"

"More like the town's heirloom." He chuckled. "Have you heard the Legend of True Springs?"

She shook her head.

"Well, it has to do with my grandparents, Miles and Adele, who fell in love during WWII." He launched into the story with his eyes twinkling.

It was obviously rehearsed and retold by every subsequent generation in the family, and she wondered how embellished the romantic tale had become over the years. It'd make a sweet movie.

"When they kissed, his bus ticket fell from his pocket and right into the fountain—fed by our own natural spring." Bert drew a breath and leaned forward. "The sun broke through the clouds, and all the townsfolk watching swore the water suddenly sparkled with more than just sunlight—with magic."

Caroline really wanted to snort but settled for raising an eyebrow. *Fantasy* movie.

"That couple atop the fountain in the center of town is them, my grandparents. And ever since, the town residents swear that drinking our water will find you your true love." Bert raised his iced tea glass in a salute—to magic or another visitor sufficiently informed of the town's advertising campaign, Caroline didn't know.

She tried to be polite. "People really believe this?"

"Oh, yes. We've seen it in action too many times not to. The town has built its reputation on it." He chuckled. "Not to mention a whole tourism campaign. Besides, Mabel, who runs the general store, was a child then and saw it with her own eyes."

Caroline kept from screwing up her face. Who was she to burst his bubble with her cynical world-view? "And the ring?"

"Ah yes. Neither Miles nor Adele had two pennies to rub together at that point, but Miles insisted she have an engagement ring, so they agreed to marry in six months. The townsfolk who'd been watching for that bus right along with them didn't want any more waiting, so they took up a collection. The local jeweler was on board and gave them a good deal, and they all tromped out to bless the ring in the fountain water, then shined it back up and presented it to the couple—allowing them to marry in just a few days' time. It's been in my family for generations—and they've all been happy unions, until my son and Neve."

Now she couldn't help herself. "But Rand must have drunk the water a million times *and* had that ring."

"Rand was in a rush and gave it to the wrong person. We knew that—didn't especially want to hand it over. We knew he wasn't ready"—he grimaced—"but if you'll forgive me saying so, he was going for looks, not substance."

She bristled. "Neve's the one with the substance." And her ex, Rand, was a selfish, immature, big-headed—

"I meant *relationship* substance. We love Neve. Always have. She's a great mother, and Bella is a blessing."

Good. On that they agreed. But Caroline still latched on to a change of subject. "I wish I could have brought Bella along."

"Me too. We don't see her often enough, being so far away." He tucked the ring back in the box. "Anyway, one of the reasons we let him have the ring is because sometimes you have to live life before life leads you to love."

Caroline smiled for Bert's sake, but her heart felt heavy. She'd had love and lost it. Now she had to just live life alone. And thanks to Neve, she couldn't even do it in the safe haven of her apartment.

Bert insisted that she join him for dinner. He grilled steaks and set her up chopping vegetables that had come from the garden for a salad. He poured her a big glass of water from the tap.

"Best water you'll ever taste," he said.

Caroline accepted it, though she narrowed her eyes at him.

He winked. "Not everybody believes. You sure don't have to."

She didn't. And it didn't matter how many nut jobs did. She wouldn't find true love again. Her gut churned with guilt, and she gulped the water as if she could drown in it.

At least now she knew why Neve seemed extra excited about her spending a little time in True Springs. *It's so charming. It'll be good for you. It's a wonderful place—really something special.*

Uh-huh. She'd have to have a word or two with her bestie.

Caroline and Bert enjoyed a pleasant meal while she regaled him with stories about Bella—though she realized that she'd been such a hermit that none of them were very recent.

When they'd cleaned up, Bert said, "I know you've got a reservation at Valeska's Inn, but we've got plenty of space."

"Thank you, but I don't want to cancel on the owners this late."

He walked her to her car and suggested they take a selfie for Bella. She pasted on as bright a smile as she could for Bella and Bert's sakes and awkwardly did the honors. It reminded her, though, of Neve's orders. "I'll take a few of the farm for Bella, too."

That was okay. Just a cell phone. She didn't allow herself to strategically frame the shots—just snap, snap, snap. Enough to pacify Neve and please Bella.

"Folks rave about Maribel and Jory's B&B. I'm sure you'll enjoy it. Now, Valeska Holzmann was an interesting woman." Bert opened the car door for her. "Married five times."

"And she lived here? Feasibly drank the water every day?" She shook her head. "Gotta say, Bert, I don't have much faith in this legend."

"Like I said, sometimes you have to live life," Bert began, and Caroline joined in, "before life leads you to love."

They both laughed, but Caroline's smile dropped the

instant she pulled away.

Sometimes life and love both led you to heartbreak.

———

Valeska's Inn was a charming bed and breakfast with lots of interesting rooms to explore. Caroline had no interest in being social in the common areas, though, and tucked herself into the airy bedroom she'd been assigned.

She turned on the TV and flipped through channels. Nothing appealed, and soon enough she turned it off.

She pulled down the covers and climbed into bed— different state, different room, but pretty much where she'd spent the last two years.

Only now she felt restless. Propping herself up, she selected a few phone snapshots of the Old Hoffman Farm and sent them to Neve.

The phone rang immediately. Caroline sighed and picked up. Neve would just keep calling if she didn't.

"Not up to your usual standards."

"Well, hello to you, too."

"Why haven't you called? Why hasn't your cell been on? Okay, okay Bella!" Neve said after a squeal. Bella in the background. "She wants to talk to you first."

"Hi, Aunt Caroline. We miss you. Mom said you are on a driving vacation. Did you leave Florida yet?"

Caroline laughed. "Yes, honey, I left Florida many days ago. I visited with your Grandpa Bert. He sends his love and was very impressed with your birdhouse."

"Did you see the goats?" Bella asked.

"I did. One tried to eat my pants."

"They are very munchy," Bella said.

She launched into all the facts she knew about goats until Caroline interrupted. "Put your mom on now, okay?"

"Okay. Love You."

"Love you too, Bella Bug." Nothing cheered Caroline like Bella did. Caroline had been there when the child entered this world, and she realized nearly a decade had passed since she'd first met Neve. A smile came to her face as she recalled their first encounter.

Outside the hospital, Caroline, on assignment and under deadline, aimed for a male stabbing victim on a stretcher. Instead, a disgruntled nurse had barged into the frame as she stormed out of triage in her scrubs, blond curls bouncing cheerily in direct opposition to the scowl on her face. The head nurse trailed behind, calling Neve every name in the book. Caroline had ended up with a shot of her too, due to the rapid shutter speed of her Nikon. But she, as well as the *Miami Herald*, had lost the shot of the victim.

Instead, she'd gained a friend. The head nurse's curses had been so inventive that Caroline and Neve ended up sitting on the curb, right outside the emergency room entrance, laughing hysterically. They'd grown closer through life's additional bumps and bruises. Successes and celebrations factored in, too, like Bella's birth. Caroline considered the pair her very own family. In fact, her only family since her parents, and now Kevin, had passed on. She sighed. She had her in-laws as well, but they resided up north and had always been distant.

"I'm back," Neve said. "Why haven't you called?"

"I was torturing you for sending me away."

"Tell me something I don't know."

"I delivered your ring."

Neve huffed. "I got a full lowdown from Bert already. What's with the cell phone pictures? The farm is so gorgeous."

Pressure swelled and pushed against Caroline from the inside out. "Cell phone pics are all you're going to get."

"I'd hoped—"

"Lay off, Neve."

———

The next morning Caroline stayed under the covers until she couldn't put off getting up any longer—not if she wanted a hot shower and some of the B&B's breakfast before she had to check out and hit the road.

All that talk of legends and true love and happily-ever-afters with Bert had made her ready to escape, but with True Springs the last—and only—stop on her agenda, she faced another crossroads. And all her choices led nowhere. Other than Neve's directive not to come home until she'd taken zillions of photographs, which she didn't want to do, she now had no plan. Zero. Zilch. Nada. Which made the thought of getting in the car again depressing as hell.

She frowned as she dug though her things—much as she had every morning since she'd left home. Neve had not packed the right stuff. Where were lounge pants and loose cargos—the ones Caroline preferred when she'd been working? Where were her cotton comfy underwear— the ones that actually covered your ass? The leggings already smelled, and she was running out of underwear. She sighed. She'd have to hit a laundromat sooner rather than later. Never again would she let Neve pack.

Clean and dressed—though not as she'd normally

choose—she made her way down to the dining room, marveling at all the gorgeous hand-carved wood in this old mansion and the fresh feeling the owners had given it.

She shot a smile at the two women seated at the long table, but was grateful when the lovely, dark-haired owner Marisol greeted her. Caroline wasn't sure she remembered how to start a conversation out of the blue.

"How was your sleep?"

Like crap, but she said, "That bed is like heaven."

Marisol beamed. "You are in one of my favorite rooms."

Caroline blurted the first thing that came to mind: "Bert Hoffman mentioned Valeska's interesting love life."

"I adore the Hoffmans," Marisol said. "Did you see the clocks in the living room? My grandmother was given one by each of her husbands."

"She was your grandmother? Were they *all* true love matches?"

Maribel laughed. "I don't know—yet. But I haven't finished combing through the attic, and I just know there'll be answers to that mystery there." She pointed out the coffee, fresh-squeezed orange juice, jalapeño quiche, and plate of Mexican pastries. "More warm sopapillas coming right out."

Caroline turned to make a plate. Maybe Marisol didn't believe in the legend. Then again, Caroline had met Marisol's partner Jory last night, and that seemed a love match if ever there was one.

With Marisol having left the room, Caroline couldn't help but overhear the conversation of the two seated women.

"Rita, you have to promise me we're going back. Soon."

Rita groaned. "I told you I would."

"But I can tell you are just placating me." The other woman took a long slurp of coffee.

"Don't drink all that, Reenie. I'm not stopping every forty-five minutes for you to pee."

Caroline cut a slice of quiche. These two, with their comfortable sniping, had to be sisters.

Reenie—the one with dyed bright red hair—set her stoneware mug down with a thud. "How are you not on board? We hiked, we drove trucks, we learned to shoot and ride, we roped cattle—and a dog!" She laughed. "And more than anything else—we spent time with Ruby."

Caroline noticed a gorgeous patterned pitcher and peered in. Water. Legendary water? Oh, who cared. Couldn't hurt you if you didn't believe. Besides, she'd had some at Bert's, she was thirsty, and there was no magical anything that would bring back her love. She poured herself a glass and moved to the table.

Rita leaned back in her chair. "You forgot we lost weight *and* we slept through the night."

"Right." Reenie snapped her fingers. "So why won't you commit?"

"I've promised. I just don't want you pinning me down on when. I have to figure out my life first." She pushed back her chair. "I'm going to the ladies' room."

Caroline snuck a bite of the sopapilla, and wow. She'd definitely be inhaling another of those homemade bad boys when Marisol brought them out.

Caroline was torn and finally set down her dishes a few seats from the sisters—close enough not to be rude, and far enough away not to be forced to carry on a long conversation.

She turned back to the sideboard to pour coffee, then sat just as Rita returned to the room, and Reenie left.

Caroline decided this pair was likely somewhere between mid-fifties and mid-sixties. Reenie was louder and bolder: besides the flaming hair, she also wore a t-shirt that shimmered with sparkles, and big, flashy earrings. Rita was more subdued. Her stacked hair was brown with blond highlights, her jeans looked worn and comfortable, and she wore a black sweatshirt with "Wanderlust" across the front.

Being on the road had highlighted for Caroline just how alone she was. She'd actually enjoyed visiting with Bert yesterday—a thousand times better than Tuesdays with Noreen—but the visit was exhausting.

"Good morning," Rita said.

"Good morning." Nervous energy prickled under Caroline's skin. Did she have to say something else? Grasping, she gestured. "I like your sweatshirt."

"Thanks. It's not what people think, though." Rita chuckled. "I do enjoy traveling, or maybe did, but The Wanderlust actually represents my home base. It's a diner my husband and I own in Pittsburgh's Strip District." She smiled, but it was tinged with so much underlying sadness that Caroline's uncomfortable edge eased.

"Owned," Rita amended. "My husband passed, and I've handed over the reins to my son."

Ah, Caroline thought, no wonder. This woman was a like soul. "I'm so sorry. I..." She hadn't shared—ever— but she felt compelled to let Rita know she understood.

She had to clear her throat and force the words. "I lost my husband too."

"Oh, honey." Rita reached over and squeezed Caroline's hand. "You are much too young for that."

"Thank you," Caroline said. She waved her hand, because where did you go from there?

Rita wrapped her hands around her mug. "I count myself lucky that we had so many good years to look back on—not that it makes it any easier. I thought we had so many more." She sighed. "Strange, but an awful lot of good has come out of it, somehow."

"Like this trip?"

Rita nodded.

Caroline said, "I wasn't trying to listen in, but…"

"My sister only has one volume: loud." Rita rolled her eyes. "And yes, this trip has been amazing. A real adventure."

"Was it near here?"

"In Montana, actually. We left over a week ago, but Reenie's still talking about it. With good reason." She smiled. "It's a special place. A dude ranch—never thought I'd be saying that—owned by the Black family. Our younger sister Ruby lives and works there."

Reenie returned and caught the gist of the conversation. She plopped herself into the chair next to Caroline and scrolled through picture after picture on her phone. Luckily, Caroline had eaten enough already.

Memory jangled when Caroline saw the ranch's welcome sign. Neve had been trying to get her to leave the apartment for ages. She'd been sending emails of beautiful places (photograph-worthy places)—which Caroline hadn't bothered to open. Neve had, of course, switched tactics and shoved brochures under her nose. A stack had grown on the coffee table, and Caroline had found them in her suitcase. She'd have to check that pile and see if Black Hills Ranch was there. She hadn't paid much attention before.

Caroline sipped her water and nodded along. Although Reenie was a little too close for comfort, the ranch truly was beautiful, even in cell phone pictures.

Maribel refilled their coffee cups and passed out more warm-from-the-oven *sopapillas*—insanely good fried pastries—and soon the two sisters rose.

Reenie said, "Nice to meet you. Check out the ranch someday. Maybe next summer."

"Maybe check it out now. It's a really good place to catch your breath." Rita gave Caroline a gentle smile, then dug in her purse. "So you remember the name, take this. It's a ticket for one free trail ride. Tell them Rita Walker gave it to you."

Caroline reached for the ticket—which shocked her with a small zing up from her fingertips right up her forearm. She dropped it like she'd touched Maribel's hot baking sheet. So odd. Had there been a pin in her purse or something? The women didn't seem to notice, so she reached for it and slid it closer to her with a fingertip.

She thanked them and wished them a safe trip home.

Caroline stared almost unseeingly at the ticket, pondering the idea of a rustic setting coupled with plenty of activity to keep the body busy and the mind at bay. Animals, dirt, and fresh air. Mountains, forests, and plenty of space. She'd always wanted to learn to ride.

A vacation? A retreat for the soul? She had all the time in the world to kill. And cell phone pictures sent from somewhere other than the highway—somewhere picture-worthy—might be enough for Neve to lay off. Then Caroline could go home.

She bit her lip. Right this minute, even going back home didn't hold that much appeal.

The other option—aimlessly traversing the country's macadam until Neve missed her enough to give up on her crazy threat—held none. Caroline set down her mug with a clunk, and the now-tepid coffee sloshed onto her hand.

Marisol bustled back into the room with a tray and began clearing the sisters' dishes. "Are you sure you don't want to extend your stay in True Springs?"

"Thanks, but it's time to go."

The only thing on Caroline's agenda was a quick stop in town to take a picture of the legendary couple atop the fountain—because there'd been a good-morning voicemail from Bella. *I need a new picture of my great-great-grandparents…it's two greats, right?*

Surely puppet master Neve had orchestrated that request.

"Are you headed home, then?" Marisol asked. "Or traveling on?"

"I'm not sure yet." But Caroline couldn't seem to tear her gaze from the Black Hills Ranch trail ride ticket.

3

——————

I f Sam Black had a choice, he would have catapulted this particular group of ranch guests down the mountain yesterday. Instead, right on the usual Saturday schedule, he hauled luggage from cabins to car trunks, barely speaking and trying hard to contain the shitstorm of emotions that had been on the verge of erupting since Carter had been medevacked off the mountain on Thursday.

In truth, he usually let the others do most of the talking on departure days when all the visitors left the dude ranch. Full of western goodness, fresh air, hearty meals, and a newfound appreciation for nature, they were always too gushy for him. Especially when the hugging started. Too intimate for his comfort level ever since his reputation got too far out of control and—

Well, he tried to keep as low a profile as people would allow him. Earlier in the week, he'd been relieved there were no single women amongst this week's guests.

Normally it mattered. Now—when Carter's health hung in the balance—that issue took a backseat.

"Those are ours." A fresh-faced woman named Sarah pointed to her and her husband's bags. Young newlyweds, who'd had a great time until Thursday. He nodded and stashed the bags in their SUV's trunk. He didn't get the satisfaction of slamming it. Damn thing had a button and a torturously slow descent.

She thanked him.

"Safe travels." He didn't smile, but knew they understood. Everyone—almost everyone—felt the weight of what had happened.

He headed off across the field to the next cabin, grass wetting his boots and bottoms of his jeans, the early-morning chill wrapping around his neck. He hadn't bothered with a coat—just his heavy flannel.

He would have gladly handled a whole tribe of flirty, pawing women every week, if only he could have prevented that self-absorbed, stupid, reckless greenhorn from ever setting foot on Black Hills property.

Vic Diamata.

The little shit who'd nearly gotten Carter killed.

Sam hadn't liked the guy from the get-go. A brash Long Islander—Staten Island, maybe? Something like that —who had a lot of money (according to him), a fancy phone that may as well have been surgically attached, and an unhealthy Napoleon complex.

Sam sneered at the pile of showy luggage on the next porch. The Diamatas' cabin. He wished he was wearing gloves.

This was the last set, though, and when he returned to

the warming cars and cluster of people, he lucked out. He didn't have to speak or make eye contact with the couple. Vic was already in the driver's seat and the Mrs. was busy thanking Will, the ranch's chef and biggest personality. Will always sent visitors off with a travel treat—foil-wrapped cookies or brownies—to keep the goodness going and make sure they didn't leave their memories at the crossroads.

Sam stashed the Diamatas' bags and moved to the periphery of this melee.

His father, Astor, was shaking hands, alternately smiling at the thanks or solemnly reassuring them that he and his wife, Anna, would make sure Carter got the best care possible.

That much was true—Sam's parents loved Carter Cross like he was one of their own, just as Sam considered Carter his brother. Anna Black was in fact at the hospital with Carter now, taking charge and issuing orders, Sam was sure. Furthermore, she'd stay until they brought him home.

"Sissy," Astor said, calling Sam's sister over, "make sure these folks have the right directions home." Marissa —nearly always called Sissy—wasn't warm and fuzzy on her good days, but she looked especially hard-assed this morning. She moved forward but didn't manage a smile. They were all reeling from Carter's "accident."

Everyone had been calling it that—and it pissed Sam off. It wasn't an accident. It was a friggin' nightmare. A preventable disaster—the worst kind. A common enough situation in the wilderness—one they *had* prepared the guests for—that had gone south fast. Dickhead Diamata was fully at fault. Carter tried to save that asshole's life— when he should have let him get exactly what he deserved.

Of course, Sam would have done the same, but he *wished*—

He clenched his fists and forced crisp morning air into his lungs. Only a few more minutes and they could get back to business—*without* guests.

Sam crossed his arms over his chest as the cars of Easterners—always in a hurry—pulled out first. Then the newlyweds. Only the family of four remained. A nice family, but he willed them gone all the same.

The preteen girl leaned against her father now, half-asleep still in pajama pants with the hood of her coat up. The fourteen-year-old boy stood alone and apart. He still looked shell-shocked. Seeing an enormous, angry grizzly maul a person—much like a dog thrashing a toy—well, the kid wasn't the only one who'd have nightmares.

The mother spoke to Ruby, who was both Will's wife and the hostess of the ranch. "You must let us know about Carter."

"I will, I promise." Ruby gave the woman a heartfelt hug.

"He'll be in our prayers."

They were going to need a lot more than prayers.

And Sam was going to need to be even more diligent than usual. Mistakes always cost him something he loved.

4

Caroline had recently entered Montana, she knew, but the towns and rest stops had begun to blend together miles upon miles ago. The road funneled to a pinpoint in the distance. Her eyes locked on the expanse of blue sky and layers of clouds like bleached cotton candy. Big Sky indeed, she thought as she zoomed forward, almost dizzy with the perceived sensation of flying.

The last of her sugar energy from lunch, a Coke and an apple pie, must have worn off.

Caroline dug through the console beside her for some chewing gum. Her zillionth piece since she'd left home. She hadn't been traveling that long, but she was already sick to death of pumping gas, digesting junk food, and sleeping in hotels. True Springs and Valeska's Inn had been the only real respite—and the only real meals. Not that she had a lot of interest in food.

She wanted to go home. She wasn't going to use her camera, and Neve couldn't make her.

Great. Now she'd turned into a pouting toddler.

But toddlers at least were good at expressing their anger. She wasn't annoyed at Neve. She was pissed off. And she was mad—goddamned angry—that she was in this situation. Widowed. Alone. Full of shame and guilt. She gripped the steering wheel tight as her vision blurred with unshed tears—but these were tears of frustration, not grief.

She just wanted to turn back time. She wanted Kevin. Alive and well, and driving this blasted car, so her hands could be free to photograph Montana's over-endowed expanse of blue and white—

She gasped. Her hands slapped her chest and her foot jerked up off the gas pedal. The car slowed too fast. Her torso surged forward.

She grabbed for the steering wheel and shoved her foot down, as a green sign with white letters zoomed past the passenger-side window.

To hell with fulfilling Neve's stupid quests. If Caroline were home, she wouldn't have forgotten long enough to have such a heinous thought.

Caroline veered right at the last second and braked hard around the curve of the exit ramp. She swiveled her head left and right, searching for the crossover to the southbound side of the highway. There, to the left, an I-25 South sign.

She jerked to a stop at the bottom of the ramp, lowered her forehead to the steering wheel, and sucked in ragged breaths. Nausea curled up from her belly and made her taste salt instead of spearmint gum.

She was truly a monster.

She squeezed her eyes shut and forced herself to breathe.

Once her heart rate returned to normal and the wave of queasiness subsided, Caroline looked around to get her bearings. To her right was a cluster of buildings gathered before a small mountain range, green-garbed and camel-backed. Just as the road had seemed to lead directly into the sky, this inviting town appeared as one with its stunning backdrop.

She sat up and rubbed a hand over her face. She should go left, get started for home. Miami was a heck of a long drive from here. She'd call a locksmith on the way so that Noreen couldn't get into her place.

Damn. She obviously needed a break if she thought new locks would stop Neve's mother.

And the hard truth was, as emotionally bruised as she still felt, she must have been ready to take a step forward and gain some distance from the past, or she wouldn't be halfway across the country right now.

She glanced around again, flipped the right blinker, listened for a few beats to the click of the signal, and pulled out. She drove slowly, straight into the center of town.

"Hopewell, Montana, Bureau of Tourism," said the sign attached to a building the size of her condo's kitchenette. The whole town would barely fill the urban neighborhood where she lived. Some storefronts sported fresh paint with bright, hip lettering over the entrances. Others looked shabby and run-down, as if they'd stood untouched for decades.

She bit her lip, afraid to be interested. Two years ago, Caroline would have jumped out of the car to shoot some close-ups of the peeling paint. The photos would have captured layers of old labor and provided a window into each structure's history. After years of photographing hard news for the *Miami Herald*, she had expected to lose some of her passion, yet she'd still found the challenge of translating a visual story to a still shot—a moment in time—almost intoxicating, no matter the subject.

Caroline peered again at a small church, scanning the details that ensured the structure shone through its dilapidation. Her pulse quickened, but she quickly squashed the familiar excitement.

She snatched up a napkin and spat out her chewing gum with disgust. But the gum was fresh. The yucky feeling came from deep inside her.

That insane urge to use her lens at every turn had ruined her life. Her camera had survived. Her husband hadn't.

Caroline pulled into a parking lot of a tavern called the Watering Hole. She grabbed her purse and jumped out of the car. As if by exiting the car, she could escape herself. *Good luck.*

She took a deep breath of crisp mountain air and pushed through the heavy wooden door. The establishment was old and dark, but clean, with lots of antique cowboy paraphernalia on the walls and a jaunty country tune playing, something about "boots made for walkin'."

Far better than the endless cookie-cutter rest stops.

A bartender with a baseball hat worn trucker-style and a shaggy salt-and-pepper mustache nodded at her, while two virile men in dust-covered jeans, t-shirts, and construction boots swiveled on their stools to see who had arrived.

She veered away from the trio and chose a beat-up wooden table near a working wood stove. She sank into a chair and shivered beneath her light cropped sweater. She'd been cold for days and had been forced to blast the heat in the car. Her Miami, Neve-chosen wardrobe had proved no match for Montana's chilly temperatures and gusty winds, even though it was only the first week of September.

"Ma'am." The bartender tipped his cap at Caroline. "You here for a meal?" At her nod, he said, "My waitress will be here in, oh, about ten minutes. Can I get you a drink while you wait?"

His long mustache waggled when he spoke. Coupled with the honest-to-goodness cowboy accent, Caroline couldn't help but smile. "Hot tea?"

"Coming right up."

The pair of construction workers returned their attention to their bottled beers. Caroline relaxed. She'd barely talked to anyone since she'd left True Springs. And she certainly wasn't in the mood now.

Would she ever be?

Caroline rubbed her arms and stared at the flickering fire behind the wood stove's gate. Maybe Neve had been right to push her out of the condo, but she didn't hold out much hope that this trip was going to miraculously dry up her grief.

And the camera thing? That was a whole other issue.

Still, she wouldn't go home. Not yet. She would keep moving forward—for now.

The bartender delivered a homestyle biscuit and a packet of honey along with her tea, and Caroline thanked him. She dumped a packet of sugar in, then swirled the steaming liquid round and round with her spoon. She stared at her ring finger—bare since she'd left home. Not by choice, of course.

When Caroline had made Neve promise that she wouldn't let Noreen touch Kevin's things, Neve agreed on one condition: Caroline's wedding band. "Everything Kevin stays home. This trip is you alone. You'll get it all back when you return."

She hadn't thought it mattered. Her memories were in her heart and her head. She held on tight to some specifics —how he'd smooth his uniform in front of the mirror, or tip his chair back on two legs on the balcony to get a better view of the setting sun, or reach for her in the morning with a summer storm pounding the skylights above…

But after two years, much was lost. Things that she grasped at but couldn't quite remember. Other things that were just…gone.

The waitress burst through the swinging door from the kitchen, crisscrossing her apron over a faded Watering Hole t-shirt as she approached. She was all business, no idle chitchat, which suited Caroline just fine. She ordered French onion soup and a salad that promised to include actual vegetables—a welcome change for lunch.

As Caroline nudged lettuce around her plate, a group of six burst in, filling the small tavern with noisy banter, rehashing their recent vacation. Relieved for a respite from her own maudlin thoughts, Caroline eavesdropped. These tourists had ridden some feisty horses, slept under the stars, eaten some rave-worthy gourmet meals. Although somebody —Caroline couldn't tell who—had ended up in the hospital. That dampened their spirits enough for the conversation to stall. Two of the women headed to the back of the place.

Caroline had been heading vaguely toward the Black Hills Ranch—loath to make a real plan but reluctant to drive without a direction—but now she was curious about this place. An alternate option? A better one?

She rose and approached the woman waiting in the hallway for her turn in the ladies' room.

"Excuse me." Caroline cleared her throat. "May I ask where you all were vacationing?"

"The Black Hills Ranch. It's amazing."

She was only a couple of hours from there, she thought, but still, what were the chances?

The other woman came out, and they both raved about the place. When the next finally entered the bathroom, the remaining woman pointedly looked at Caroline's empty ring finger.

"We're all married," the woman said, leaning in conspiratorially, "but supposedly, all the single women leave the Black Hills Ranch sat-is-fied. Sam Black holds a reputation as a serious ladies' man." She winked, before the bathroom door popped open and they returned to their table.

Hah. If they only knew that Caroline's quest was photography—not that she planned on fulfilling it. The *last* thing on Caroline's mind was a roll in the proverbial hay. She couldn't even imagine.

She used the bathroom, splashed some water on her face, and then retreated to her table as quickly as possible, to avoid any more conversation.

The Black Hills Ranch it was, she guessed.

She'd have a better chance of getting Neve to give up if she chose a real place to stay for a bit. Bonus points that it was someplace Neve had suggested with that brochure.

A mountain retreat would definitely provide some respite from the tedium of driving and nasty highway fare. It'd buy her time. And maybe, just maybe, it'd be…nice.

Caroline pulled out the brochure and the directions she'd jotted down from her phone's GPS to review them again. The trail ride ticket was folded inside, so she set it on the table. She ordered a slice of cheesecake in order to sit by the fire a while longer.

Her waitress appeared and poured more hot water from a beat-up tin pot. She slanted her made-up eyes toward Caroline.

"Rumor has it that Black Hills stables a stud cowboy rather than a breeding stallion." She suspended the stream of water and looked pointedly at the ticket before eyeing Caroline. "Don't be fooled. Sam's a good man."

"I'm not—"

The server clunked the teapot onto the table and stalked off.

"—interested," Caroline finished. Sheesh. Was the woman warning her off or egging her on?

She shook her head. It didn't matter. Good or bad, hot or not, Caroline truly wasn't interested.

5

Sam Black shouldn't be wasting time chopping wood today of all days, but this particular task had soothed his mind hundreds of times over the years.

Place, swing, *split*. Place, swing, *split*.

His body knew the drill, while his subconscious processed other things. Right now, hacking away his fear, worry, and frustration took priority. Carter Cross, his best friend, had been mauled by a bear just a few days ago. He'd live, but he was in bad shape.

Sam switched to hauling all the chopped wood into the bed of the ranch's dually along with the splitter and ax. He climbed in and drove the vehicle off the road and through the grass, where a lodgepole pine had fallen right out of the forest. Sam used his boots and jean-covered legs to bend the needles away from his face and set to stripping the limbs.

Whack, whack, whack.

He was anxious to make the five-hour drive to the

Billings hospital, but Sam's mother insisted there was no point just yet. The doctors didn't know squat, and Carter wasn't lucid enough to appreciate the visit. Sam was willing to sit bedside and wait, but if Carter awoke to find Sam lounging on his duff, he'd never hear the end of it. That, or Carter would drag his bandaged body out of bed and ask for his boots, open gown be damned.

Sam grinned. He could only pray that Carter got that much fire and mobility back. Sam would like to wring Vic Diamata's neck—if it wasn't for that asshole, the grizzly might well have realized they were no threat to her or her cubs.

Sam stuck the ax in the tree trunk and hung his head. For years now, he'd been teaching their clients every safety rule he knew. But how did you force city folk to pay attention—stop with their damn phones—and then subsequently control their terror when faced with hundreds of pounds of bluffing bear?

He and Carter had both done what they'd had to. It had been dumb luck that he'd been the one closer to the larger group of hikers—forcing them together into a cluster as calmly as he could, while Carter had the better position to intervene when the separated guest had panicked and run, basically painting a target of raw meat on his own back.

Sam's blood pumped with adrenaline all over again, and he shook his head hard to dispel the memory. He stripped off his shirt, snaps popping open as he wrenched it over his head.

Logically, Sam knew that he couldn't foresee or control every disaster. But ever since the fire, he'd felt accountable for every accident that occurred around here.

He'd sworn to do everything in his power—and he had, every damn day since—to prevent harm or calamity.

He mopped sweat from his face and tossed the balled-up shirt over the side of the truck. Retrieving his ax, he slipped into a comforting rhythm once again, until the hum of a car engine sounded from the eastern bend.

Sam glanced over his shoulder. Foreign car. White subcompact. No guests would arrive today, and nobody local would drive that shoebox.

That likely left only one other option. A woman seeking stud service. Would that damn rumor never die?

Shit. He slammed the blade into the tree, a piece of bark shooting off. Quick as he could, he crossed back over to the truck, jammed his arms into his shirt, and hastily did up the snaps. Immediately, he got back to work.

The car stopped on the road behind him. A female called, "Excuse me?"

He stood nearly forty feet off the road. Apparently, that wasn't nearly far enough. Maybe, if she thought he couldn't hear her, she'd give up.

Sam gritted his teeth and swung, again and again. He'd finish stripping this sucker in minutes if he kept up this pace.

"Excuse me!" Even raised, her voice sounded sultry. The sexy sound wedged into his chest the same way the ax split wood.

As Sam lifted the tool high above his head, he heard a car door open and gravel crunch. Damn it. The thick branch split clean through.

Sam turned, pointing the blade at the ground, even though he gripped the handle hard. A woman in short, tight white pants and an orange sweater that didn't reach her wrists or her navel, yet stretched enticingly across her rounded breasts, tiptoed gingerly through the tall grass toward him.

He moved in the opposite direction, toward his truck. He grabbed his canteen of water and slugged, spilling crisp water down his chin. He tossed the jug aside then turned to watch the female's tedious progress. As she stepped up onto a wide log, her flat-soled shoes slipped, and Sam tensed. She landed safely, however, if not gracefully.

Intent as she was on watching her feet, she seemed faceless to Sam. She'd remain that way too, he vowed, like he always did whenever a new woman showed up. A sloppy ponytail sat on top of her head, although the rich chestnut hair appeared soft and silky in the early September sun.

Sam spread his legs wide and braced himself for the onslaught of sexual innuendos he was sure would come as soon as she opened her mouth. Women who traveled here with sex on their minds normally didn't waste any time.

When she finally glanced up, only a few feet away from him, her gaze locked on to his chest, and she stopped cold. Sam cleared his throat. Her eyes jerked up to his face. His heart lurched, and his blood rushed, hotter and faster than he thought possible these days. What a knock-out. Her cheeks were gaunt, her coloring too pale, and yet there was something about her. Big, pretty eyes, dark, long lashes, full pink lips—all the more striking because she didn't appear to be wearing lipstick or any makeup at all.

She looked surprised. Her mouth formed a small circle, and moist pink lips beckoned to Sam. His stomach somersaulted.

The woman wet her lips with a quick dart of her

tongue. "Is this Sam Black's place? Black Mountain Ranch?"

Fourteen friggin' years—he was thirty-seven, for God's sakes—and women still showed up looking for him. Women just like her—sporting very little clothing, exposing lots of skin, and asking for him by name. Not so often now, but it happened.

Sam raised the ax to his shoulder, blade facing out, and then launched it through the air. The woman gasped and jumped. The blade sank into the earth six feet to her left.

"You're looking for Black Hills, not mountain."

"Right, sorry." As the sexy female shaded her eyes against the lowering sun, her shirt inched higher, showing the smooth curve of her waist. Sam's hand itched to sit just there, atop her hip.

Now why hadn't he lied and sent her back down the mountain?

"I'm on the right road, then?"

A curt nod—he didn't trust himself to be courteous if he spoke.

"Good to know." She hesitated. "Well, okay, thanks."

She started back toward her car, ridiculous summer shoes flapping against her heels, but she moved faster than before. Too fast.

He surged forward just as her feet scrambled for traction on smooth bark and she started to flail. A stray thought darted through his mind as he came upon her bent form: no way was she wearing panties. The lightweight pants stretched too tightly over her high rear end. She was definitely one of *them*.

In her mad dance, the woman managed to twist toward

him, providing an up-close-and-personal view of her navel. Sam hauled the woman from the high log. His face just missed her bare belly, but her breasts slid right past his nose. Despite being too skinny for her frame, she was damned attractive. And she smelled like something familiar…wildflowers? And maybe honey, too?

Feet now on solid ground, she panted lightly against his bare chest, setting all his nerve endings on high alert. He relaxed his hand but didn't remove it from the curve of her waist, the very spot he'd longed to touch only moments ago. Up close, Sam was faced with plump lips, warm brown irises, and flawless skin—except for circles that were too dark under her eyes. He ached to fit his bottom lip to each of those two half-rings.

Instead, he released her forearm and placed his other hand on her waist under the guise of steadying her.

The woman's left hand fell to his chest and rested lightly over his heart. Her palm might as well have been a stun gun. His muscles refused to cooperate.

What the *hell* was wrong with him?

"Thank you." Only two syllables, but her voice shook. With adrenaline and fear from the near fall, or the same shock he felt when they touched?

As the beauty gazed into his eyes, her pupils dilated, black overriding flecks of gold, topaz, and a deeper brown. Heady confirmation.

"Much obliged," Sam said, digging his thumbs into her prominent hipbones—a defensive move to stop them from stroking her of their own volition. "You're all right?"

The woman's gaze, and hand, slid slowly, sensuously down his chest. "Yes."

Skin on skin. It felt so—

He jerked his gaze down. *Shit.* In his haste, he'd missed half the snaps on his shirt, inadvertently offering up that ogle-me vibe he tried so damn hard to avoid.

He dropped his hands from her warm, bare skin and tore his gaze away. No matter that she possessed skin as soft as butter, eyes as rich as dark caramels, and a backside, sans panties, that made him picture—

Stop. Kill the imagination. Just block it out.

"Let's try this again," Sam said, taking her forearm and avoiding the desire he'd glimpsed in her eyes. Just as he handed her up and over the log, his mind registered the approaching noise of another vehicle.

The minute her floppy shoes connected with the fans of needled branches covering the ground, she faced him.

"Good day, ma'am," he said, then tipped his head and stepped away.

He cleared the fallen tree in one step, picked up his ax, and glanced up the hill. The approaching truck belonged to Sissy. She accelerated downhill.

"You should move your car," Sam said. "That truck'll be wantin' to pass."

For a moment, she remained rooted, staring at him. So many emotions crossed her face that Sam couldn't pick out even one. Then she turned and fled.

He took a few seconds to right his shirt and then followed. He tore his eyes from the woman's panty-free backside to watch Sissy's barreling arrival and skidding stop.

Dirt and rock spat at the visitor lady's feet as she wrenched open her car door. She'd mentioned him by name, so if Ruby didn't get rid of her, he'd be forced to deal with her sooner or later. But not now, at least.

The stranger dove into the driver's seat like a skittish rabbit disappearing into its burrow. She raised a hand toward the other vehicle, threw the car into reverse, plowed back at few feet, then whipped to the right and forward, clearing the Ford by only a couple of inches.

Sissy was out of the driver's seat like a shot. "Who was that?"

"Don't know."

"What did she want?"

"Directions."

"To the ranch?"

"Yep."

"Why?"

"No idea."

Sissy put her hands on her hips and glared. "You could have saved her the drive up."

He shrugged then approached the passenger side of her truck, where his dad sat. Astor Black, their father, was still a handsome man, but lately his lips remained drawn tight and the lines crossing his forehead had deepened.

He frowned at Sam. "We're headed to the ranchers' convention now. Your mother won't hear otherwise."

Sam rested his free hand on the open window frame. "I'm sure she'll call you the minute there's any change in Carter's condition."

"I know." His dad's hand fisted on his lap. "I just don't like it."

Sam glanced at the ax he held. "You're not the only one."

Astor looked toward the cloud of dust that hadn't quite

settled yet, and his shoulders sagged. His blue eyes slid to Sam. "You'll be extra careful while we're gone?"

A muscle in Sam's jaw spasmed, but he held his father's stare until the older man looked away.

"Sorry, son. I know you always are." Astor rubbed a hand over his face. "I'm just not sure I can take another accident."

"We had no control over that bear—or that goddamn greenhorn." Sam said it for his father's sake, yet he kept beating himself up, wondering what else he could have done.

"I know." Astor motioned to Sissy. She rounded the car and vaulted into the driver's seat.

"Can't wait to retire, I'll tell you that," Astor said with a halfhearted smile.

"You won't worry any less then, Dad," Sissy said.

"Probably not."

"Well," Sam said with a wink, "I reckon I'll be mighty happy when you retire."

"I'll just bet." This time his father not only smiled but barked out a laugh as well.

Sam's breath eased out of his tight lungs. He slapped the truck, and Sissy hit the gas.

The worry over Carter was really getting to them all. But Sam would do his damnedest not to let anything else happen. With all the guests gone, that should be simple.

He frowned, thinking again of the mystery woman who'd just gassed it up the hill. It was unsettling how strongly he'd reacted to her. But it didn't matter.

He'd steer clear. Women were distracting. And distractions were dangerous. He'd learned that the hard way.

He'd never risk endangering anyone, ever again. Not for anything.

Sam stepped through the pine branches, not as soothed by the thought of more physical labor as he wished. He balanced over his feet and hefted the ax. A familiar mantra crossed his mind as he swung.

No distractions. No distractions. No distractions.

6

The encounter with the sexy, bare-chested ranch hand—or more specifically, the flare of attraction she'd felt for him—had left Caroline unsettled. So unexpected and…uncomfortable. So when she pulled her filthy white Honda Fit to a stop outside the main lodge of the Black Hills Ranch, she turned the engine off, but made no move to get out.

Dust billowed around her windows as she surveyed the building to her right. The two-story log cabin with homey curtains on the windows and a wide wooden porch sprawled as if to embrace all the beauty that sat before it. Caroline's gaze swept past a series of barns and a maze of fences and out past man-made structures to a breathtaking view of lush, rolling meadows and swaths of trees backed right up to layered mountains. Other than one oddly symmetrical stretch of weedy grass, with a misshapen, upright black beam poking out of the ground, the place was perfectly picturesque. She couldn't have found a landscape less similar to Florida if she'd tried.

Caroline reached under the dash to rub at her ankles where she itched from the trek through that tall grass. No longer insulated by the steady whish of the car's heater, she noticed other sounds through the silence: the faint whinny of a horse, the tinkling music of a wind chime, the rustle of the wind…but no human noises.

Since she'd left True Springs, the flicker of hope she had felt upon hearing about the ranch had swayed and sputtered. It had surged anew though with the second recommendation in Hopewell. Now that she'd seen this place, it became a steady burn in her chest.

Caroline breathed deeply and opened her car door. Her muscles protested. She'd been mostly cramped in the driver's seat for the better part of two weeks, and flailing on top of that tree hardly counted as stretching. She crossed the looping driveway and gingerly climbed the wooden steps to the front porch.

Before she could talk herself out of it, she knocked. While she waited, she did a little jig to dislodge the pebbles and dust from her leather mules. Another knock, but still, no answer.

When Caroline tried the handle, the door opened. She leaned in and called, "Hello? Anybody here?"

The chatty woman at the tavern had said that the place rotated guests in and out on the same day. But besides the two trucks down the road, where the hottest man she'd ever seen wielded an ax like he was possessed, she hadn't noticed any other cars.

She heard footsteps on the old plank floors, and a woman's voice echoed. "Come on in. I'll be right there."

Caroline entered the foyer and turned toward a huge living room, noting the western theme and overstuffed, well-worn furniture. No fire lit the stone hearth. Nonetheless, the room emanated warmth.

A woman entered from the hall, peeling thick yellow rubber gloves from her hands. She was in her late forties or so, trim and attractive under a short crop of spiky, highlighted hair. She seemed surprised to see a new face, but she wore a gracious smile.

"Evening. I'm Ruby Jenks, hostess here at the Black Hills Ranch." She shoved the rubber gloves into a big apron pocket.

"Hi. I'm Caroline Murphy—and I believe it's your sister who sent me."

Ruby's smile grew even larger. "Rita or Reenie?"

"Both, but Rita mainly." Caroline couldn't help but smile.

"I can't wait to hear how you know them, but first, tell me what brings you all the way up here."

"I'm hoping you have room in your next session for me," Caroline said. "I, uh, hadn't planned on having this time off, so I didn't make a reservation."

"Our next session?" Ruby frowned.

"This is a dude ranch, isn't it?" Caroline asked.

"Yes, but our season just ended. The last group of guests packed out this morning. I'd be glad to make you a reservation for the spring," Ruby said.

"No, thank you. I won't be..." Caroline pulled her thoughts together. "Does that mean that all the other ranches out this way are going to be closed now, too?"

"All those within driving distance, anyway."

Caroline slumped as her spirit took a nosedive. She had thought if she enjoyed riding as much as she expected she would, maybe she'd hit several dude ranches. What better way to get some quick, intensive lessons? She'd even gone so far as to consider—if she found a town or area that felt right—maybe staying a little while. *Idiot.*

"Where are you from?"

"Miami."

Ruby smiled. "No wonder you didn't consider the seasonal restrictions we face up here in Montana."

Indeed, Caroline thought. She hadn't thought about the weather. She hadn't thought, period. She'd grasped at the straws of a recommended destination that gave her listless weather vane a direction. "I sure didn't."

"And," Ruby said, "being from Pittsburgh, my sisters wouldn't have considered our weather up here either."

Caroline suddenly felt as lost as when she had left Florida. She had somehow pinned all her hopes on this place. She gripped the strap of her purse more tightly in her fist. "Can you recommend a hotel in town, or between here and there, where I could spend the night?"

"There's nothing in between, but come with me to the kitchen and we'll call town."

Ruby settled Caroline at the end of a giant pine table, fixed her a seltzer with a slice of lime, and dug an actual phonebook out of a hutch drawer. Caroline told her about briefly meeting Rita and Reenie, but she felt rather awkward. Her fate, for the time being, anyway, rested in a directory the size of a pamphlet, and a woman she didn't know.

Mounted on the wall was a chalkboard that still read, "Western Omelet. Fried Eggs. Apple Pancakes—Sam's Favorite."

Well, Caroline supposed, she guessed she wouldn't be meeting the infamous stud. No way could Sam Black be as hot as that ranch hand she'd met, anyway. Before she'd even stopped the car, something about the way the man had moved, swinging that ax in a circular dance, rhythmic and sure, tugged at her insides. Then that chiseled face and those penetrating blue eyes; no question about it, he was sexy as all get out—even to someone like her, who wasn't the least bit interested.

Ruby spent more time punching numbers on the cordless phone than speaking into the receiver. Obviously, Caroline's chances of finding accommodations for tonight were slim. Apparently, there was some sort of event that had booked up all the hotels anywhere nearby.

Time to get back in the car again and see where her tires led her. *Ugh*, more driving.

Regardless, from now on when she traveled, she'd keep her eyes and her mind open to possibilities.

"Caroline, I'll tell you what." Ruby replaced the clunky receiver. "You're going to stay here for tonight."

Caroline shook her head. "I couldn't impose. I can see you're busy." She gestured to the army of cleaning detergents on the kitchen counter.

"I insist," Ruby said in a voice that left no room for argument. "I won't have you driving out of the mountains in the dark without food or rest. These roads can be treacherous even for those of us that know them well." She clasped her hands together. "So, what can I get you to eat? My husband Will is an excellent cook, and we've got plenty of delicious leftovers. It'll just be you and me."

Despite having eaten a few hours ago, Caroline didn't want to be rude. And she sure didn't want to drive all night because she couldn't find accommodation.

Ruby hadn't exaggerated: her husband was a very good

cook. They enjoyed some idle conversation, but Ruby didn't press Caroline, for which she was grateful. Afterward, when Ruby turned to the dishes, Caroline—feeling awkwardly idle—grabbed a cloth and some stainless-steel cleaner and went to town on the appliances. It felt strangely good to be productive.

Soon enough, however, the hostess led Caroline across a field of grass to a cluster of small log cabins to get her settled in for the night.

Once alone, Caroline freshened up, then dug through her suitcase and layered on some stretchy workout clothes. She was accustomed to carefully regulated central air rather than the chill of a mountain evening. And almost everything Neve had packed was meant for significantly warmer weather. Not to mention, more social occasions.

"Ridiculous," Caroline said, wishing for some baggy pajama bottoms and a thermal t-shirt.

She'd promised to check in with Neve, so she texted a brief message: *Staying overnight near Hopewell, Montana. Not sure the name.*

The phone rang almost immediately. Neve, of course.

"That's all I get?"

"That's all you get." Much as she loved Neve, Caroline was still kinda mad. She didn't feel like sharing. Pouting? Maybe. But she figured she was entitled. "By the way, I don't appreciate you sending me to drink some True Springs fictional love potion. Talk about pointless."

Neve laughed. "It wasn't about the water. It's about your camera."

Caroline shook her head and took a step back—even her body resisting, despite the fact that Neve couldn't see her. "You can forget about that, too."

"Not a chance."

Caroline heaved a sigh. They were going to keep having this conversation unless she put a stop to it. "Seriously, Neve, cell phone pics are all I can handle."

Was that true? Or was it all she was *willing* to handle?

"Take your time."

Her feet were cold on the wood floor and thin rug. She pulled down the bedding and climbed onto the simple box-frame bed. "It's not going to matter. I may never shoot pictures again."

"The fact that it might take you a while is exactly why this is going to work."

"Think of Bella. You are denying her auntie." No matter that they weren't related, Caroline loved the child as if she were her own.

"I hate to tell you," Neve said gently, "but you haven't been the best aunt lately."

That hurt. Really hurt. And yet Neve wasn't wrong. Caroline used to take Bella to the zoo and spring for face paint, to the theater for Disney movies and big buckets of popcorn, for sleepovers and ice cream sundaes with far too many toppings…

"If you ever want to see me again, you and Noreen will have to give up this cockamamie roommate idea."

"Hate to tell you," Neve said, "but she's really looking forward to it."

Caroline swore and hung up on Neve.

She pulled the thick Indian-patterned blanket up to her chin, shut her eyes, and shook her head. Dammit, when Neve took the gloves off you had to be ready.

Sorry, Bella Bug. If Caroline made it through this trip, she'd do better when she got back home.

Caroline found comfort in the fact that she wasn't in a roadside motel with a noisy heating unit spewing air so stale and moist that she couldn't help but think of all the bodies that had slept there before her. This little cabin smelled of cedar and pine, warm wool, newly laundered sheets, and, most of all, fresh air that chilled the tip of her nose as she inhaled.

She wondered if she could capture the smell and feel of this place. Certainly, she could turn out a series of four-color shots that would blow away anything that the Black Hills Ranch currently showed in brochures or online. The pictures they'd used hadn't done it justice.

Her stomach knotted at the thought of lifting the cool weight of her camera to her eye once again. Her camera bags were in her car, courtesy of Neve. Caroline had shoved them to the back corner of the trunk and thrown a beach towel over them. For a split second, she considered getting rid of the equipment. Except she'd worked too hard to buy her camera and her lenses, and she'd built her career with those same pieces. Granted, she didn't want to use them, but she couldn't bear to part with them either.

Caroline bit her lip. Not yet.

Seeking distraction, she looked around the room illuminated by moonlight. The cabin was rustic and sparse, but still managed to appear cozy with its understated western decor.

Her gaze was drawn through the small paned window. Following a line of fir trees up to their cone-shaped tops, she could see a blue-black sky, exploding with the white twinkle of stars.

The sky was one made for wishing, but Caroline didn't

know what to wish for. She couldn't change the past, and now, once again, had no ideas for the future.

The ranch-hopping plan had hinged on what-ifs, but at least it had been a course of action with purpose. Caroline hadn't expected the idea to be kaput even before it had gotten underway. She couldn't wander indefinitely. So now what? Now where?

Unfortunately, Caroline's gut instinct felt null and void. She wished she could cry herself to sleep, rather than lie staring into the night with no answers, but after ages of tears like floodwaters, she was finally dry as the desert.

Caroline bolted upright in bed. "That's it!"

Why not head south—to Arizona or Texas? Surely ranches spanned a longer season in the southwest. And warmer weather, too—score.

She flopped back onto the pillow. She smiled, then sighed and turned her head toward the window. The glowing stars shone as bright as a certain cowboy's crystal-blue eyes.

Star light, star bright...

"I wish for an open dude ranch and..."

Unbidden, a vision of the cowboy, ax in hand and his large frame backlit by early evening sun, flashed through her mind.

"No idea..."

She had no idea what came next.

7

"Who the hell drives halfway across the country to the mountains of Western Montana without calling first?" the man asked, his voice raised over the sizzle and spatter of what smelled like bacon.

Caroline cringed and halted just outside the swinging door to the kitchen, torn now between thanking Ruby and just taking off.

"And you two," the man continued, "taking pity on this loony bird, fixing her dinner, cooking her breakfast, having to re-clean that cabin after she's gone, when we've already got enough chores for twenty!"

Another male voice, this one with a heavy twang: "I'd be cookin' breakfast anyway."

"You know he's right," Ruby said. "Will's not happy unless he's filling bellies. Besides, Caroline and I had leftovers for dinner, and one extra cabin to clean isn't going to make a bit of difference in the amount of work piling up around here." There was a pause, then Ruby's voice again. "What's really got you so riled?"

"I'm not riled."

Out in the hall, Caroline raised an eyebrow, even as the familiarity of his deep voice tugged at her memory bank.

"Sam always gets worked up when there's a woman underfoot." Will cackled. That was right, Caroline thought—she'd almost forgotten about the infamous stud.

"Plain and simple," Sam said tightly, "with Mom away watching over Carter, and Dad and Sissy away at the conference, we are severely short-handed."

That grabbed Caroline's attention.

The frustration in his voice was evident as Sam continued. "The minute Mom says so, I'm gone too. Even if this place doesn't get battened down before the first snow, I have to go."

"Of course you do," Ruby said.

"I know you two are gonna want to visit him as soon as possible as well," Sam said. "So, in the meantime, I need you fillin' in outside, not making additional housework."

Caroline hovered in the hallway, her heart pounding as an idea began to take shape. She had considered the possibility of staying in one spot for several weeks. Why not work, too? Kevin's life insurance and pension had sustained her thus far, but only because she hadn't been spending. Considering she hadn't earned any money herself since then, however, some income would be a good thing. Granted, she didn't know the first thing about ranches or horses or any of it, but she was an extra, willing body, and Sam Black was obviously short-staffed.

Caroline took a rallying breath and pushed through the swinging door, but rammed into it when it stopped short, blocked by something solid. A very large, very broad man's back in a denim shirt that had nearly all the blue washed out of it.

"Oh, I'm sorry!" She stepped back, pulling the door with her. "Are you all right?" What a ludicrous question, she thought. It would take a person twice her size to cause him injury, and a much heavier door as well.

"I'm just fine, ma'am," Sam said as he turned around.

As her eyes caught on his face, recognition of his voice slammed into place and her careening thoughts jerked to a full stop.

"You're Sam?" she asked, face to face with the man she'd approached, and—*oh no*, accidentally caressed— yesterday. The same one who'd made a steamy appearance in her dreams last night.

He remained silent, looking her over insolently from head to toe and back again. Caroline suddenly felt self-conscious in her skintight, low-riding black stretch pants, cleavage-baring fitted tank top, and cropped bright blue sweatshirt jacket. Her body temperature skyrocketed, and she knew her face must be flushing scarlet.

"Why didn't you tell me you were Sam Black?" she demanded.

"Why didn't you tell me your name?" he countered.

Caroline narrowed her eyes and fumed. Insufferable was a good description. He was also, undoubtedly, the most arresting man she'd ever seen, with deep tanned skin, a strong jaw, and a wealth of black hair as dark as twilight. His eyes shone crystal blue: flat, cold, and positively scowling at her. Nothing like the sparkling stars last night after all.

Ruby intervened. "Caroline, this is Sam Black, the manager of the ranch. Sam, this is Caroline Murphy."

"Pleased to make your acquaintance, ma'am," he drawled, mocking the polite introduction.

"Liar," Caroline muttered, but she grasped the outstretched hand he offered anyway. She caught her breath. Just like yesterday, she felt the warmth of his callused hand spread clear to her toes.

Her eyes locked with his as she slid her tingling hand free.

Ruby said, "And this is my husband, Will Jenks. He's the chef here, among other things."

"Right fine to meet you, Caroline," Will said, grinning as he turned from the range. His eyes twinkled and his overgrown mustache stretched as far as his deep dimples.

She smiled in greeting.

"So." Will rubbed his hands together. "How do you like your eggs? Scrambled, fried? An omelet, or Benedict, maybe?"

"Hold on." Sam glared. "I'm sure Ms. Murphy is anxious to get on the road."

Caroline returned his glare, feeling a bit of her old self spring to life, then switched to a sugary smile for Will. "Scrambled, please."

She snuck a look at Sam. Narrowed eyes, clenched jaw.

Next thing she knew, she was seated directly across from him, their plates steaming with heaps of scrambled eggs and crisp bacon. As good as it had smelled earlier, her stomach churned from bringing up the possibility of employment on the ranch. She'd found it easy to be pushy in Miami, but of course, her camera had done all the work, not her tongue-tied mouth.

When she'd wished on those stars for an open dude

ranch, she sure hadn't envisioned this situation, and it was about to get more uncomfortable. *Very funny, universe, very funny.* A giddy laugh born of nerves threatened, so she clamped her lip between her teeth.

She'd barely touched her breakfast when Sam stood with empty plate in hand, interrupting the Jenkses' attempt at small talk.

"Excuse me, but I've got to get back to work," he said.

"I, uh, wanted to talk to you about that," Caroline said. *So much for tact.*

Sam stopped cold, his eyebrow lifting like a question mark. "You wanted to talk to me about my work?"

"No, it's just that, well…"

Caroline couldn't face off with him towering over her. She stood and suddenly felt as if she were entering a hot spot on assignment for the newspaper, with an adrenaline high and her well-being in jeopardy. She reminded herself that he was just a man, and this was just a filler job, and a long shot at that. "I overheard you say you were short-staffed. I hoped that you would consider hiring me on as an additional pair of hands—just for, I don't know, a month or so, until you have your help back."

"Lady, we are not in the habit of taking in strays, especially those that eavesdrop," he sneered. His plate clattered into the deep double-basin ceramic sink.

"You were practically shouting." She braced herself with her hands flat beside her dish and leaned over the table toward him. "Listen, I admit I don't know anything about ranches or horses, but I do know housework."

"I can vouch for that," Ruby said. "She insisted on tackling the kitchen with me after dinner."

Sam didn't look away from Caroline. "Sweetheart," he

said with a harsh chuckle, "even our guests are required to have some experience."

"I'm a hard worker and a quick learner, and I'm willing to do anything you need done."

Sam copied her position, until they were practically nose to nose across the table. His grim lips hovered less than a foot from hers, and those intense blue eyes seared her very core. He said, "Mmm, *anything* is tempting, but it would take me longer to train you than it'd be worth."

Will said, "Maybe you should consider her proposal."

"She's a *greenhorn*." Sam emphasized the word like it was the devil. "Think of Carter. The last thing we need is another—"

"Okay." Will raised both hands. "Just saying we sure could use an extra warm body around here."

Sam's lip twitched. "Although I'm sure Caroline's not opposed to being a warm body—"

"Sam!" Ruby said sharply.

Caroline jerked back, her face flaming. Even though she'd palmed his hard chest yesterday—yikes—she was shocked he'd make such an insinuation—multiple times, and in front of an audience, no less.

Sam turned away, bracing his arms on the counter. His head hung low and his shoulders hunched, causing the collar of his flannel shirt to tease his dark hair. Caroline crossed her arms and waited. His broad back expanded with a deep intake of breath. He blew it out and straightened.

Then he strode around the end of the table until he stood directly in front of Caroline. Her insides quivered— dread or excitement?—as their gazes locked.

"I was way out of line," he said. "I'm sorry."

"Apology accepted. Although maybe I should hold out for a conciliatory job offer." She tried to smile, but she still felt off-kilter.

Sam's brows lowered, but she caught a slight twitch of his lips. His gaze held steady. "I couldn't pay you nearly as much as an experienced hand."

She nodded. "Could you throw in free room and board and some riding lessons?"

"Lessons?" Sam scowled. "Now I'm supposed to take time out to train you and give you lessons?"

Ruby said, "You could teach her to ride and anything else around here in the blink of an eye. So could Sissy or any of us."

Inwardly, Caroline cheered. The votes tallied three against one now.

Sam stared her down, considering his options. She managed not to squirm. She couldn't, however, keep her skin from heating under his gaze.

"Damn it all." He spun and crossed the kitchen toward the door to the back porch. His broad shoulders filled the doorframe before the screen door banged shut.

Will jumped up, grabbed Caroline, and spun her around with a whoop. "I was rooting for you, girl!"

A grin spread across her face. "Does that mean I'm hired?"

8

An hour later, Sam told Caroline, "First, you'll muck out the stalls." He slid one of the aluminum barn doors open, smooth and quiet on its metal track. Just like new, after fourteen years.

And yet he'd still give darn near anything to have the old barn with its rickety, sticky two-ton door back.

"Muck out?" Caroline asked.

He cocked his head and leveled a look at the gorgeous woman. The very one he'd tried not to think about all last night. "Just how green are you?"

"Uh, neon or lime? I've only ridden a horse once at a birthday party in Miami. I was six."

Sam swallowed a curse and immediately lifted his hand to dig his fingers into the muscles between his neck and shoulder. That was some serious green. He drew a cautious breath. There were only two outcomes here. She couldn't cut it—in which case she was gone. Or she would —because he'd make sure she was trained like she was bred for ranching.

"All right, then, watch and learn." He maneuvered the wheelbarrow into the center aisle and snagged the four-pronged fork from its corner.

Caroline, who stood a few feet inside the door, covered her nose with her hand. Her tight tank top rose, and a creamy swath of skin showed above the tight, low-riding workout pants. It was going to be a long morning for the both of them.

He leaned on the fork. "If you can't handle the smell, you ought to pack up that Matchbox car of yours right now. Before you waste any more of my time."

She dropped her hand and straightened her spine. Sam figured she was probably close to five foot ten. Tall enough so that he wouldn't be forced to bend over to kiss her, small enough so that she'd still feel delicate in his arms—

Whoa. Rein that train of thought in.

"What smell?" Caroline asked. "The dust just tickled my nose, that's all."

Sam narrowed his eyes. He'd seen plenty of dudes go green over the smell of manure. Never fazed the ones who truly loved the animals, though. He'd just wait and see where Caroline fell.

Luckily, Sweetness, one of the laziest horses he'd ever met, occupied the end stall. Sam rubbed the animal's nose. His own horse, Bedlam, was stamping and snuffing, and making a fine racket from the other end of the row.

"Come on over here," he said to Caroline. Then he focused on the horse with coloring like Will's famous cookies: warm beige base with both white and dark choco-late chips. "Sweetness, this here's Ms. Murphy. She's going to clean up your mess. She's new, so don't kick her."

Caroline raised an eyebrow at him but spoke to the horse. "Is he always so quick to put people at ease?"

Sweetness whinnied.

"Thanks a lot, traitor." Sam gave the horse another pat and entered the stall. Time to teach. "Fork. Horse slop. Wheelbarrow." Sam thrust the tool into the hay, then emptied it into the basin a few times. "Nothing to it."

He handed her the fork. "Today, just pick up the mess. We'll do a complete clean—removing all the hay, hosing down the stall—in a few days. When you finish this stall, move right down the line."

Caroline hefted the fork, grimacing slightly. "How many stalls are there?"

"Just eight in use at the moment—though I'll do the two down at the other end." Bedlam wouldn't hurt her, but he was intimidating. And Palo, the young palomino, was a pain in the ass. Far too unpredictable for a newbie to handle. "The other six shouldn't take you long." Sam tipped his hat and smiled. Guests were always surprised at how much a decent pitchfork weighed, and given just how green she was, it would likely take her quite a while.

On his way out, he slid the double doors at the other end of the barn open for ventilation so she wouldn't pass out on him her first day. He shook his head. Made no sense that he felt a little protective of her, when the acid creeping up his throat meant he had some serious misgivings. Short-staffed or no, he'd love nothing more than for her to pack up and hightail on out of here.

Once he'd pulled the dually around, he entered the old barn and climbed hand over hand up the ladder to the loft. Then he hoisted the first of the forty-pound feed bags and sent it sailing out the loft door to the bed of the truck below.

Every heavy thud felt as ominous as nails in a coffin: he'd just hired a greenhorn. He knew better than most that ignorance bred accidents. Carter's shredded body spoke to that.

He braced his hands on his knees and bowed his head. Mentally, he said a quick, fierce prayer that accidents on this soil would never again claim lives, that he hadn't made a dire mistake in hiring Caroline Murphy.

Grimly, he returned to his labor until the truck bed was full.

Caroline might be a barely dressed newbie with no experience, no clue, and no muscle, but given their verbal sparring over breakfast, she was obviously intelligent and quick. He'd just have to make sure she learned an awful lot real fast, for everyone's safety and his own peace of mind.

Sam pulled off his heavy work gloves and threw them down into the truck as well. He rubbed the back of his neck, wishing he could get her flushed cheeks and fiery eyes out of his mind's eye.

He usually preferred a woman with more meat on her bones, and Caroline looked as if she'd blow over in the mildest of Montana winds. Sam grimaced, thinking of how little she had eaten at breakfast. No way was she going to watch her calories on his ranch. Besides, no matter how hard she tried, she'd never manage to look like a straight-as-a-board model. Oh, she had the mile-long legs. But even undernourished, Caroline's curves were full and enticing under those body-hugging clothes.

Yessiree, he sure would enjoy seeing her ripened up a bit. Naked would be good, too. He wished he didn't feel like whistling at the thought, and he really wished he hadn't gotten that tingle at the base of his spine that signaled arousal. He'd had the same problem facing off with Caroline across the kitchen table, her brown eyes spitting liquid fire and her rich chestnut hair swinging forward, so close he'd wanted to slide it through his fingers, even with both the Jenkses present.

It baffled him. Shoot, he'd not been this randy in ages. Years ago, there had been many women. Far too many. Young, cocky, and horny, he'd opted for quantity over quality.

But it wasn't just him. His younger brother Owen and his friend Carter were hardly saints—carrying on where he'd left off. The old rumor had taken on a life of its own. In reality, a lot of the women who visited were quite satisfied with a little harmless flirting or praise for a job well done. Thank Frank, compliments were no chore. And in the service industry, it was pretty much a given that you kept guests happy at all costs.

Luckily, Caroline was no guest.

Maybe his instant attraction to her had something to do with her eyes, challenging him, reaching out to him across that table. Or maybe it was her guts. Few people stood up to him.

He groaned. Who was he kidding? He'd been hot for Caroline the minute he'd seen her startled eyes in the lower field. No doubt he'd simply gone too long without a woman.

Didn't matter anyway. Sweetness would win barrel races before Sam Black laid a finger on Caroline Murphy, especially on Black family land.

Sam stared out the door of the loft. He'd always loved

the view from up here, but today the majestic scenery felt tainted. He massaged under his collar again. A flaming support had fallen on him during the fire. It was long healed, but he still bore some scarring there, and the muscles always clenched up when there was trouble.

Between Carter's mauling and Caroline's arrival…

He shook his head. Disaster wasn't going to avert itself. The sooner he trained Caroline, the sooner he'd feel things were under control. Bonus—the sooner he could start avoiding the too-sexy woman.

Sam jumped down from the loft to a stack of hard-packed bales of hay, and immediately spun off to jump the remaining distance to the barn floor.

As Sam crossed the clearing, he allowed himself a grin. If he wasn't so worried, he'd be enjoying the joke: sexy city girl shoveling out the horse stalls. She'd said she'd do anything, hadn't she?

He stepped quietly into the barn, halted just inside the door, and pushed his Stetson up a notch. He didn't hear any scraping or rustling as he waited for his vision to adjust in the darkness. Was the woman farting around admiring her manicure?

Sam gritted his teeth, reminding himself that he didn't much care what kind of woman Caroline was, and he'd be glad for an excuse to fire her.

As Sam's vision improved, he saw that Caroline was only three stalls down from him. She had removed her zippered sweatshirt, if you could even call it that, baring that little tank and plenty of skin. The pitchfork leaned against the sideboards of the stall. Sam admired the flex of her bare shoulders as she brushed the sweat from her forehead with one hand. Caroline was watching Old Granddad, a tame, whiskey-colored horse. Tentatively, she reached out to pet him. Sam couldn't see her hand any longer, but he could see her face. A sweet smile slowly lit her up in the same soft way the moon illuminated the night sky.

He hadn't even realized he'd moved toward her until the sound of his booted footfalls snatched the curve from her lip. She bent to grab for the weighty fork and, with nervous jerks, stabbed at the hay. Thank Frank, Granddad was old and jaded enough not to be startled by her sudden movements.

"How's it going?" Sam asked, peering into the wheelbarrow.

"I was just taking a quick break," Caroline said. "This thing is really heavy."

"Mmm hmm."

"It is," Caroline insisted, thrusting the fork handle toward Sam.

"I know exactly what it weighs."

"Right. Of course." Caroline bit her lip, looking sheepish—and far too kissable. She propped the fork against the slats of the stall and turned toward the horse.

"Sudden movements aren't a good idea around horses, or any animal, for that matter," Sam said, then regretted it. If he kept scolding her, she'd never tuck that luscious lower lip back in. "Luckily, Granddad here is too old and bored to spook."

"Sorry." She avoided his gaze, seemingly concentrating on stroking the horse's flank. Her pink nail polish was seriously chipped. "I was nervous."

"Why's that?" *Here it comes,* Sam thought, his shoulders inching up.

He'd suspected he'd seen every female ploy for sex in

existence. Normally he wasn't the least bit tempted, often feeling repulsed instead. But given that the ranch depended on positive word of mouth and repeat clients, he always rebuffed their advances as delicately as possible. Yeah, he occasionally indulged when he wasn't anywhere near ranch property, but only with women he'd known for years, women he trusted not to wag their tongues, women who weren't aiming for a certain notch on their bedposts.

Caroline shrugged.

"Come on, spit it out," he said, just wanting to get this over with.

"Because today's my first day on the job." She peeked up at him through a veil of dark lashes. "I had hoped to prove my work ethic, not get caught scratching ears."

Sam's mouth twitched upward, and his muscles relaxed. He reached out and tipped up Caroline's chin with a finger. "Hey."

She reluctantly lifted her eyes to his—and Sam was shocked at the heat that flared between them the instant their gazes connected.

"Don't worry about it," he said. "I wouldn't take kindly to a new hire who didn't enjoy the horses."

Sam brushed a thick strand of silky hair that had fallen from her ponytail off her cheek. Her thick lashes lowered, and Sam pulled his hand away like he'd been stung by a bee. He'd touched her—her chin then her hair. What in the hell was wrong with him?

Caroline swiped at her hair and bit her lip again.

He moved into the aisle behind the wheelbarrow, seeking a barrier to put between them.

Caroline's gaze seemed to be magnetically opposed to him. Spotting the fork, she lunged for it like a lifeline. She scooped at a particularly messy batch of hay and then spun to the wheelbarrow. She gave the tool a good single thrust.

The mound shot out, past the rim of the wheelbarrow, and smacked squarely into Sam's thigh.

Sam simply lowered his hat and settled in. The mess of horse manure slid slowly, agonizingly down the leg of his jeans, until it reached the knob of his knee. Then it splatted unceremoniously and directly onto his booted foot.

Caroline dropped the fork, her hands flying up and then hovering as if she didn't know what to do with them.

Sam regarded the pile on his foot. What had he gotten himself into? Caroline had no more control over her muscles than a newborn colt, and no more sense than that either. She'd just dropped a sharp, tined tool an inch from her toes—toes that were covered only in canvas. Sam shook his head. Of all things, he thought, she'd worn tennis shoes that were open at the heel—to shovel out muck. Might as well have gone barefoot.

Sam crossed his arms, waiting for the last of the stuff to fall from his leg. When it did, he met her wide eyes with his narrowed ones and let her stew. Allowing new hires to quake in their boots for a few minutes never hurt. Kept them from getting lazy later.

Caroline lowered her hands, "I am so sorry. It was an accident." Her eyes pleaded with him. "Really, I didn't mean to—"

Sam held up his hand, cutting her off. He did, of course, intend to give her the old heave-ho if things didn't work out, but he wasn't tyrannical enough to misinterpret a minor accident. She would stop pelting people when she'd built up some strength, naturally gaining more control over the fork.

Sam gave a powerful shake of his foot, dislodging the mess onto the floor. Although her face was the color of summer tomatoes, she lifted her chin defiantly.

Sam was impressed, but he said, "You know, I think we'd all be safer if we put you on housekeeping duty instead."

"Please—I want to work with the horses," Caroline said. "I'll do anything."

Again with the anything. If she knew the anything that kept popping into his mind, she'd already be on the road back to Miami. Or would she invite him into the stall? *Don't go there.*

Sam looked pointedly at his pant leg. "Does anything include…laundry?"

"Of course." Before he could hide his smile, she glanced up. The lines of worry on her forehead relaxed, and she smiled too. "I suspect I've just been had."

Sam grinned. "I've always despised that particular chore."

Caroline's face erupted in a smile as bright as the noonday sun. Sam's heart thumped with pleasure. He imagined tasting the corners of her smile with his tongue —and just as fast wondered what the hell was wrong with him.

"All right, back to work with you. Be careful until I get back."

He'd use the hose on his boot and take five to change his clothes. And if a little breathing room didn't restore him to sanity, he'd take another five for a cold shower.

9

———————

When Caroline finished mucking out the stalls, she added clean bedding. Enough hay in each stall for urine to drain through while still remaining fresh on top. More hay still for each horse to eat. Sam informed her, after the fact, of course, that she should have used twice as much hay. She supposed he believed in learning the hard way.

Muscles shimmying with fatigue, Caroline dug in with the fork and began again at the first stall. As she worked, Sam—in fresh work pants—explained the differences between corralled horses and barn-kept horses and their care.

Caroline had a hard time concentrating on his words. She couldn't understand her strange feeling for this man she'd just met. She felt both comfortable and uncomfortable around him. When he was being a grumpy boss, nervous energy zinged. When he acted like an asshole, anger boiled. When they were trading jibes, she felt almost like her old self—confident and sure. When she held his eyes or got too close—a flutter of anticipation and need. She'd worked hard at not feeling anything for so long that this was…unsettling.

She slid her eyes toward him and caught an expression of consternation.

"When the snows get too thick for the grass to poke through, we'll bring some of the corralled horses down to the open barn and some of them here to the stalls. By then you'll be able to handle a few more stalls." He smirked. "And that fork."

Caroline paused from shucking the hay long enough to screw up her face at him in retaliation. Although still embarrassed, she was thankful he was able to joke about the incident.

He laughed and continued the lesson. "The horses that are kept in the barn all year round either need more attention or were stall-raised to start with…"

Sam didn't look nearly so harsh when he laughed. His smile rounded out his hard edges, making him seem less like a steely, humorless cowboy.

Caroline returned the fork to its designated spot along the wall.

"Now you feed them," Sam said.

"You mean I still didn't give them enough hay? Why on earth didn't you tell me earlier?"

"Take it easy," Sam said. "Some of the horses get feed in addition to the hay."

"Oh."

Sam walked over to a series of tall bins with wooden tops. "The strawberry roan mare, Sally Girl, and the black mare with the white star on her nose, Midnight, are both going to give birth in the spring. See the slight swell of their bellies?" Sam looked into her eyes for confirmation. She held his gaze, nerve endings humming, and eventually remembered that she was supposed to be answering a question.

"Yes." She nodded. "But I just thought they were a little chunky."

His brows lowered, and his face emanated displeasure. What was that all about, she wondered? He was allowed to make jokes on the job, but she wasn't?

"The pregnant mares need supplements to the hay, so they get two scoops of this, and two of that." Sam picked up two feed buckets and handed her the metal cup from the bin labeled "Oats."

"Now, Granddad over there, he's just plain finicky." He smiled at the old horse. Strange, but Caroline wished he'd smile at her again instead.

———

The next couple of days passed in much the same manner. Sam put her through her paces during the day, teaching her the ins and outs of different chores. He always made sure she understood the importance of every little thing. Safety was some kind of hot button for him, she guessed. Likely because they so often had guests on the ranch. Lunches usually meant making a sandwich or grabbing some leftovers—though Will was always in the kitchen making sure she found the good stuff. At dinner, she learned, everyone in residence was expected to sit down together. Will and

Ruby always suggested she and Sam join them in the living room in front of the fireplace for a cup of cocoa or tea or nightcap. Sam always begged off, citing paperwork to catch up on in his cabin or some chore he hadn't finished.

Caroline declined as well, being completely exhausted in mind and body.

Just as well she and Sam didn't spend additional time together. While she'd helped Ruby clean and winterize cabins, she'd also spent quite a lot of time with Sam in the barns.

He continued to act hot and cold with Caroline. She wasn't exactly smooth and steady herself.

She'd been as accommodating as she could be, and her sore muscles spoke to the fact that she'd been working her tail off. So, she didn't understand why he didn't seem to like her.

She supposed it was for the best, though. Because at this point—although it shocked her—she could admit she was attracted to Sam. That shocked her, threw her, baffled her. She'd never, ever expected to feel anything for anyone but her husband again.

But here she was (worlds away from her home and her life with Kevin) with the most impossible choice in a man (a difficult new boss), and damned if he didn't draw her to him like a moth to a flame.

Caroline purposely hadn't talked to Neve since she'd been hired, sending only brief texts saying she was fine. It wasn't some sort of withholding for payback, it was just…

Well, she wasn't sure. Being here felt like a delicious secret. Something she almost couldn't believe. Her body was busy, she was gulping fresh air like she'd never tasted it before, and she was getting comfortable around people again. The Jenkses were easy to be around, and yeah—even with Sam she felt strangely at ease a lot of the time. At least when he wasn't being a jerk.

The best part was that she fell into bed each night so bone-tired that she didn't have any energy to think.

When she returned to her cabin the third night of working, she showered, sat on the bed, and called Neve.

Bella answered her mom's phone.

"Where are you? Mom is dying to know."

Caroline laughed. She just bet she was. "I'm in Montana. You would love it here. I'm on a real ranch, with horses and everything."

"Horses! Can I come visit you this weekend?"

"If I stay for a while, I promise I'll bring you out."

"I have a horse," Bella said, and Caroline heard a clunk and a scurrying.

Neve's voice next. "Where the hell have you been since True Springs?"

"The Black Hills Ranch in Montana."

"A ranch! That's awesome!" Neve sounded elated.

"I'm actually working here."

Neve gasped. "Oh my God. You're not coming back? What have I done?"

"It would serve you right." Caroline flopped back on the bed and propped her feet on the wall. Damn that felt good—she'd been standing the whole day. "Of course I'm coming back. I've got indefinite leave from the paper. Although my editor has been harassing me. I just figured…"

"Yeeesss," Neve said.

Caroline sighed. "Well, out here, everything seems a bit easier to bear. You know how much I love animals. And the mountains, the sky, I swear even the air…it's entirely different, you know?"

"I hear ya, Heidi. Sounds like a healing place," Neve said. "And you sound good, really good. I'm so glad."

"Yeah, a little better—*just* a little," Caroline admitted. "Maybe you weren't totally insane to make me leave home. Anyway, the ranch is short-staffed at the moment, so I sort of forced the manager to hire me. Pretty sure he's just waiting to fire me. I've been a total klutz, even threw horse manure on him, so that's not a plus."

"You did not! You'd better spill every detail."

The next morning, Caroline headed for the barn bright and early as usual. When Sam joined her, he didn't launch immediately into some lesson like he usually did.

Instead, he faced her, long legs spread, muscled arms crossed, and seemed to be assessing her.

Uh-oh. Had she forgotten to close the barn door last night? Or the one on the chicken coop? Had she—

"When I went to my cabin, I got a call from my mother," he said.

"There's been a change?"

"Nothing major, but sounds like it's time for me to head on over there." His expression was grim. "I'll be leaving as soon as possible, and I don't know how long I'll be gone. My father and sister are still at that conference, then they'll hit the hospital, too."

Caroline wondered what the family of this imposing

man might be like. She was glad she'd have some time to get her feet wet before meeting them.

Sam ran a hand through his hair and blew out a hard breath. "Will and Ruby can care for the horses in the corral, but I need you to help them out around the lodge."

"Of course," she said.

"Caroline." He pinned her with his eyes. "I need to know if I can count on you. You'll have to clean out these stalls daily, feed the horses like I told you, and groom them, too. For now, Will and Ruby will exercise them."

She had learned that both the animals and the ranch meant the world to Sam—not to mention how he felt about his people. It took some of the sting out of his overbearing teaching methods.

"You can count on me." Caroline noticed his shoulders dropped a fraction of an inch. "But you are going to take me through grooming once or twice, aren't you?"

"Before I go, you'll know grooming like you've been doing it all your life." He looked her over, then quickly averted his gaze. "You don't have more appropriate clothes?"

"Unfortunately, no."

"Borrow something from Ruby, maybe?"

Caroline snorted. Ruby was a really tiny woman.

Sam grimaced, surely realizing the same.

"As soon as I get some time off," Caroline said, "I'll definitely be heading to town for some…warmer clothes." She wasn't going to admit that she felt exposed under his gaze, but more coverage would be a very good thing.

Sam nodded even as he reached up and massaged the muscles of his back and shoulder—a move he made often.

"Good. Okay. Grooming." He didn't look at her again, just turned to leave. "This afternoon. Might take a while."

What was the problem with grooming? Or did he just not want to spend that much time in close quarters with her?

10

———————

"Harder," Sam ordered Caroline.

"Slower," he said. Then, "Smoother stroke, yes, like that."

Caroline's face flamed and parts she'd forgotten she had woke up and paid rapt attention. There was so much sexual connotation behind Sam's words.

Was he thinking the same thing? He had to be. She would swear his sexy voice rumbled more deeply with every instruction.

"That's good," he said, "but more pressure on the glide."

Caroline nearly groaned out loud. Thankfully, he stood behind her in Lucky's stall. Otherwise, she couldn't possibly have hidden the direction of her thoughts—or the uncontrollable hardening of her nipples.

This was—wow. Just crazy intense. She had only just met Sam, an unexpected employer. And she wasn't looking for a relationship, or even sex. But her body didn't care. With each word that escaped his lips, her breathing quickened and her core tightened.

"Not quite," he said. He covered both her hands. "Like this."

And now, in guiding her, each time the grooming brush slid against the horse, Sam's hard body pressed along the entire length of her back. Between strokes, he pulled back a fraction of an inch.

An intense quiver erupted between her legs and heat built in her belly.

Again, forward and back, delicious contact and needy withdrawal. The repetitive action mimicked sex, and *holy moly*—Caroline even felt the intimate press of Sam's arousal.

"Can you feel the difference?" Sam's mouth was near her ear, his voice deep and coaxing.

Purposely seductive, Caroline decided, which was when her mind gave up the battle. Her body took control. A shiver ran along her spine, zipping from her lower back to her neck.

That was her answer. She knew Sam felt the ripple and understood, because she heard a low growl from deep inside him.

So crazy intense.

He continued to move against her backside, heat then emptiness, contact then want, while his arms remained stretched along the bare length of hers. Caroline shut her eyes and imagined that, instead of against barriers of clothing, his hard cock stroked inside her, in and out, in and out. Her knees wobbled.

"Now," he said, stepping back, breaking the contact, "let me watch you."

Caroline didn't turn around; she only nodded. Who cared if she couldn't have imagined this a few days ago? Who cared if there was a horse present? This was the most erotic game she had ever played; she didn't even consider breaking the spell he had cast.

She moved slowly, deliberately, and sensually, simulating each movement he had taught her with his body, knowing that he watched her. The horse's muscles reminded her of Sam's chest, rippling in the evening sun. She closed her eyes again. In her mind, it was Sam she stroked under her fingers, and yet, also, Sam watching her from behind as she performed only for him.

Her hips swayed in time with the strokes of her arms. She rolled her head along her neck, causing her ponytail to dip, the ends of her hair sliding over her shoulder blades. Caroline knew, instinctively, that he stood just as enthralled.

Caroline continued to groom, slowly. She waited for Sam's deep rumble to direct her—for what next, she didn't know. She shied away from imagining what might come next. She didn't want this, shouldn't want this—and yet, oh God, she did.

But for too long he didn't speak. He gave no suggestions, no reprimands, no encouragement, no participation…

Doubt flooded her, and when Caroline's strokes faltered, the horse whinnied. Embarrassment seeped in, supplanting desire. Arms still braced against the animal's flanks, she peeked at Sam over her shoulder.

His eyes smoldered, devouring her, and she ignited all over again. She didn't—*couldn't*—think. She dropped her arms and turned, stepping toward him—face raised, ready.

Sam shut his eyes for a long moment. A shudder rippled through him and then stilled. Seeing the physical effect she had on him heightened Caroline's desire to a feverish pitch.

She stood rooted, waiting for him to reach for her, but when he raised his eyes, the heat and fire had vanished. Even the color seemed to have disappeared. He was…gone.

"You dropped your hand," he said in a flat, cold voice. "If the horse doesn't know where you are, he can't relax."

Caroline spun back to the horse and nearly scalped the poor beast, so hard were her first strokes. Tears seared her eyes, and she could barely draw a breath. She had never, never been so humiliated.

———

Sam watched Caroline practically attack Lucky. He should tell her to ease up on the animal, but he didn't trust himself to speak. If he opened his mouth, if she faced him again…

He'd reach for her. He'd loosen her ponytail, bury his fingers in her stunning hair, and press a wet kiss into the salty curve of her neck. And he wouldn't stop there. He'd nip her earlobe and lick the rim, and he'd probably shoot himself in the foot by whispering in her ear that he'd never, ever, wanted anyone the way he wanted her.

Sam ran his hands through his hair in disbelief and frustration. What had just happened was *insane*. There was no other word for it. He'd friggin' lost his mind.

He noted her rigid back and white knuckles. He hadn't meant to hurt her. But no matter how out of control things had gotten, in the end, he needed her to believe that he didn't want her.

Yeah, right. He'd never laid a hand on any other employee, never even considered creating such a…a…

Dammit. Call a spade a spade. The fact was that he'd pretty much dry-fucked her from behind under the guise of teaching her to groom.

Christ. What was *wrong* with him?

And why *her*?

Heck, he barely knew her. She'd only been here a handful of days. And yet—she'd turned his world upside down. Sam felt as if his body was attached to a giant pulley drawing him to her. He'd been smashing that feeling every chance he got—acting like the cranky bastard he was or avoiding her completely.

But today? Once he'd actually seen the effect of his words on her body—her taut nipples, her flushed skin, her glazed eyes—his instinct for self-preservation had disappeared.

He couldn't understand what had possessed him. He hadn't touched a woman on ranch property in over a decade, rarely even been tempted while he stood on Black family ground. But this woman… Well, he must have gone loco. He'd actually pressed himself, rock-hard erection and all, against her soft backside, here, in their barn. He'd been split seconds from grabbing her breasts, tearing off her clothes, and actually burying himself inside all that heat.

He had no idea how he'd managed to stop, to shut everything down inside him after she'd turned to him—because he still burned, still fought against a raging desire.

Was he that hard up? Hell, he'd spent an enjoyable night with Melinda in Billings only a couple of months ago. Or had it been longer? He and Melinda had enjoyed plenty of sex over the years, but he'd never heated up with just a glance from the buxom redhead.

Sweet heaven, had he *ever* reacted to a woman the way he had with Caroline?

Sam skimmed her form with his gaze. She furiously groomed the indifferent beast, making her sweet rear end wriggle.

Sam wiped his brow with his forearm. What was he doing standing here, still watching this temptress? Setting himself up for disaster, that was what.

Sam bolted out of the barn and fought an incredible urge to run right down the driveway and keep on going. Or make a U-turn and run straight into Caroline's arms. The first option was unthinkable, the second—a suicide mission.

———

Caroline had a brief respite to get herself together when Sam bolted out of the barn. Then she set to work grooming the next horse—anger, desire, and confusion giving her a burst of energy. By the time she'd finished that horse, though, Sam had returned to teach her everything she'd need to know in his absence.

Now, Caroline was grooming Sally Girl, the fifth horse in succession, and her energy was long gone. Her arms were so overused that they shook. Her back muscles screamed. She had grime embedded in her fingernails and all the way up her forearms to the crevices of her elbows. Worse, her feet squashed in her shoes with muck she didn't even want to think about. She'd like to belt the idiot designer who had dreamed up backless tennis shoes. Her tank top was drenched, her nipples now surely visible through the white, stretchy fabric. And she'd bet there was a really attractive blotch of wet spreading under her butt cheeks, right through her stretch pants.

No matter, Sam continued to correct her. Easy enough to be patient—or stubborn, she thought—when you weren't the one doing all the perspiring. Hell, he hadn't even removed his flannel work shirt.

As she worked, Sam insisted that she recite the safety rules for handling horses, procedures of grooming, and his earlier instructions on feeding. In other words, everything that he had taught her thus far.

"Never stand directly in front of or behind a horse," she said. "He has nearly three-hundred-and-sixty-degree vision, but those two spots are blind, so he'll rear or kick if he gets scared by something he can't see."

She switched to the body brush and started over at Sally Girl's head, moving her hand in a circular motion and following the direction of the horse's hair. Her muscles shimmied—she wasn't sure she could keep this up long enough to reach the animal's hindquarters. "Leave one hand on the horse as you move around so he'll always know where you are."

She droned on, exhausted physically, exhausted emotionally from the strange push and pull with Sam. Finally, she couldn't think of anything else she'd learned.

Still clenching the terrycloth towel she'd used to shine the horse's coat, she faced Sam and propped her hands on her hips. "So?"

Caroline prayed to whatever God watched over impulsive women, obnoxious cowboys, and oversized four-legged beasts that, this time, her newly acquired skills had passed muster.

"Good enough," Sam said. "I'll do the last two. Go wash up for supper."

Not resounding praise, Caroline thought as she tossed the brushes on the shelf and nearly ran out of the barn. Still, if it meant she was free from grooming, she'd take it. Any more of Sam's overbearing teaching methods, and she'd scream.

Caroline shook her head as she pounded up the steps to her cabin. She could barely believe what had transpired. She'd gone from a woman who couldn't imagine sleeping with someone this morning to wanton, needy, and burning —actually aching for sex.

No—aching for *Sam*.

Had she ever felt as aroused as she had this afternoon? As uninhibited? Sex with Kevin was good, but they'd been together a long time. She couldn't remember it being so hot, so wild, so…

She didn't want to think too much about Kevin right now. Not when her body craved Sam.

In the bathroom, she cranked the hot water. She couldn't wait until after dinner to shower tonight. She was far too dirty and sweaty.

She stripped off her disgusting clothes and dug out a plastic bag for her disgusting shoes. The main house's laundry room had a slop sink. She'd soak and sanitize her shoes after dinner. Wearing them wet tomorrow would be better than wearing them like this.

She stepped under the spray, and her whole body sighed with relief. Her mind spun back around that crazy episode in the barn. She tried to convince herself she'd imagined it. But her body kept her honest—tingling with the mere memory of Sam's deep voice, his hard body covering hers, his breath in her ear.

God.

It had been truly unbelievable and—despite being cut short—totally amazing.

Sam had made her lose her reason. Better yet, she marveled, he'd made her forget for a while. She tipped her face into the spray and refused to let herself feel guilty.

11

Now that Sam had left, Caroline finally decided to confide in Neve. With Sam away, it felt less real, less intense.

As usual, she waited to call until after she'd showered and was sitting cross-legged on the bed in her cabin.

"Remember that prickly new boss I have, Sam?"

"The one who sounds like a real piece of work. Of course."

She picked at the fuzz of the Indian-pattered blanket. "Well, he's hot."

"Hot? Did I hear that right?"

Caroline could almost feel Neve ballooning with excitement. This may have been a bad idea.

"How hot are we talking?"

That nervous feeling fluttered in Caroline's chest again. "Incredibly hot. Drop-dead hot. Total cowboy—tall, broad, rough, and rugged. He's got a sexy smile, not that he uses it often. Even his voice, when he…"

"When he what? Did you kiss? Oh my God—wait, I

have to cover Bella's ears—did you sleep with him? Hurry up, tell me everything."

"Don't get so excited. He's the manager of his family's ranch, remember? My boss. I'm here because the ranch sounded amazing and I needed somewhere to be. I did hear a rumor, however. Sam supposedly has quite a rep for keeping the single women customers smiling. You know the term for a horse that's kept for breeding, don't you?"

"A stud?"

"Right, well, that's what they call Sam, and let me tell you, when he turns on the charm, the name fits." When he hid the charm, he was more like a big, cranky bully. He definitely had a softer side, but he seemed to reserve it for everyone but her.

Neve whistled and demanded to know more. But there wasn't that much to tell—because Caroline left out the part where she had experienced one of the most incredible sexual escapades, or non-escapades, as it were, of her life while grooming a horse. Even Neve wouldn't have believed her, and she herself wasn't ready to dilute the episode by speaking of it just yet.

Neve seemed far too pleased.

"Hang on, he's got an issue with me, and I've only worked for a few days. Seriously, I doubt anything is going to happen here." Caroline could insist all she wanted, but her traitorous body still pleaded for a very different outcome.

Neve snorted. "He just hired you, he wants to fire you, he bullies you, you irritate him, he's hot, you're hot, you're in the wild, wild west—sounds like it's got all the necessary elements for a full-throttle romance to me."

"Neve, you tasked me with using my camera—which

I'm still not even willing to do. Don't even get any ideas about a relationship. It's out of the question."

"No pressure, my friend," Neve said. "I'm simply saying: you never do know."

———

A couple days later, Caroline watched while Will held a metal bucket full of apples to entice the horses who needed a light grooming. A plastic lid fit over the pail, with a hole cut out of the top—a hole big enough for a man's hand, but too small for the horse's muzzle. A pony knocked over the bucket in his exuberance to reach the sweet treats, and Caroline laughed.

"The beasts never learn that they only get one apiece," Will joked.

Caroline had finished her own tasks early today— already her new skills had improved in effectiveness and speed. So, this afternoon the Jenkses had included Caroline in their favorite ritual. She fed each horse an apple, winning a handful of pure slobber as a reward. Will and Ruby quickly brushed down the horses, talking all the while. Midnight was a hog, and Sweetness a true lady. And apparently, some years ago, a young colt named Frank had clenched the bucket's handle between his teeth and darted off with it, spilling the bright red fruit as he crisscrossed the paddock. The others had formed an apple-eating train behind him; hence, the plastic lid was born.

"So you can *Thank Frank*," Will emphasized, "for the plastic lid—and anything else that needs thanking around here."

Caroline smiled. Now it made sense. She'd heard that

phrase more than once already. Tall tales grew taller with each telling, Caroline knew, but she enjoyed the stories all the same. Plus, it helped her match the horses' names with their personalities, while the animals learned her scent and her voice.

She soon found herself smiling and laughing like it was the most natural thing in the world. And it was. Here she stood in a breathtaking landscape with the warm breath of a horse mingling with her own, and people who made her forget why she'd come.

She wished she could hold this moment forever. She itched to shoot some pictures, see what she could preserve with her trusty lens.

As soon as the urge surfaced, however, she squashed it back down. She searched for a distraction, and her eyes fell upon the rectangular clearing with the burned post in one corner.

"What happened over there?" she asked.

The pair exchanged a glance before Will spoke. "There was a fire, years ago. Burned one of the original buildings down to the ground."

"That's terrible. I hope no one was hurt."

"No people, thank goodness," Ruby said. "But unfortunately, they lost a number of horses and a few stable cats."

Caroline gasped. She hadn't even been here a week, and already, she couldn't imagine losing a single animal.

"Do they know what happened?"

"A lantern was knocked over." Will nodded toward the new barn with the metal doors. "You'll notice they've got electricity everywhere now, even in the barns."

Ruby stopped brushing the horse and smiled. "When

we first started coming here, it was pretty rustic. Even the cabins had minimal amenities."

"All part of my plan." Will winked. "I wooed her in the dark, otherwise she'd never have fallen for my ugly mug."

"Another tall tale," Ruby said, and laughed. Then she frowned. "Really, though, as vacationers, it was so strange. One year, everything was just like always, the next, we arrived and voila. The old barn had vanished, the new one had appeared, and everything was wired. Sam was injured but healed by then, yet he'd changed somehow. The whole dynamic had."

"They were spooked, is all," said Will.

"I imagine Black Hills must have been even more charming pre-wiring," Caroline said.

Ruby nodded. "It was, but then, most folks still fall in love with the place at first sight, and once they spend some time here, they're hooked."

"Say, honey." Will put his arm around his wife's tiny waist. "The lady's nose is getting burned. Why don't you help her choose a hat from the costume gallery?"

"Great idea. Why didn't I think of it before?" Ruby linked her arm through Caroline's. "Come with me, madame. We're going shopping."

The costume gallery turned out to be a walk-in closet off the mudroom that had been transformed into an eclectic dressing room. An open trunk was heaped with boots and shoes of all kinds. A bookshelf held rectangular woven baskets of gloves, bandanas, belts, and other miscellany, while two hanging racks supported shirts, jeans, vests, and jackets of all sorts and sizes. Pegged racks hung on the walls. Some had chaps, some scarves, and there were hats galore. The walls sported a deep crimson paint, the trim a pale yellow. Framed western prints—Remington and Russells, according to Ruby—hung beside the ornate mirrors.

"Wow," Caroline said. "This room is a perfect mix between an old-time boudoir and a tasteful dressing room."

"It used to be a dingy dumping ground, but I thought if it was done well, folks would feel better about wearing hand-me-downs," Ruby admitted.

"Well, you were right." Caroline was excited at the prospect of "shopping" here.

"Even still, more people seem to leave stuff than take it, although some of our guests come in just to play dress-up." Ruby swept her arm to encompass the small room. "Take anything you want."

"Really? This is great—now I'll only need to buy half a new wardrobe." Caroline poked through a rack of clothes, selecting a couple of shirts. "I figured I'd head to town for some appropriate clothing, but I didn't want to take time off so soon."

"Nonsense—you'll go tomorrow. Just make sure you get some boots." Ruby looked pointedly at Caroline's now thoroughly disgusting tennis shoes.

Caroline laughed. "Believe me, boots are number one on my list."

The hostess chose several hats for Caroline and turned her to the mirror.

When she modeled a caramel-colored one with a dark brown band that matched her hair, Ruby said, "Ooh, that's the one."

Caroline regarded her reflection. Electric-blue Lycra top with a bold black stripe across the chest, black leggings, no socks, disturbingly filthy tennis shoes, and now, a squat cowboy hat. The brim was closer to round than oblong and rather flat, and the crown was short and circular, instead of high and peaked.

"Looks awfully goofy at the moment."

"The hat really does suit you," the petite woman said.

Caroline smiled. "Better yet, it fits."

"It's flattering," Ruby added.

"I'm not trying to impress anyone."

"Maybe you should."

Caroline took off the hat and twirled it around a finger. She shook her head slowly.

Ruby held up her hand. "Right off, I noticed the sparks zipping between you two."

"Ruby—"

"Most women are all over Sam. With good reason—he was quite a gigolo when Will and I began visiting over fifteen years ago. Had quite the reputation."

So the stud rumor was true.

"I'm not sure what happened, but nowadays he's pretty closed off." Ruby shrugged. "With you, though, I see something different in the way he reacts."

Caroline's heart gave a joyful—ridiculous and stupid—leap, even as she told Ruby, just like she'd told Neve, "A romance is out of the question."

After yesterday, she could maybe see being tempted into some very hot sex—but if and when that insanity ever happened, it'd be between her and Sam.

Romance? Love? Not a chance.

She set the hat aside and sagged onto a brocade antique piano stool. "I think it's time I tell you what brought me here." She gestured for Ruby to sit.

"You don't have to tell me anything."

"I'd like to," Caroline said, and realized it was true. "Really." The hostess pulled up a stool, while Caroline took a few deep breaths. "I'm a recent widow."

Ruby's hand flew to cover her mouth, but her quick intake of breath was audible anyway.

"Oh, Caroline, I'm so sorry."

Caroline smiled wryly. "Yeah, well, me too." How to begin? "My husband was a police officer, but he didn't die on the job. He was with me in a car accident on vacation two years ago. It was…a freak thing. He died upon impact." She shuddered. She still found the event hard to think about without getting sucked back in time and over-whelmed by guilt. And she wasn't about to tell Ruby all of it.

She reached for an ornate belt buckle and traced its grooves with her index finger. "I've had a really hard time."

"Of course you did," Ruby said. "You're so young. It's not fair."

Caroline needed to tell her new friend what she could. "I'd still be at home in bed if it wasn't for my friend Neve. She forced me to take this trip." She smiled, thinking back. "She actually packed my bags, pried my wedding ring off my finger, shoved me in the shower, and even painted my nails." She wiggled the chipped specimens for Ruby's inspection—barely any polish left.

Ruby frowned.

"I didn't set out to find this place," Caroline said, "but I'm glad I did. It's magical, and I'm healing every minute." She looked down at her hands, and then back up.

"I didn't plan on getting close to anybody again either, but you and Will, well, you make me feel like I belong."

Caroline's eyes began to well with tears, while Ruby swiped at her own.

"You'll love the rest of the family, too. I promise. Just like they'll love you," Ruby said, and stood to hug her. "And honey, if there's anything we can do…"

"Well, actually," Caroline said, "you could lay off the matchmaking."

"Of course. I'm so sorry. I had no idea."

"You wouldn't have. And although I surprise myself, I do find Sam attractive." She blushed. Why in the world had she said that out loud? "But a relationship is out of the question."

"Say no more."

Oh, I won't, thought Caroline. And yet a lump formed in her throat—a hard longing for what she'd lost. A relationship. A soul-to-soul connection. Love. A future with a partner at her side.

All the things she'd never have again.

12

Sam had been gone three days when Caroline remembered that she hadn't yet tackled the laundry—the price of tossing manure on your boss. Despite having extra chores in his absence, she'd found she had some extra time—probably because she wasn't spending hours being trained on new tasks. Instead of taking on another chore, however, she'd chosen—with Ruby and Will's assurance that she should—to hike in the afternoons.

Caroline stopped dead in the doorway of the laundry room. *Wow*.

From the sheer volume of dirty clothes—overflowing baskets and a few mountainous piles on the floor—it was a miracle they weren't all walking around naked.

She grimaced and picked her way over the piles. She might have been smarter to keep her hot date with the washer and dryer, rather than explore the grounds and trails.

No—she'd find a way to fit in both.

The walks were healing. Each turn of the path appeared more beautiful than the last, and every gorgeous spot sparked her photographer's mind. She couldn't bring herself to use her camera, yet she couldn't keep her brain from doing what it knew best either. Mentally, she clicked away, cataloguing the scenery at every angle into photographs she'd never develop.

This landscape, its trees and sky, weather and wildlife, felt fresh and invigorating. Lush fields rolled into an explosion of trees. Split-wood fences bordered the paddocks in a maze, but somehow the man-made structures seemed married to the earth rather than imposed. A backdrop of snowcapped mountains seemed to rise out of the land like an offering to the gods. She couldn't imagine ever tiring of this view.

Speaking of tired, Caroline was whipped. She had lain in bed, or on the couch, for the last two years. No spin class, no weights, no jogging, no mad dashes on the job, not even a stroll to a nearby restaurant. And then she'd plopped her tush in the car for a marathon drive. Pretty much until she had set foot on the ranch, squatting over toilets in rest stops was the maximum stress to her muscles in a long, long time.

Now, thanks to an overdose of physical labor in her first week on the ranch, her arms and back were dreadfully sore. She still couldn't believe how heavy that pitchfork felt. Hadn't titanium reached Montana?

Sitting sedentary through the evening meal hadn't helped either, as her muscles had stiffened up.

She thunked a full laundry basket on top of the dryer and draped herself over it to stretch out her tight back and shoulders. She exhaled slowly, waiting for the discomfort to subside. Inhaling deeply, she received a jolt to her senses.

She could smell Sam. Here, in his clothes.

She lifted a crumpled plaid shirt to her face and inhaled the slightly musky scent. Then a navy bandana, the color faded nearly to purple and its white pattern dingy, with its more pungent smell of sweat and hard work, dust and rich earth. Her chest constricted and her body felt a different kind of ache, one of want and need.

How was it possible that she recognized his scent from that one physical—and yet not fully intimate—encounter? How could she actually long for that smell, and the man that came with it? Caroline's logical mind rebelled, but apparently her body was a different matter altogether.

Caroline reached for another shirt and brought it to her nose. She sniffed but launched into a coughing fit.

"Stinks, huh?"

She spun toward the door. Ruby stood, her arms crossed over her chest. How long had she been there?

"That's Will's shirt, you know."

"I know, I, uh… I caught a whiff of the cologne and…" Noticing Ruby's raised eyebrows and corresponding smirk, Caroline decided the less she said, the better. She tossed the shirt into the washer.

"I know perfectly well that shirt reeks." Ruby sighed. "My husband seems to think real cowboys drenched themselves with aftershave."

Caroline forced a smile and tossed clothes into haphazard piles on the floor.

"You're mixing the whites with the colors."

Caroline yanked a sock and an undershirt out from under some darks and searched for the white pile. Darn, whites were in the washer, and she'd thrown Will's red button-down in there. Her back to Ruby, she fished out the evidence of her inability to focus.

"I came to see if you'll join us again tonight for some tea and Scrabble." Ruby paused. "But if you're sniffing my husband's clothing for a reason, maybe you should pass."

"No! I thought I was smelling—"

The hostess grinned like a cat with a mouse's tail trapped under its paw, while Caroline felt heat rush to her cheeks.

"I'll have Will light a fire in the living room hearth. Join us when you're through. Careful—don't turn the socks pink." Ruby winked and left.

Caught red-handed, or more like red-nosed—how mortifying. So much for Caroline's earlier insistence that she wasn't looking to attract anyone. Ruby must assume she was hard up.

Caroline put her hands on her hips. She supposed the facts spoke for themselves. Despite herself, she was indeed hard up. Desperately horny, all thanks to Sam.

At first, she'd tried to deny his effect on her. But since the grooming session, she'd had to face facts. Now? He wasn't even in the room, wasn't even on the ranch, for God's sakes, and his smell alone had her longing to touch him—to see how silky the hair that curled at the nape of his neck was, how rough the dark stubble on his chin was in the evenings, and, most of all, how his lips felt against hers, how his hands felt on her skin. She wondered if she could make him groan with pleasure—or, even better, draw one of those rare, genuine smiles from him.

The good news was that she had ceased thinking so incessantly of Kevin. Unfortunately, her mind jumped so frequently, and with such startling sexual connotations, to Sam that she feared she was only transferring one obsession for another.

Call it simple, healthy lust. Chalk it up to a couple of years without a man's touch. Deem it a natural need in retaliation to too much pain, too much grief. She'd been hiding out for so long—maybe something as basic as a man's scent could cause sensory overload.

Surely, if she and Sam Black ever ended up in bed together, the heavy-duty physical attraction she felt would disappear as abruptly as a Florida rainstorm.

"Fat chance," she muttered. Because she'd seen what happened when the heat between her and Sam surged hotter than Miami's blacktop in August. Out of nowhere, he flipped a switch and became as frigid as a street vendor's freshly scooped Italian ice—the kind that gave you brain freeze no matter how long you let it melt. If he had his way, they'd never do the deed.

Furthermore, Caroline was positive that Sam hoped she would up and quit, given enough dirty jobs. Too bad for him that she discovered she actually enjoyed her chores, even the dirty ones.

She grimaced and plucked a crusted sock from the floor. Okay, the laundry was an exception.

Caroline was learning something new at every turn, all of it completely out of the context of her old life. Everything was different here. The orange in the sunset, the green of the grass, the blue of the sky. Between the fresh mountain air and the healthy physical exhaustion, she was even thrilled to drop into bed each night. No tears, no insomnia, no disturbing dreams filled with crunching metal and her own screams. Just blissful, deep sleep.

She loved feeling close to the land—dirt under her fingernails, earthy dust on her clothes. Loved, too, being able to reach out and touch the animals, so warm, so full of life.

That's it, she thought, wanting to smack herself on the forehead with the revelation.

It wasn't Sam alone that she was attracted to—after all, he was just a man, like any other—it was his vibrancy and what he represented. He was like the animals and the outdoors all rolled into one—full of heat, beauty, health, strength…and life.

She had begun to awaken in this place. She found small bits of joy in simple things, like the feel of soft earth under her feet, the steam from hot coffee curling from her cup into the chill mountain air, the subtle vibration of stomping hooves that traveled through the ground to her toes, and even her fast-blossoming friendship with the Jenkses. She delighted in using her body, sore as it was, and felt pride for each new chore mastered and task accomplished.

Sam was wrapped up in all that. As she came alive again, it was only natural that she'd be attracted to those things and people who represented her reemergence into the land of the living. If she and Sam did see this crazy attraction through, maybe she'd awaken even further. Maybe she wouldn't just transform from black and white to sepia, she'd emerge in full color, rich and alive.

Caroline stuffed the rest of Sam's shirts and their smells into the washer, added soap, and slammed the lid shut. She pushed start and nodded once.

She wove through the rambling house to find her new babysitters—Will and Ruby. She smiled. The couple had been careful to occupy her time in the evenings, not that she minded. She enjoyed their company and already valued the quality family time, as she'd come to think of it. She wondered if Sam would mess up the nightly ritual when he returned.

Truth was that he already disturbed her peace of mind. Her thoughts spun round and round like the spin cycle on the washer, returning to him far too regularly. The good news was that after tonight's revelation, she felt far more at ease over this crazy pull toward Sam.

13

S am braked for the single red light in Hopewell when he spotted Caroline. She walked away from her little Honda across a parking lot. Silky material printed in bright flowers hugged her rear then flared out to swish well above the backs of her knees. Her hips swayed in a sexy cadence that seemed to match the beat of the old Travis Tritt song blaring from his speakers. *Here comes T-R-O-U-B-L-E.*

Sam gulped as he raked his eyes over the rest of her form. Dammit. Hadn't the days he'd been gone helped him shake her loose at all?

Rather than the ponytail she usually wore, her hair hung loose, directing his eye down her back to her hot-pink bra strap. Yes, her bra was visible beneath a sleeveless, see-through magenta blouse. Trouble, indeed. The second the light flipped to green, Sam cut a hard right from the left lane. He whipped the truck into a parking spot and killed the engine, the strains of the honky-tonk stopping abruptly.

Caroline fluffed her hair and straightened her skirt on the threshold of Moe's Department Store. The place wasn't exactly a mecca of fashion. He doubted she could get another pair of those backless sneakers. Still, Sam swore, they surely had the items she seemed attracted to, the revealing, tight, sexy stuff…

Who knew what she'd purchase in there. He jerked open his door and stepped out of the truck. Shoot. If he had any hopes of getting through a workday without further incident, he had to be sure she purchased clothing with coverage.

Sam pushed through the double glass doors and scanned the space. Moe's wasn't all that large as far as department stores went, but the retailer supplied clothes for everyone within a fifty-mile radius. Sam walked around handbags and jewelry toward the back of the store, where socks and hats led to men's clothing.

He headed for the women's section via the single elevator. Three floors up. The building was narrow, but tall, as close as Hopewell had ever come to a skyscraper. The bell dinged. Sam held his breath and waited for the doors, slower even than the ride, to slide open. Clothing racks and mannequins. No hot pink or flowers smoothed over lush curves and soft skin. Sam stepped out, boot heels clacking on marble, and found Caroline perpendicular to him, deep in the racks, her head bent.

Her thick chestnut hair already sported a few streaks of blond, evidence that she'd spent plenty of time in the sun while Sam was holed up in the fluorescent glow of the hospital.

She looked up expectantly. Faced not with a salesperson, but instead with Sam, she dropped the item she'd been inspecting like a hot coal and snatched her hand to her side. Her cheeks suffused with color. Sam looked at the lingerie rack she'd been touching and felt his body heat as well.

Lord help him.

He cleared his throat. "Uh, hi."

"Hi." Caroline tucked her hair behind one ear. "What are you doing here?"

"Shopping."

"For women's lingerie?" She relaxed, and her lips curved into a delightful smile.

"No, I saw you come in and followed. Thought I'd say hello." He wasn't sure he could stand around joking with Caroline. Not here, surrounded by female lacies. Caroline's own bright pink bra drew his attention, its delicate edges beckoning to his fingertips.

Sam reached for the collar of his shirt, aiming to loosen it, but dropped his hand halfway. He might as well shout his physical reaction through a bullhorn. Besides, his overshirt wasn't even buttoned.

"What are you doing here?" he asked.

"Shopping," she said, and grinned.

"What for?"

Caroline bit her lip and cocked her head as if she were considering. Then she bent and picked up what she'd dropped. She draped it over her front—damned if it wasn't a black teddy, low cut in front, dangerously dipped in back, and every bit as sheer as the blouse she was wearing. A flower-shaped cutout between the breasts zeroed in on her cleavage.

Sam groaned out loud. He couldn't help himself.

"You asked." She grinned—apparently delighted at his discomfort.

He grabbed the hanger with its weightless item out of her hand, threw it in the center of the rounder, and pulled her into the aisle.

Her laugh floated over his shoulder as he marched to the elevator. Her shoes flapped double time to the hard clunks of his heels.

Sam jammed the button. Releasing Caroline's arm, he faced her sparkling eyes and forced words between clenched teeth. "You need practical clothes."

"Is that so?" she asked, as the elevator doors slid open.

"Yes." He motioned her through the metal frame. As she waltzed in, his eyes fell to her sweet rear end.

He plastered his own ass to the wall farthest from Caroline, who stood in the middle of the small space. Not nearly far enough away.

Caroline tilted her head. "You don't like my clothes?"

The elevator doors slid shut. Sam gulped. He'd been aiming for the men's shirts downstairs. He hadn't considered the private quarters of the elevator.

"They're inappropriate, that's all."

She bit her lip. God, he hated—loved—when she did that. He didn't know what it meant—was she unsure? Debating? Trying not to laugh? He only knew what it did to him. Plump lips being squeezed by her white teeth.

He couldn't look away.

The bell dinged and the doors slid open slow as molasses. No one was there. Caroline turned and began to step out.

"Wrong floor," Sam said, but she was still in motion. He lunged to grab her arm. Only he yanked too hard—or maybe the floor was too slippery—because her feet went out from under her as she spun back around.

He still had a hold of her arm and yanked her up.

He held her in a dancer's dip—bent over his arm. Her eyes were wide, her mouth parted in surprise, her breasts so close to his mouth. He pulled her up—but it only served to press her flush against his him.

They were both breathing hard. She stared at him for a long moment. Then, slowly—cautiously—she rose on tiptoes. Again she paused, then finally she leaned in and brushed her lips softly over his. She pulled back, waiting.

Sam froze, his arm still clamped around her, his legs almost straddling hers.

She dropped her gaze to his lips. A moment, two, then she leaned in, again, but this time she licked the underside of his upper lip.

That was it—he combusted. He grabbed Caroline's bottom with both hands, yanked her up, flush and hard against him, and attacked her open mouth in a searing kiss.

She raked her fingers through his hair, and then pulled his head even harder toward her. She tasted him as fervently as he inhaled her.

Sam spun them to push her up against the metal wall, and pinned her lower half with his, freeing his hands to press her breasts upward, his thumbs automatically searching out her nipples.

She moaned, a guttural, instinctive noise that made him grind his erection into her. Sam kissed her, hard and fast, then tore his mouth away to attend to her breasts.

"Caro—"

Good Christ, but he wanted to taste her everywhere at once. Sam nipped at her with his teeth, right over her sheer blouse and delicate bra. He slid his palms along her bare thighs, bunching up her short skirt. One hand squeezed her sweet tush; the other traced along the edge of her panties.

"Sam," she said.

He slipped his finger under silk fabric, into silkier folds, and his thumb into her hot button.

"Caro—"

She jerked against his hand and pulled his mouth back to hers. He didn't have words anyway—all he could think was *pure heaven.*

Sam groaned into her, both with desire and frustration. If only—

Ding.

Sam raised his head, trying to reconcile the noise, but his mind remained focused on Caroline. Swollen lips, flushed cheeks, mussed hair. And where his hand still lingered, wet heat.

When had he started thinking of her as Caro? The minute she licked him, exploding his restraint into frenzied, desperate action. Caro. The nickname suited her far better than the formal Caroline. But holy shit—they were in an elevator.

Sam slid his finger out of her heat, and her lashes fluttered open, unveiling her own deep wells of desire. He held her gaze but pulled away to help her to stand and right her skirt.

Caroline's gaze locked on something behind him. She bit her lip—that lip again.

"Sam Black," came a shaky voice, "will you never learn?"

Sam cringed and swore under his breath. He dared a look over his shoulder.

Mrs. Bandemeyer shook her head, her old-lady hat slipping slightly on her nest of gray hair as she clucked her tongue.

"Ma'am. Excuse us." Sam nodded and bolted out of the elevator, dragging Caroline along behind him—though he could feel that she had a hold of his shirt. She laughed.

Sam tugged her deep into men's shirts.

"What? No introductions?"

"Hell no. She'd have the scene printed up on posters and hung all over town before the sun sets." He rolled his eyes. "The less fodder that woman has, the better."

His pulse hadn't yet slowed from the intense desire he'd felt for Caroline in the elevator, but Mrs. B had cleared his head instantaneously.

Caroline dropped her hold on his shirttail, and Sam reached for her hand. He stroked the back of it with his thumb, partly to soften his next words, partly because he was reluctant to let her go. He had to, though.

"We can't do this." He squeezed her hand, then dropped it.

Her face fell. His heart panged.

"You work for me. Employer/employee trysts are completely unacceptable."

"Yes, but—"

"No." He shook his head. "What just happened—it can't happen again. End of story."

Caroline opened her mouth, then shut it. She twisted a tassel on her purse around her finger then let it be. She looked him in the eye. No smile, no flirting. "Couldn't we just keep it quiet?"

"Something like this would never stay under wraps."

She held his gaze, searching for something—he had no idea what. Finally, she nodded.

Then she bent over slightly, reached under her shirt, and slid a finger around the underside of each bra cup. She shimmied and pushed up her breasts with both hands.

Hot need rushed him. "For God's sakes!"

"Well, you got me all out of whack in there." She smoothed her sheer shirt over her perfect breasts as she straightened. Damp circles stood out prominently where his mouth had found such pleasure only moments before.

Sam shut his eyes for a second. "Listen, Hopewell is not the beach or a cosmopolitan city. Hell, it barely registers on the map. You've got to stop acting so outlandish, doing these things."

"What things?"

"What things?" He lowered his voice to a rumble and ticked items off his fingers. "Wearing see-through clothes that show off your underthings, kissing men in elevators, touching your breasts in public."

Caroline beamed.

"What?" he scowled.

"This is the most fun I've ever had." Her eyes actually twinkled.

Sam groaned and bit down hard. He'd count himself lucky if he didn't grind his teeth into sand before they finished this conversation.

He surveyed the racks of men's dungarees and coveralls. There, one rack over, flannel shirts. Thick, baggy plaid shirts that would reach all the way to Caroline's knees. Sam thrust a few into her arms.

"What's this for?"

"Clothes." Duh.

"You really were shopping," she said.

Sam blew out a hard breath. "They're for you—to cover you up."

She burst out laughing. "Oh, Sam. I knew you cared."

"Caroline, you cannot work the ranch in floppy shoes, shirts that show your navel, or"—he looked heavenward—"lingerie."

"Why not?"

"Because it's not safe."

She grinned. "For whom?"

"I'm warning you."

"Oh, all right," she said. "I'll try to tamp it down a little."

"Start with those shirts," Sam said.

"No way."

He glared at her.

"*Women's* clothing."

He rubbed a hand over his eyes. "Only if I can help you choose."

Caroline raised her eyebrows. "Lingerie?"

"Snowsuits," he growled. "Come on."

14

Over an hour later, shopping completed, Sam and Caroline decided to catch a bite before driving home. As they entered the Watering Hole Tavern, Sam asked, "Bar or table?"

"I'm freezing. Let's sit near the wood stove," Caroline said.

They sat close, catty-corner to the room, the wood burner in the corner. Caroline smiled at the mustached bartender—C.J., Sam had called him—who stood front and center under the moose head and tipped his hat.

Only a week had passed since she'd dined here the first time, but she felt like a completely different woman.

Sam looked different, too. He pushed back his chair to stretch his legs, tipped up his hat, which he'd retrieved when they moved their cars, and rested his hands across his chest. He seemed to think he'd established a boundary, both with the table planted between them and his earlier words, but Caroline was sure that the crazy attraction that sizzled between them would flare up again.

"So tell me about this party Ruby and Will keep talking about," Caroline said.

"It's an annual end-of-season bash," Sam explained, "in honor of our employees and those on neighboring spreads. Black Hills hosts but everybody pitches in, except the seasonal help—they're not allowed to lift a finger."

"Why do you host?"

Sam smiled. "Partly because we're the biggest, partly because Will flatly refuses to give up control over the food."

"Ah." Caroline frowned. "I'm not a seasonal worker, am I?"

"Nope. Since you live on the premises, you're expected to work the party."

"So you're no longer on the proverbial fence as to whether you're firing me?"

Sam laughed. *Wow.* He looked good with his lips curved up instead of down over strong white teeth.

"Depends," he said. "You forget I haven't been home yet."

"I assure you the horses are happier running wild."

Sam's grin stretched a bit further. She ached to kiss those lips again, taste him. What a rush the elevator encounter had been—and yet it wasn't nearly enough.

"Sam," said the waitress, the same cryptic server Caroline had spoken with during her first visit. She hadn't noticed her approach.

"Darlene." Sam rose and kissed her on the cheek, then performed introductions.

"I see you made it to Black Hills," Darlene said.

"Just followed directions," Caroline replied. The woman's lip twitched upward.

Sam ordered the ribeye. She chose a smaller strip steak but added onion soup. She'd enjoyed the thin broth before, plus, as the temperature dropped outside, she realized she'd forgotten a sweater.

She'd intended to buy a heavy jacket, long, durable pants, thick shirts, cozy PJs, and, of course, practical boots today. With Sam along pushing for baggy fleece from head to toe, she'd decided she needed some non-practical items as well. Oh, she'd succumbed to his pressure and her nearly constant goosebumps, but she'd snuck in the teddy and insisted on some sheer silk long underwear, along with the thick printed ones Sam had chosen. Sam's eyeballs had bulged some at that.

"Ruby and Will told me what happened to Carter. How is he?"

"He's out of the woods in terms of all the blood he lost," Sam said. "He really is going to be all right. Physically, at least. The broken bones and torn muscles will heal. He should be able to walk, to run, to ride just fine, eventually."

Sam slugged some beer. Caroline sensed there was more to come, and not all of it such good news.

"The real concern is his face and neck. Those bear claws swiped deep." Sam shuddered. "He's had surgery, may need more. The doctors are optimistic, but it's bad, so what does that mean? I don't know."

Sam's features were tight, his eyes shuttered. Carter was a handsome man. Caroline had seen him in several framed photographs throughout the lodge. Blond, good-looking, and, according to Ruby, a real charmer with the ladies. Sam, Caroline supposed, could relate. How would a major stud deal with the loss of his looks and maybe some of his physicality too?

"I'm so sorry, Sam."

"Thanks."

"Ruby says he's strong and confident, that this won't keep him down for long."

Sam's brows drew together. "Normally, I'd have said the same thing. After seeing him in that hospital bed, though…" He fingered the damp wrapper on his longneck bottle. "I cracked a joke. Something about 'No wonder you're still lying here; the doctors and nurses don't give you a second to rest.' And Carter said, 'A conspiracy, how the hospital stays in business.'" Sam's face was grim as he glanced up at Caroline. "The words were in character, but the joke never reached his eyes."

"I know what that's like," Caroline said. She'd been much the same when Kevin died, and for most of the time since. When she had to engage, she'd pretend, saying the right things because it was expected, but she was pretty much dead inside. She asked, "You two are close, huh?"

Sam smiled, looking younger and lighter at once. "We sliced ourselves with an arrowhead at age eight." Sam laid his arm across the table, opening his palm to Caroline. "Sworn blood brothers."

She traced a scar from the base of his middle finger right off his large palm. "A little overzealous, weren't you?"

"The stone cut differently than the pocket knives we were used to." Sam grinned, just like a naughty boy. "That, and infection set in. I hid it from my mother." He pulled his hand away just as Caroline's steaming crock of soup arrived.

"Actually," he continued after he'd smothered his salad in blue cheese dressing, "I'm closer to Carter than my real brother."

"Where is your brother?"

"He prefers a solitary life."

"And how did Carter come into the picture?" Caroline asked.

"We unofficially adopted him. Years ago, we ran cattle—this was before we started taking guests—and therefore needed more manpower. His father was a seasonal hire who normally had his kid in tow. Always ended up disappearing drunk. My dad despised the guy but kept him on for Carter's sake." Sam stabbed a tomato. "One year he didn't return for his son after a cattle drive, so Carter just stayed."

"Wow."

"Yeah, once Carter realized he was gone for good, he never looked back. Besides, my mother dotes on him far more than the rest of us." Sam smiled, and Caroline could tell how fond and proud he was of his mother.

Sam ordered another beer, but Caroline declined. Just talking with this handsome cowboy in the flickering golden glow made her head feel light.

"I'd like to hear about your mother, too," Caroline said, realizing that she wanted to know all about Sam Black. She wanted to keep him talking. She didn't want all this wonderfulness—from the hot and heavy to laughter to hearing his stories—to end.

Their main courses arrived amid piles of French fries. Caroline bit into a crispy fry and promptly lost her train of thought. She grabbed her knife and fork and dug in.

"Mmm," Caroline said, licking her lips, "this tastes

amazing." Her appetite had returned with gusto since she'd arrived at the ranch.

She paused mid-bite when she felt Sam's eyes on her. "I'm starved." She shrugged, then popped the morsel in her mouth.

He grinned, and Caroline smiled back as she chewed.

A shadow crossed his face. Abruptly, Sam looked down as his plate.

Caroline watched him avoiding her, and thought, no way. Not again.

"How's yours?"

"Great," he replied, bent over the table.

"Fix me a bite," she said, lowering her voice a little. "I want to taste you…"

Sam's head snapped up.

"Your steak." She was satisfied. She'd gotten his attention.

Sam cocked his head to the side, gauging her, she thought.

Then he sliced slowly through a juicy hunk of ribeye, speared it, and reached across the table to offer Caroline a bite. His fork hovered before her mouth.

"Mine's better."

She raised an eyebrow and opened her mouth. He didn't move it closer, though. She rose out of her chair a bit to lean in. She closed her lips over the meat and slowly slid it off the tines of the fork.

A warm drip hit her chin. Sam's hand still cradled the fork, but his index finger scooped the warm liquid upward. Sam quickly leaned toward his hand, sucking his wet knuckle. Caroline was sure the move had been instinctive, not planned, until he slowly rubbed that finger across his lower lip.

Immediately, she throbbed where she sat.

Caroline nearly groaned when the realization struck her: this man could easily make her explode with pleasure without so much as touching her.

Sam's gaze shifted from her lips to her eyes. His eyes held desire, maybe even promise…

And this time, he didn't look away.

Caroline could barely breathe. She wanted nothing more than to stand before Sam, naked and willing, completely at the mercy of his heady power.

Was she brave enough? Could she take what she so desperately wanted? Live fully and boldly—at least tonight?

"Sam," Caroline said, "I was wondering…"

15

———

S am shook his head and held up his hand to cut
Caroline off. He did *not* want to know what she was
wondering.

Something had shifted while he'd been away. Before,
the attraction between them had been strong and mutual,
but neither of them was actively pursuing it. If anything,
they'd both pushed against it.

But today, she'd flirted with him in Moe's, kissed him
in the elevator, and when he'd told her they couldn't go
there? She'd pretty much suggested they have an affair on
the down-low. And what kind of magic did she wield that
he'd just flirted back?

And since he seemed to have little self-control when it
came to her—*no.*

No, he couldn't know what she was wondering now.

"No more questions about me," Sam said. "Tell me
about you."

She sucked in a deep breath, then she shook her head

—as if clearing it. "There's not much to tell." She avoided looking at him.

"There must be. You're from Miami, right? Do you live right in the city?"

"Yes."

"Do you like it?"

She bit her lip again, and as usual, there was no artifice in it. "For many years I did. It was full of energy, vibrant, and colorful."

"What kind of place do you live in?"

"A condo."

"Alone?"

Caroline cocked her head to the side, considering, before she answered, "Yes."

Sam checked her ring finger, although he already knew it was bare. "What do you do for a living? Besides ranching." He smiled.

She returned the smile for an instant, but then it faltered. "I was a newspaper photographer, but I'm not anymore."

"Why not?"

"You know, I'm really cold," she said. "I'm going to grab some of those new clothes from the car and change." Caroline stood and slung her purse over her shoulder.

"Did you want dessert?" Sam asked.

Caroline turned toward the front door. "Sure." She glanced back over her shoulder. "Maybe we could share."

Innocence or innuendo? He couldn't tell.

Between the fire in the wood stove and the sexual tension that never seemed to ease between them, Caro couldn't possibly be cold. Then again, Sam thought, as he watched her shirt slide across her bra strap and her skirt swish against the backs of her thighs, she was barely dressed.

Oooeee.

He lifted his bottle to his lips. Crisp bubbles tickled the back of his throat, but just like Sam, the liquid had grown warm.

Only a couple of hours ago, he'd gripped that very bottom in his hands, stroked Caro's feminine heat, and kissed the hell out of her sweet mouth. He wasn't sure he'd ever recover.

He stripped off his overshirt and hung it over the back of the chair, but he still felt overheated in his thermal undershirt. He set his beer bottle down with a thud and signaled Darlene.

Whenever Caro touched him, the gesture impersonal or provocative, she set him on fire. Every time she spoke, the tone serious or joking, he found he liked her more.

If only he'd met her somewhere else, he'd have bedded her immediately and satisfied them both with a wild, but brief, fling. Then he'd have tucked her number into his wallet for the next time celibacy had him hightailing it out of the mountains.

Darlene arrived, and Sam ordered coffee and dessert for them both.

Just as well she'd run when he'd begun to pry. He shouldn't want to know more about her. Besides, there would be no point. That slip in the elevator—that was as far as this could go. Worse even than a guest he'd need to dance around for a week, Caro, a woman who seemed to get under his skin with almost no effort whatsoever, was staying on. Instead of a waltz of avoidance, he'd be doing a never-ending polka.

Sam sighed. He was so sick of running from women. Maybe he'd brand some letters into his Stetson: Out of Order. Wouldn't matter. The ladies who came looking for him would ignore that sign, sure as all the others he'd posted over the years.

Sam wished that, just once, a woman would show interest in him, as a man, because she truly liked him, not as a stud to be used for servicing a need. Then again, it was a pointless wish.

A mug of black coffee suddenly appeared before him. Darlene waited for Sam to glance up, then angled her head toward the door.

"She's different, huh?" the waitress asked.

Sam shrugged his shoulders, while his heart lurched. The woman had always been far too intuitive for comfort.

Darlene shook her head and walked away, just as Caro scooted through the door with one of Moe's large, handled paper bags crinkling as she moved.

Caroline stopped at the table.

"Mmm. Coffee." She shivered, goosebumps visible on her arms. "I'll be right back."

Sam slumped back in his seat and breathed a sigh of relief. Soon she'd be warm and covered from neck to toes in shapeless flannel and denim.

Just as soon as he'd relaxed, Darlene's comment resurfaced in his brain. He sat forward, propping his elbows on the table. *Was* Caroline different from all those other women?

She'd asked for him specifically when she arrived. Since then, she'd flirted on occasion. In the elevator, she'd kissed him first. But he'd been the aggressor. Hell, he'd practically ravished her. Which meant he had to discount the subsequent innuendos she'd made this evening. Unlike most women who came looking for him, Caro hadn't cornered or begged him—except, of course, for employment.

She hadn't shown up naked in his cabin or cried wolf in her own. She hadn't left a trail of clothes into the bunkhouse for all the world to see or handcuffed him to the lead pole and dropped the key into the depths her bra. Sam shut his eyes for a second, jaw clenching, as he forced away those awful memories.

He looked up again, his eyes landing on Caro's glass. Pink lipstick curled below the rim. Now that he'd tasted those lush lips, it was so easy to imagine what they'd feel like in other places.

Hell, if he was honest with himself, he'd been insane with need for her long before she first pressed her lips to his.

Did any of that mean she was different?

Sam's gut said yes. His hardened heart said no.

He shook his head. Why did he even bother? Caro could be an angel come to earth and he still wouldn't pursue a relationship. He couldn't. He didn't have room for that.

Caroline appeared next to the table, pulling at the tails of her shirt. She held her arms out and spun in a circle.

Sam swallowed hard. The corduroy overshirt wasn't what he'd hoped. She'd left the thick button-down open, her breasts still prominent under a fitted t-shirt. Although her waist was partially hidden, her rear end was not. Shirt-tails ended just above her delectable ass, revealing heavy khaki that hugged her shape.

"Certainly looks warmer." He reached for his ice water

and gulped. What he really needed was to dump it in his lap.

Caroline sat, pulling her button-down together in the front and reached for her fork.

She licked her spoon free of hot apple cobbler and vanilla ice cream, first the front and then the back, before her eyes rose to Sam's.

If she had set out to torture him, the minx was doing a damn fine job. His hands ached to touch her, and his temperature hovered consistently near the boiling point.

"Perfect choice. Want some?"

"No, thanks. I'll stick with my ice cream." Sam had purposely chosen the same vanilla that came with her cobbler. If he'd had to share, to lift his fork again to her mouth, he'd never be able to stand up from the table without the whole place knowing exactly the effect she had on him.

Her lips slipped over the rim of her coffee cup; her mouth slid every bite slowly off her spoon. Sam tried not to watch, but he was drawn like a kid to candy. No sense of what was good for him, and a memory for rules about as long as a flash of lightning.

Caroline finished every bite and obviously enjoyed it. He'd been pleased to see her scarfing that steak. No dieting remarks or tiny nibbles. Now dessert as well. He could see that Caro's face had filled in somewhat. Had Will's full suppers and rich desserts already begun to fatten her up?

He wished he could inspect every inch of her himself. He'd start just below her earlobe, and take his sweet time reaching first her lips, then her collarbone, then…

Sam laid his hands flat on the table, ready to call the meal quits. He *had* to distance himself from this woman.

Caro chose that moment to run her finger through the remaining cream and cinnamon in her dish. She popped her finger in her mouth and sucked, sliding her finger sensuously out. She shut her eyes.

"Wow, that was good," she said.

Sam jumped up, bumping the table and sloshing water onto the wooden surface. "It's really getting late. You ready?" He'd already paid and left Darlene a generous tip.

Caroline's face fell, but she nodded. Sam grabbed his shirt and moved to her chair, ready to take her arm, escort her quickly to her car. She twisted to pull her purse from the back of the chair. When she bent and reached to retrieve her shopping bag from the floor—stretching her pants even tighter—Sam bolted for the exit, leaving her to follow.

Once crisp cool air filled his lungs and the dark of the night wrapped around him, Sam slowed. He heard Caro behind him, rummaging through her purse.

"Where the hell are my keys?"

By the time they crossed the dimly lit parking lot to their vehicles, she still hadn't produced them. Frowning, she set the shopping bag down on the hood of the car. She removed each item of new clothing, plus the sexy outfit she'd worn earlier. The bag empty, she glanced at Sam with a worried look.

He was just relieved that she hadn't put the bag on the ground and bent over again.

"You don't have to wait. I'm sure I'll find them," Caro said.

One at a time, she removed items from her leather

purse, repeatedly leaning across the hood to dump each one in the clothes bag. Her pants tightened across her rump each time.

Sam's control teetered, ready to crash. All he could picture was a naked Caro, draped over the hood, creamy skin against white metal, his hands pulling her back toward him.

Sweat beaded on his upper lip.

"Let's dump your purse," Sam said, snatching it from her. He turned it upside down. A lipstick tube bounced off metal and rolled to the ground. A pack of cinnamon gum and a bunch of receipts fell out. He shook the bag almost violently.

A few square foil packets, with circles raised in the centers, smacked the hood of the car. Condoms. Sam groaned.

She had to find those keys. Quick.

He had to escape. Now.

"Uh, Sam?" Caro said. Her hands were splayed on a back window as she peered through the glass. "I found them."

Sam glanced in the front window. All four doors locked, and the car keys peeking out from a mess of clothes on the back seat. Sam swore.

"What should we do?" Caroline asked.

"Were there any hangers in that bag?"

Caroline shook her head.

"I'll call the sheriff." Sam strode to his truck for his cell phone, and she followed.

As Sam dialed, Caro put her fingers to her mouth. He was sure she was going to suck them. Thank Frank, she only nibbled nervously at her nails.

"Wade, it's Sam Black. Just fine, although there's a lady, one of my new employees, here at the Hole with her keys locked in the car... Oh, yeah? ... Figures... That long, huh? No, no, thanks, Wade. Yeah, maybe I'll call AAA."

Sam hung up. "They've got the whole force breaking up a barroom brawl. It'll be a few hours."

Sam began to dial another number.

Caro said, "I think my AAA membership has lapsed."

Sam narrowed his eyes. "You drove all the way from Miami with no AAA?"

"I didn't exactly expect to be taking this trip," she muttered.

He turned his back on her, popped open a case attached to the back of his truck, and began rummaging around.

"Damn, nothing in here will do the job either." Sam pushed the lid back down with a firm snap. Looked like he'd be spending another couple of hours in close proximity to Caro—which pleased him far more than it should have.

"You'll have to ride with me, and we'll come back for your car first thing tomorrow."

Caroline checked her watch. "It's already after nine o'clock." She took a deep breath then pointed up the street to the Rodeway Inn. "Why don't we just stay?"

16

———————

Stay overnight—off ranch, no less—with Caroline? Temptation shot heat through Sam, as he stared hard into her face. Guileless expression, but eyes alight with… hope. Sam bit down a curse and punched a button on his phone. He explained the situation to Will, then said, "Rather than drive back down tomorrow, we're figuring we'll just get some rooms."

Will said, "You could just get one room."

"Will," Sam said. He hoped to hell Caroline couldn't hear him.

"Just saying," Will said.

Sam cut Will off, tossed the phone on the seat of the cab, and turned toward Caroline.

Caroline stepped close and placed her hand on his chest between the lapels of his overshirt. Even through thermal, her hand seared his skin. "Will has a good point. And I feel like the universe is telling us something." She looked up at him—those big brown eyes he wanted to drown in. "How about it? One room?"

Sam laughed, a harsh, guttural noise that he knew sounded completely unlike him. He yanked off his hat, trying to get air, despite the fact that they were surrounded by crisp, fresh air.

Here he stood with the most attractive woman he'd ever met. And dumb luck—he refused to deem it fate—was actually in his favor. Perfect timing seeing her on his return trip home, now keys locked in a car, and, best of all, they stood on ground that wasn't his. No responsibilities way down here.

Sam hung his head. Caro had changed into boots, too. When had she bought those? Heavy-duty kickers. Boots made for work. And that was just it. Caro worked for him.

Sam returned his hat to his head and met Caro's eyes. She hadn't backed off. The hand that she'd rested on his chest slid south, stopping just shy of his belt.

"Sam," Caro whispered. She licked her lips. "I'm serious. Share my room, my bed, tonight. Just tonight. If you want, tomorrow—we go back to a working relationship."

The idea of spending the night skin to skin with her was—

Hell, the swell of his erection spoke to him as loud as thunder, drowning out his will to resist.

"You have no idea what you ask."

"I know exactly what I'm asking for." Her voice got stronger as she talked. "Sex, Sam. Hard, fast, hot, and wild." Her gaze was more direct, more compelling—like she was gaining confidence as she went. "Nothing more, nothing less."

He was already completely mad for her. If she kept talking like that, he'd be taking her right here in the parking lot.

Sam shut his eyes, attempting to tame the fire that surged through his veins. "Caro—"

Her fingers against his lips stopped him. He dared to open his eyes again, and immediately encountered her heated, yet deadly serious, gaze.

"Shh," she whispered, her breath fanning over his lips. An image exploded on his brain—the same cinnamon and honey warmth wrapping around the pulsing length of his penis. He had to have her. Sam nearly groaned.

"I know you're my boss, and that's a problem for you, but this thing, this feverish heat between us…it's crazy intense. We're going to have to tame it sooner or later. And I'd rather it be now. Here, where no one other than us has to know."

Sam looked past Caro, over her shoulder, trying to think, to gain control over his body and his mind. The neon light of the Rodeway Inn glowed, beckoned.

"I would hope you know that I would never tell anybody," Caro said, disrupting his thoughts. "In case that's what's worrying you."

Swirling wind chose that moment to lift the ends of her hair, blowing it around her face. A thick strand stuck to his flannel shirt. Sam looked down, the brim of his hat nearly resting on the top of her head. Sam lifted the lock of silky hair and rubbed it between his rough fingers, imagining the dark softness, spun now with gold, teasing him where he was most sensitive, while her mouth drove him insane.

Sam twisted a thick hank of hair around his forefinger, met her eyes, and tugged. Hard. Hard enough to pull Caro flush against him, right where his traitorous body wanted her. Brown eyes, also flecked delicately with gold, flared. She slid her hands along his sides to caress his back, while her breasts pressed against his front. His back and chest muscles clenched—hell, his whole body was strung tight as could be.

Desire shone so fiercely in her eyes that he could have been looking at a reflection of himself.

He forced himself to speak. "You realize I'd be setting myself up for sexual harassment, and God knows what else."

"You really think I'd pull something like that? You—" She tried to wrench herself away, but stopped abruptly. Sam held her hair fast.

"Hold on." He clamped his other arm around her waist. "Some things just have to be said, that's all. It'd be your pretty word against mine, and I'd deny it till the day I died."

Disgust crossed Caro's face, and she shook her head as well as she was able. She glanced at her car, and then out at the road.

"I do believe you, though," he said. For reasons he couldn't sort out, he actually did believe she wouldn't kiss and tell.

She nodded solemnly and seemed to search his eyes.

Irrationally, he found himself willing to take a chance on her. For an opportunity to put the pure physical torture he'd been feeling to rest. And for one night that he knew would be so memorable that he'd savor it forever.

If they did this his way, he could honor his vow to himself *and* ensure no one would know.

"We'd have to go a ways to get to a place where nobody would see us," Sam said.

Caro's gaze snapped back to his. "How far?"

"Under an hour. I've got a place in mind."

She inclined her head but looked past him.

Sam wanted—even needed—those eyes on him, hot, ready, and connected like they'd been only moments before.

"I have some terms." That got her attention. "One night only."

Caro's eyes shadowed for a split second, then flamed.

Sam waited.

He needed assurance that this thing between them could be tamed, that tomorrow he'd be in safe territory. He used his knuckles, wrapped partly in silk the color of rich earth, to gently trace her jaw line.

Caroline nodded. "What else?" she asked, and nipped at his fingers with her lips. His blood pounded at the small gesture, at the larger implication.

"We don't sleep. Not a wink."

17

Sam had driven not to another town, but farther into
the hills. Caroline hadn't asked, hadn't spoken. She
didn't want to break the spell, choosing to watch the trunks
of the pines slipping past her window against a dark blur
of evergreen. She pushed thoughts of Kevin away. She was
far enough from home and so far outside of her normal
world that her past felt like another life entirely. She gathered nervous desire to her, building it up inside, letting
anticipation percolate into a steaming pot of need.

Finally, the truck came to a stop, its headlights
beaming on a run-down cabin. If they had the kind of sex
she hoped they were going to have, she wasn't sure the
rickety shack would still be standing around them in the
morning. She raised an eyebrow at Sam.

"It's private." He shrugged, with a cockeyed grin.

Sam stepped out of the truck. By the time she'd gathered a big, deep breath and her courage, he'd opened her
door and helped her down, his hands tightening on her hips
before he turned away.

Caroline followed him to the door. The lock, a wooden slat, was on the outside of the structure, so Sam lifted it and went right in. The cabin was darker inside than out, so the roof must be sound, Caroline thought. Sam found matches, an old oil lamp, and a few thick candles from a rough shelf over the sink. There was a small wood-burning stove in one corner, and Caroline prayed it worked. She knew Sam would warm her under the covers, but she wasn't planning on snuggling. What she had in mind was — Wait—where were the covers?

The bed—if you could even call it that—was nothing more than two cots, wooden and rough-hewn, pushed together and topped with a loose plastic sheet.

Caroline shivered. She'd taken the tags off her new, insulated barn jacket on the ride up and wore it already, but still the night air bothered her. If she and Sam even managed to get their temperature up in this icy cabin, their sweat would pool around them on that plastic. And if they panted in the wrong direction, the cobwebs dangling over it would fall and smother them.

She caught Sam's eye, and he smiled.

He grabbed an old broom from the far corner and swiped at the cobweb she'd been studying. He ignored the others, however—maybe he was in a bit of a hurry.

Caroline had planned on attacking Sam with her lips and hands the minute the door was open. She had imagined them being so mad for each other that they couldn't wait. She wouldn't have thought she'd even notice her surroundings, but Sam was busy setting up house.

He moved with the same strong fluidity here as he did in the barn or the paddock. So sexy.

Sam opened what looked like a broom cupboard.

Inside were fresh sheets, comforters, quilts, pillows, and a jumbo box of condoms.

Sam grinned and opened his arms wide, as if to display his wares. "The high school kids are still at it."

"And I thought you were the one stocking the place," Caroline said.

Sam unfolded an air mattress over the bed and hooked up a battery-operated pump. Her heart seemed to pound as loud and fast as that motor, so she stepped outside to wait.

Caroline leaned against the front end of the still-toasty truck. All of a sudden she didn't need the extra heat. Her goosebumps vanished and her skin warmed thoroughly, just from thinking about a whole night of unadulterated sex with Sam Black. Stud extraordinaire. A man with that kind of reputation—

Caroline jumped at the snap of the sheets. Sam was making their bed. She looked up at the stars above and sent a mental message off to the universe. *I have no idea what I'm getting into, but here goes.*

Sam stepped through the door. He paused there, where he was silhouetted by the glow from inside, his face a blank to her. She didn't want a blank—she wanted Sam.

He moved slowly, advancing to a few feet in front of her. His blue eyes were intense under forbidding dark brows, his face taut, his posture tight, but he reached out, slowly, and waited patiently for her hand.

Caroline met his gaze. This was Sam. A good and handsome man she'd come to enjoy being around in a very short period of time. She wanted him more than she would have believed possible—and there was nothing wrong with that.

Caroline placed her hand into his, and everything else

slipped away.

The minute Sam shut the door behind them, he pulled Caroline against him. And then his hands were in her hair, his lips devouring hers. Caroline's knees nearly buckled in response to the onslaught.

Sam's warm hands slid down her neck and into her coat. He had slipped it off her in seconds, yet his mouth never left hers. He stroked across her collarbones and down her sides, his thumbs just barely brushing her breasts. He dug his hands under her layers, searching for skin, finding only corduroy and cotton. He groaned, and Caroline smiled into his lips at his frustration. Because she was cold, she'd worn the silk long underwear under her t-shirt.

When Sam yanked up all three layers and finally reached the taut, soft skin of her belly, Caroline moaned, her hands automatically seeking his body in return. His fingers slid toward her breasts, and Caroline whimpered. Her body reacted to Sam's every move instinctively, and she knew then, with only a kiss and a touch, that she was in for the best sex of her life.

"Shirt," she murmured into his mouth. He understood and stepped back, just enough, to slip his soft button-down off his shoulders.

"Thermal," she said next, when he began to return to her. This time, he was forced to remove his lips to pull his shirt over his head. All the while, he held her eyes.

"Better?"

Caroline tore her gaze from his face to his chest. His skin glowed in the light from the candles and stove, and dark hair led her eyes straight to the button on his jeans—under which there was a distinctive bulge.

"Much," she said, moving to run her hands along the hard muscles of his chest. He was a big man, larger somehow without clothes. Almost intimidating. Caroline considered herself tall at five feet, ten inches; not many men seemed overbearing compared to that. Yet he felt perfect under her roaming hands, and she definitely felt safe.

"Not so fast," Sam said, removing her palms and lifting them over her head. He slid his hands slowly down the length of her arms, again past her breasts, down her sides, and lifted the hem of her partially buttoned shirt right over her head, past her outstretched hands. His height allowed her to keep her arms locked, straight overhead, breasts pressed forward. She remained in this position, telling him in no uncertain terms to release her from all her clothing.

Sam repeated the action. Cotton tee, over her head, past her hands, gone. Sheer silk long underwear, gone. Caroline began to lower her arms, but Sam shook his head, putting them back in place over her head.

His gaze lowered to her chest, only her bra left. Never had such a small piece of clothing felt so restraining. Sam took his sweet time, teasing each nipple through the scant fabric until she began to sway. And then, when Caroline wasn't sure she could take any more, up and over went her bra. Her breasts spilled forward, and Sam's roughened palms caressed every bit of her skin all the way to her fingertips.

He reached up and wrapped a hand around her wrists, her bra caught between them, as he lowered her arms in front of her. Caroline's wrists remained imprisoned in his fist and her silk undergarment, while the index finger of

Sam's other hand touched the hollow beneath her ear and traveled down, tracing, tracing nonsense patterns that caused her skin to erupt in goosebumps. Finally, he took one nipple with his tongue, torturously circling it until she fought to get her hands free.

Sam would not release her, however, but gave her more, sucking and nipping. Caroline's shoulder blades made contact with the planks of the door. The contrast between the chilly, rough wood and Sam's warm, soft mouth caused a delicious shudder to rip through her. Sam switched to the other breast, and Caroline's moment of relief built instantly to pressing need. She began to writhe against the door, but Sam pulled her against him and spun her toward the freshly made bed.

With her hands finally free, Caroline was mad to touch him, her hands sliding over everything she could reach. She barely noticed that Sam was skimming her khakis and long underwear bottoms down, until he caressed bare bottom and groaned into her mouth.

She hadn't wanted to change into the new panties she'd bought until they were washed, so she was still wearing her thong. "You like?"

Sam didn't speak, just took her mouth more fiercely, his tongue diving over hers in an urgent dance. He pulled her thong from behind until it created pressure on the center of her desire. Caroline nearly climbed up him, but he pushed her away, lowering her to the bed, tracing the tiny patch of pink lace at the juncture of her thighs with his fingers. *Now*, she was glad Neve had packed for her.

Caroline still reached for Sam, but he moved to her feet, wrapping a strong hand around her ankle as he pulled off first boots, then her brand-new, thick socks, and finally her pants that were now bunched up with the long underwear. He dumped them all unceremoniously on the floor.

"Never seen so many layers."

"I've been freezing ever since I arrived."

Sam's eyes jerked to her face. "Are you cold now?"

"I'm far too hot for you, to be cold now." Why not put it all right out on the table? She wanted him. Plain and simple.

Sam's eyes smoldered. He immediately set to work unbuttoning his jeans, his eyes roaming over her body. Caroline felt his gaze as if it seared her, but lowered her eyes to watch his hands.

His jeans came down, navy boxer briefs with them, in one quick thrust. He immediately bent to pull off his boots and bunched clothes. Caroline saw the play of lean muscle over his shoulders, the flex of his thighs. He was cut. Every muscle in bas-relief. The hard, lean lines of a man who used his body all day, every day. He blew away those exhibitionist meatheads she saw so often strutting along the beach.

When he stood up, Caroline's breath caught in her chest at his length jutting forth from a nest of dark curls. He was oversized there, too. Not to mention hard, proud, and utterly glorious.

Sam chuckled. Caroline wondered if she'd been drooling.

She smiled up at him. "Come here."

He grinned. "Yes, ma'am."

He leaned over her, his hands braced on either side of Caroline's head, one knee beside her hip, his lips inches from hers. Caroline held her breath, waiting. Sam stared hard into her eyes. She saw his pupils dilate, his irises still that churning sea. Watching his desire affect his physicality was an aphrodisiac of the highest order.

And then Sam's mouth was on hers, his body stretched above her, her hips rising to feel him against her, where she wanted him most. Sam gave her his whole weight, and she wrapped her legs around him, aching for far more. Sam shifted to lie beside her and pulled her to him, smoothing his hands down her back. He looped his fingers through the strings of her panties again, pulling them up until she writhed from the delicious tease, then skimming them down past her knees. She worked it off with her feet, while Sam tore his mouth from hers and devoured her breasts.

Caroline stroked and teased his cock with her fingers, flicking the ledge of the soft tip, circling an escaped bead of moisture, wrapping her hand hard around him for long, slow strokes. Sam stopped kissing her breasts, resting his forehead against her skin, his breath puffing against her sternum. Caroline could see that every muscle in his back was straining as he fought to hold it together against the attention she lavished on him.

Caroline wriggled beneath him, trying to scoot down to reach him with her lips.

"I want to taste you," she murmured into Sam's hair.

He raised his head. Caroline could tell he liked that idea, but he said, "Me first."

He trailed kisses along her neck, between her breasts, and along the lines of Caroline's ribs. His hands spanned her waist as he pushed her flat. The kisses he gave her belly and the curve of her waist made her stomach muscles clench. Sam nipped her hipbone with his teeth, and then sat back on his heels.

One look from him, and she opened her legs, knowing implicitly what he wanted. Sam stared, seemingly devouring every detail. Caroline's whole body hummed with anticipation that neared desperation, as she watched him ever so slowly reach out and, with one finger, trace her from front to back. He repeated the movement numerous times, until finally, he slid inside her. He bent his finger, putting delicious pressure on a spot she hadn't thought about in a long, long time.

She groaned, and her knees lifted of their own accord. Sam bent down. His tongue flicked her hard nub while his fingers worked their own magic. As soon as Caroline cried out his name, he withdrew.

"Oh no you don't," Sam said, kissing her tenderly along her jaw line.

Caroline moaned. Her core beat with frustration, but she knew in the recesses of her mind that she wanted to feel this man inside her far more that she wanted release for herself.

"Please, Sam," she said.

"Please what?"

"Please stop torturing me." Caroline smiled and looked at him directly. "Please put that condom on fast, and enter me hard, because…" Sam was already complying, tearing at the foil square. "I need you. Now."

Sam growled and rubbed the tip of his shaft along her, slicking the condom with her juice, stopping finally at the indentation that would lead him to her very core.

She quivered with need as she stroked down Sam's back to his tight buttocks.

"Make me yours tonight, inside and out." She pulled him into her. She wanted it all. Now.

As her body accommodated his length and breadth, she thrilled with satisfaction. But he stopped once he was seated. "Sam, please," she said. She raised her eyes to his and saw the challenge there. "Move now." She let all the need she felt show in her voice.

He pulled almost out, holding her gaze.

"Stroke me."

He slid in, so slowly, and out, pausing just as he was about to leave her.

"More."

Again, he moved. In, then out. And stopped.

"Harder."

Again.

Caroline held his eyes. "Faster."

They recreated the hotter-than-hot episode in the barn, but this time, the roles were reversed. He wanted her words, her voice, to direct his actions. This time, face to face, she was in charge, telling him exactly what she needed—so they'd both get what they so feverishly desired.

"Longer strokes," she urged him.

Still, he stopped between every order, driving her mad. Soon she wouldn't be able to form coherent thoughts.

"Sam, I've wanted you since… Please… Sam, oh…"

Sam picked up speed, edging her forward, and nearly pushed her to the brink. But she held on, thrusting with him, matching his rhythm, until his body tensed.

"Yes," she gasped. "Now."

"Caro," Sam called as he lost himself in her.

Her core exploded, and she was beyond words—so much so that she didn't even realize what had happened.

18

"Uh, Sam." Caroline's voice reached Sam through a thick haze. "I'm suddenly lying against something very hard."

Sam abruptly rolled off Caroline, his hipbone landing against wood. Instantly, he realized what had happened and erupted in laughter. Caroline stared at him like he'd lost his mind.

Eventually he managed to choke out, "We—popped—the—bed."

"What?" Caroline asked. She sat up to investigate. "Huh. I'll bet those high school kids never managed that."

Sam burst out laughing again, and Caroline joined him. He loved her laugh. It was so rare that she acted carefree. She lay back and stretched her arms over her head. A wide smile remained on her face.

Sam wiped his eyes, reveling in sharing such a feel-good emotion with her. Not to mention how incredible he felt simply lying naked next to her.

He smoothed his hand over her belly, and her

laughter subsided. Hell, Sam thought, growing serious, entering her had been mind-blowing. Years ago, he'd had women galore, but he couldn't ever remember being inside a woman who'd made him feel like that. Who admired him so frankly, with pools of desire in her eyes, who fit him like a glove, who matched him for every thrust, who told him in no uncertain terms exactly what she wanted.

What had she said? *Make me yours tonight, inside and out.* Sam groaned, that thought making him hard for her all over again. He refused to consider the meaning behind his reaction. Instead, he moved his hand over her hip to cup her left butt cheek.

"Caro," Sam murmured, lifting his eyes to her face, "I need more of you."

She arched her eyebrows, as if to ask, *So soon?* but she rolled against him willingly. Passion flared as they stroked and kissed and moved against one another.

Sam rolled to his back, to spare her the hard wood beneath them, and pulled Caroline astride him. She rose to her knees and leaned forward, taking his tongue inside her mouth as she took his shaft within her body.

Sam encircled her hips with his hands, pulling her hard against him. She bucked, needing to lead him herself, so he slid his hands to her breasts and tugged at her nipples until she rode him as fast and hard as he wanted.

Caroline's hair flowed around her shoulders, her head tilted back in ecstasy, the firelight making her glow. Sam had never seen a woman as beautiful as Caroline. He willed himself to wait, to give her everything she desired and to watch her face through it all. They only had tonight. He had to remember every moment of this.

She rocked faster, arching sensuously, rushing toward the pinnacle.

No longer in control, Sam raced with her. He kept his eyes open, just barely, and on her face. Their orgasms collided, exploded together again, no less intense this time.

———

Caroline was near boneless after round two, and collapsed on top of Sam. Now, her cheek rested against his chest, and she idly spun her fingers in the dark curls there. He smelled of pine and spice, a smell she imagined she would forever associate with strength and passion. She wanted never to move, but finally she roused herself enough to speak.

"I'm getting cold."

"Mmm, I'd like to take care of that myself"—he felt beside him for the blanket—"but I think I'd better see what can be done about this mattress."

Caroline climbed off the bed, wrapping herself in the blanket. Sam pulled on his jeans and then dug under the sheets to inspect the mattress. She got a look at the rough patch, some scar tissue, over his shoulder that she'd felt when she explored him. Had that happened when—

"Looks like we just popped this plastic cap out." Sam pushed the plug back in and turned on the pump, the steady whir competing with the crackle of burning logs in the stove. "Hopefully there are no leaks."

"I suppose there's only one way to find out."

"Darlin', I like the way you think," Sam replied.

Caroline cleared her throat. "So who stocks this place? And who owns it?" she asked, buying time. Although she was ready for Sam physically, her mind had started clambering for a little breathing room. Sex with Sam was even more intense than she'd expected.

Oh, she knew it would be incredible, but she hadn't bargained on feeling so close to him so quickly. Whether they were making love or just laughing together, she felt *connected*. It had been so long since she'd had that. Her past suddenly felt so distant that she worried her memories were in danger of being displaced. That scared the daylights out of her. She needed to put sex—for that was all this was—back in perspective before Sam set her on fire again with his big hands, sensuous lips, and powerful hips.

"This place used to be a hunting cabin," Sam said. He turned and added a log to the wood stove. "But old man Tiller never used it, and now, he's not well. I doubt he even remembers it's here. So the kids stock it themselves, or at least we did in my day. Honor system. Whoever was here last washes the sheets, restocks condoms and shelf-stable snacks, makes sure there's wood outside, or whatever. Brings everything back on his next trip."

"Or her next trip," Caroline teased.

"Or her next trip," Sam said, but he shook his head.

"What?" Caroline asked. "We're a prime example of a woman taking the bull by the horns."

"So we are, but I'm not sure high school girls have had time to garner that kind of confidence."

"Confidence had nothing to do with my offer. I was horny."

Sam laughed. "I'm awfully glad you were."

"Actually," she said, "I've never propositioned a man before."

"No?"

"No, but I'm sure you've got loads of propositions to compare it with. How did I do?"

Sam's brows drew together as he shrugged, effectively dismissing the topic.

He turned his back on Caroline, pushing on the air mattress with his hands. He spread his legs wide and crossed his arms, making his broad, bare back seem even larger. His worn jeans hugged his rear end and emphasized his long legs.

Caroline didn't like the awkward silence that had ensued. If he didn't want to talk about old girlfriends, random hookups, or the millions of offers he must have received over the years, fine. But this was her night, and since he'd insisted there only be one, she refused to allow him to ruin the mood.

"I can't believe none of the parents caught on to kids washing strange sheets all of a sudden."

"Most kids around here are fairly self-sufficient. Besides, there's a self-serve laundromat in town. Open twenty-four hours." He glanced over his shoulder and smiled.

Good, Caroline thought, she was getting somewhere.

"I'm surprised this place isn't jam-packed with bunk beds. Must have been a pretty popular place."

"There was a time when those two wooden cots were separated, and don't forget when a kid's sixteen and grew up sleeping outside on the hard ground half the time anyway…" He turned to face her and shrugged. "You can see just how popular it was if you look at the underside of those cots."

Caroline twisted the blanket she wore in both fists and

squatted down to peer at the wooden structures. Carvings, scratches, and burns marred the old surface and covered nearly every square inch of both beds.

Sam knelt down as well. "They've been busy."

"Are your initials here?"

Sam grinned. "Dumb young men feel the need to brag on the major milestones of life."

"You lost your virginity here?"

"Yep." Sam smiled. "Kim Reese."

Old girlfriends must not be taboo after all. "You were sweet on her." Caroline scrambled into her long underwear, then climbed onto the bed. She adjusted the blanket around her and sat cross-legged against the wall. She felt snug and at ease.

"I was. She was the girl-next-door type. Cute and sweet, and as inexperienced as I was."

Caroline enjoyed Sam's voice, deep and rich, and loved to watch his sexy lips move, especially now that she knew just what chaos they reaped when they slid over her body.

Hard to imagine he was ever inexperienced. "Where is she now?"

"Next door."

"Still interested?" She said it teasingly, but inexplicably, her chest constricted.

"No," he said with a chuckle. "She's married to my neighbor. We all grew up together. They're happy. Already have four kids."

"What about you? How come you're not married with children?" Caroline asked, wanting to know this man.

"Just not in my cards." Sam looked uncomfortable.

"Haven't you ever been in love?"

"Twenty questions, huh?" Sam climbed onto the bed next to her. "Yes, I've been in love."

"And?"

"You don't quit, do you?"

"I think we already established that," she said.

"So we have." Sam smiled, admiration in his eyes.

Caroline's heart beat with pleasure.

"Becca was the sister of the neighbor I just mentioned. She was a year younger than me, only sixteen when we got together. And boy, oh boy, did we get together. We climbed out our windows nearly every night, met in the barn, or on the trail, in empty cabins."

Sam seemed lost in thought, but he continued after a moment.

"She claimed she was a city girl at heart." He smiled and touched Caroline's nose playfully. "Like you. Turned out she was. Soon as she graduated, she took off for New York. Barely said goodbye, and never looked back."

"Ouch."

"Yeah, it hurt. But I got over it eventually."

"How?"

"Lots and lots of women," Sam said. But again, he switched the subject, shivering exaggeratedly. "Some draft in here. How about you sharing that blanket?"

Sam tugged Caroline so that she sat between his legs, her back leaning against his chest, his legs enveloping hers. He wrapped the blanket around them both and slid his arms across Caroline's middle. She could feel his rough jeans and even his crisp chest hair through the sheer fabric she wore.

"So," Sam said, "what about you?"

"My first partner sexually or my first love?" Caroline asked.

"Both." Sam stroked her ribs with his thumbs.

"There's not much to tell. My husband, Kevin, was my first love and my only partner."

Sam's fingers stilled.

She said, "There were plenty of guys I thought I was in love with before him, but after I met Kevin, I knew those had only been crushes."

Caroline waited, but Sam didn't speak. Caroline had worried that she would seem inexperienced to Sam sexually, given that she'd only had one partner, and he'd had so many. But she'd thought she'd done more than fine, thank you very much.

She twisted to look at him. His expression was hard as stone. And his eyes were as empty as they'd been in the barn after she'd reached for him. He looked not at her, but past her toward the wood stove.

She nudged him with her elbow. "What's wrong?"

"You're married."

"Widowed."

Sam shut his eyes for a long moment. When he raised his lids, he looked directly into her eyes. He extracted a hand from the covers and traced her jaw line. "I'm sorry."

"Me too. I didn't mean to…" She faced the cabin again and leaned back against him. "I feel as if I've known you, somehow, for a long time. I didn't even think about the sequence of what I just said—the fact that you would have preferred the outcome first."

Sam slid his hands back around her middle and squeezed her in a tender hug, before he tucked the ends of the blanket under their legs.

They sat quietly for a time, watching the flames dance and flicker.

"He must have been quite a guy, for you to save yourself for him."

He was, but she didn't want to talk about Kevin tonight. "I wasn't purposely saving myself. I just never got anywhere close to losing my virginity before that."

"Why not?"

"Because I was tall, flat-chested, and super awkward. Nowhere near the prettiest girl in school. Let alone the sexiest. I grew up in Miami."

"What's Miami got to do with it?"

Caroline sighed. Did she really have to spell out all her faults? "I was brown-haired and pale. That ranks exactly nowhere when you're competing with dark, sexy Latinas and beachy, tanned blonds."

"You're kidding, right?" Sam chuckled.

"Don't laugh." Caroline swatted his forearm under the blanket.

"You're serious, aren't you?" Sam said, turning her so that he could look into her eyes. "Caro, you are one of the most gorgeous women I've ever seen."

"Well, at least I grew some curves," she said, but the compliment evoked a warm blush.

"You're incredibly beautiful, every inch of you," Sam said as his eyes roamed over her face. "Especially here," he said, then kissed her near her eye. "And here, and here," he murmured as his lips moved along her face.

Caroline shivered and hoped like mad that he meant to kiss every inch of her.

19

They had dozed in the early dawn, temporarily sated after the incredible sex they'd shared. When Sam awoke, with cracks of sunlight slicing through the darkened cabin and Caro's hair streaming across his chest, he felt a few seconds of the most intense joy he'd ever known.

On its heels, an ice-cold pain rushed in to encase his chest. He couldn't keep her. It just wouldn't work for him. No matter how bad he wanted—

No.

While he struggled for calm, Caro smoothed her warm hands over his body, trailing them with her lips. Not wanting her to see the depth of his need or the scope of his pain, which he hadn't had time to sort through, he shut his eyes.

Sam savored each touch of her magical fingers, every press of her lithe body against his, while they made sweet, slow love one last time. Afterward, they lay alongside each other, and he stroked her silky hair, until the dreadful weight he felt became unbearable. Then he extracted himself from her embrace, avoided her eyes and any small talk, and dismantled the physical evidence of their passion piece by piece.

Caro was leaning against the Ford's driver's-side door when he came out. She still watched him, hoping for what, he didn't know. He'd meant it when he said this could last only one night. That night had been exhausted. So, he prayed, had their passion.

Sam stuffed the rumpled sheets into the case behind the cab and pushed down the lid. There were other sets of sheets, plenty of candles, bottles of water, and loads of condoms, so he wouldn't worry about returning these to the cabin right away. Also, he'd tucked a twenty-dollar bill in the cupboard, hoping the kids would be smart and use it for additional prophylactics, and not on alcohol.

He walked past Caro to do one last check inside— mainly to escape her gaze.

Then he threw the wooden bolt on the cabin's door so that bears and other scavengers wouldn't trash the place. "Time to go."

Caro's forehead creased in a quick frown, before she smiled. "One last hurrah, perhaps, before we get in the truck?"

He shook his head, even though his body called for a different answer.

"Sam—"

"It's over."

She flinched but pushed off the truck, opened his door, and slid across to the other side.

Sam hopped in and started the engine. He felt like such an asshole. He couldn't face her.

Apparently she felt much the same, because she stared out the window most of the trip with her fists bunched in her lap and her jaw clenched.

Sam felt the wind buffet the panels of the truck even though the winding dirt road was cut into the mountain and surrounded by dense trees. The sky was gray and forbidding and the temperature had dropped, which seemed fitting.

Caroline was hunched down into her jacket, so Sam upped the heat, aiming the vents toward her once it had warmed. Her body language remained stiff.

He kept his hands locked on the steering wheel, fighting an overwhelming need to reach out for her hand, to ease her disillusionment. He longed to return the playful light to her eyes and a sexy smile to her lips.

She'd been under his skin since the minute he met her —but last night, she'd burrowed deep. The fact that he wanted to put her needs first? Jesus, that terrified him.

Guilt—coming at him from all angles—made acid crawl up his throat. His back and shoulder muscles ached deep.

This was bad. This was really, really bad.

She was an unacceptable distraction. An impossible possibility. And, most of all, dangerous—to all he held dear.

By the time they arrived in Hopewell, his mood was as dark as the clouds. He hated this silence between them, yet there was no point in breaking it. He'd laid out the terms: one night only. She'd agreed. Period. Done. Finished.

Over.

He swung into the tavern's parking lot, empty except for Caro's Honda Fit.

Shoot, he'd nearly forgotten that her keys were locked in her car. Sam hoped the rain would hold off until the sheriff or one of his staff could get them out of the fix. He reached for his cell phone and began to call the station. Caroline grabbed the shopping bag and her purse from the floor and slid out of the car.

"Don't bother," she said over her shoulder, and slammed the door.

Sam watched her stalk to her car. What was she talking about?

He got out, slowly, while dread edged into his mind.

Caroline dropped her bags to the pavement and knelt down by her back tire.

Hell no.

She reached under the car and snapped off a little black box.

His lungs froze as his heart folded in on itself.

She worked the lid off and moved to the driver's door.

His mind was screaming, but his feet felt like lead.

She'd just hit the button to unlock all the doors when Sam finally sprang forward. He grabbed her forearm and wrenched her away from the car.

"You did it on purpose?" He already knew, and yet he desperately wanted her to tell him no.

Her eyes spat fire as she tried to pull away.

"Answer me," he growled.

"You had your *one night*, so what do you care?"

"Because you tricked me."

"It was more like a nudge. I wanted—I needed—" She made a face. "It doesn't matter. You would have gone on forever with your can'ts and shouldn'ts." She waved her free arm wildly.

"That's my right."

She glared. "What's between us needed to be addressed."

"There's *nothing* between us." Sam dropped her arm, suddenly loath to even touch her.

"Oh, you've had so many women that the phenomenal night we just shared was nothing out of the ordinary, is that right?" Caroline asked.

Lying, rotten, fake, two-faced…

Sam's stomach twisted with the sourness that tasted exactly like betrayal. "You're just like all the others."

He stalked to his car, slammed the door, and took off with a squeal of tires. She could get home safely on her own.

Home, hell. Black Hills was *his* home, not hers. She'd deceived him, used him. Orchestrating and manipulating until she'd gotten what she wanted. Sex, purely for her own pleasure, at any cost, with no thought to what he wanted.

Caro—Caroline, dammit, her name was Caroline—was no different than all those women who kept showing up for what they called stud service, except for one thing: she'd succeeded where the others had not.

And he'd fallen for it. Hook, line, and cement block.

Sam swung around mountainous curves faster than he should, his tires losing traction in the dirt now and then, but he barely noticed.

How in hell was he going to work alongside this woman?

He could send her packing—he'd fired people for far less. But dammit, now that he knew what she was capable of, he could no longer be sure she'd keep her word. Especially since she'd been hurt by his cold dismissal this morning and likely further incensed by his angry words. Would she have produced the spare key if he'd been less harsh, or would she have kept up the charade?

Sam slammed his hand into the steering wheel and swore.

He couldn't fire her. At least as an employee, she'd be reluctant to bring embarrassment on herself. If he pushed her further, there'd be no telling what she might say or do before she gathered her things and drove off.

Drops splattered on his windshield.

Maybe, just maybe, now that she'd gotten what she wanted, she'd disappear. Point that ridiculous car of hers southeast and not stop until she reached Florida.

The rain poured down and thunder rumbled, but Sam didn't slow. He just flipped on the wipers and gripped the wheel.

If Caro took off, then he'd never have to see her again.

Somehow that thought didn't ease him, as it should have.

Caroline crossed from her cabin to the barn, her boots sinking slightly in the mud. When she arrived, there was no sign of Sam, so she'd put her purchases away, stood under the shower for far too long, and agonized over ever facing him again. By the time the rain stopped, she'd come to terms with things. She couldn't delay any further. She owed Sam a massive apology.

She hadn't meant for things to get so out of hand. She'd just been so mad. And now, she admitted, so hurt.

Their night together had been stunning, but it wasn't just the sex. Even when they'd been talking or laughing or just lying quietly next to each other, she'd felt *right* somehow. At ease, content, even happy, and, most importantly, connected.

She simply couldn't believe that Sam hadn't felt something similar. The way he'd treated her, tuning into her sexual signals so easily, attending to her pleasure so thoroughly, touching and complimenting her so freely…when he certainly hadn't had to. After all, she'd clearly requested only hot, wild sex—yet he'd given her so much more.

She hadn't tried to deceive him. She hadn't thought of it that way. The blaze between them had grown so hot that she absolutely knew they'd end up in bed together. She'd only meant to give the situation a nudge. She hadn't even had a guarantee that the ploy would work. The night could easily have resulted in two rooms at the dingy motel in town, which she would have paid for, or a ride home and a ride back in the morning, though if that had happened, she could have "remembered" the hide-a-key at any time.

Truly, she hadn't meant to hurt him. She'd simply hoped to perhaps speed up the timetable and ease them both sooner rather than later. After hibernating for so long… Well, she'd been desperate to live, to connect, to feel—with Sam.

Caroline took a deep breath as she stepped into the barn.

Sam stood to her left, ripping tools off their hooks and shoving them into a beat-up leather pack. He wore a plaid shirt with the sleeves rolled up over a long-sleeved t-shirt, work pants every bit as sexy as his jeans, and his hat pulled low. The bit of hair she could see curling around his collar was wet and gleamed as black as night. She wished she could touch it freely, as she had last night, but she'd lost that right—if she'd ever really had it in the first place.

She wrapped her arms around her middle and moved toward Sam. No matter her reasons or how unsure her scheme, she had, indeed, deceived him, and he had every right to be angry.

"Sam."

He tensed and then continued packing the sack as if she hadn't spoken.

"I—"

"The horses need to be fed." His words were clipped and his voice harsh. He refused to look at her.

"I know. I want to apologize," she began.

"Don't want to hear it," he said, as he snatched up his bag and slung it over his shoulder.

Caroline opened her mouth. Sam crossed to the other wall, yanked his saddle off the rail, and headed for the wide-open sliders at the other end of the barn. She'd seen his horse, Bedlam, in the paddock.

Caroline scurried after him. "Please, listen. I was wrong to do what I did." Sam stepped over the threshold. "I never meant…"

Long, angry strides took him quickly away from her.

Dammit. Caroline felt tears spill from her eyes. She spun and kicked hard at the hay, sending up a cloud of dust. "I'm so sorry," she whispered, but only the horses were there to hear it.

20

———————

The day she blew things with Sam to hell, Caroline was so upset that she'd broken down and told Neve everything. *Everything*. The amazing sex. The tender moments. The laughs and the crazy cabin. How much she liked him. How alive and wonderful she'd felt. How she'd tricked him. How it had all come crashing down.

When they spoke a few nights later, Neve asked how the tension level was.

Caroline grimaced. "On a scale from one to five? A six. It sucks."

"Still not speaking to you?"

"Not speaking to me, not talking to me, not looking in my direction, not referring to me. He's ghosted me." She sighed. "Honestly, it's fine. I don't even blame him. I just wish… I don't even know. I wish so many things. But more than anything, I wish we could have ended that night on good terms."

"It is what it is now."

"Yeah, because I screwed it up so fantastically."

"You're going to have to let it go."

Caroline shook her head despite the fact that Neve couldn't see her. "The whole reason you sent me away is because I'm not so good at letting things go." She'd wrapped herself in a blanket and was tucked up in the rocker on her little cabin's porch.

"This is different, though."

"I know, I just keep thinking… I can't have Kevin—not ever." She stole a glance at Sam's cabin across the clearing. His lights were still on too. "But Sam's here—not that you can compare the two—and I could have had him, but he doesn't want me. I had my chances and I ruined them." She sighed, and the puff of her breath was visible in the night's chill.

"First of all, you didn't ruin things with Kevin, you just lost him. It's just shit luck."

Caroline shut her eyes. She should have told Neve ages ago what really happened. She just so desperately wanted it not to be true, couldn't bear if Neve—

"You don't know that Sam won't come around eventually," Neve insisted.

"He won't."

"Well, if he doesn't, then he's not right for you anyway."

"I like—liked—him a lot, but he isn't right for me. Not really. He's not Kevin."

There was a slam on Neve's end. "Goddammit, you have got to stop that."

"Stop what?"

"This impossible ideal you've created in your head."

Caroline sat up too quickly, the rocker tipping too far forward. "Kevin was—"

"I said stop," Neve snapped. Then her voice softened some. "He was just a man. He wasn't perfect. You were good together—but you weren't perfect together. There is no such thing."

Caroline was at a loss for words, but Neve wasn't finished.

"Remember when he'd decide to go for a drink with the guys after shift and he'd forget to tell you? Nothing made you madder than when he made you worry unnecessarily. What about when he was furious that you didn't take that other job offer, even though it was more money? How about—"

"Stop," Caroline barked. "I get it."

"I'm sorry," Neve said. "But somewhere along the way, you built up this idea in your head—"

"I said I get it. Enough, Neve."

"I just want you to be open to—"

"I *knew* you were going to bring this back to Sam." Caroline stood up, grabbed the blanket in a death grip, and stomped inside. "But you can forget it. It's not just my hang-ups here—he's not going to budge."

———

Caroline was relieved when Astor and Sissy returned home after a week and a half away between the conference and the hospital trip. The initial awkwardness of meeting them —her a stranger that had made herself at home during their absence—had nothing on the tension of the last few days. Especially at dinnertime, when Sam refused to even look at her, and Ruby and Will traded worried glances. Two more people around the table—and working the ranch—

was definitely a good thing, although it did make for a longer meal.

Astor had been plenty welcoming to Caroline, if understandably distracted. When they'd just about finished dinner, he announced that they would call his wife, Anna, right from the table. It was clear he missed her, and this way, he said, everyone could hear the Carter update.

Caroline tried to excuse herself.

"Stay," Astor said, pulling his cell phone from his shirt pocket and switching to speaker mode as it rang.

Anna was nothing but warm and gracious despite the phone introduction. "We're so glad you found us right when we needed help, Caroline. Ruby has told us so much about you."

Sissy rolled her eyes. Sam's sister was a tough nut— curt, cold, sarcastic, and either she didn't like an outsider taking up residence with her family while she'd been away, or she sensed the tension between Caroline and Sam. Probably both.

"Good thing, too," Anna said, "because Sam doesn't say boo."

Caroline darted her eyes at Sam, who looked away and clenched his jaw. She squashed the pang of hurt and regret that constantly surfaced around him and managed to concentrate on the conversation with Anna, who asked, "How are you settling in?"

After that, Sam's mother gave them a brief update on Carter's progress and then turned the topic to the upcoming end-of-season bash—as if focusing on something good and normal helped them take their minds off Carter.

The next night, after they'd cleared the dishes and sat

back down with coffee and tea, Will passed around a plate of chocolate chip cookies. "A classic."

Caroline grinned—she'd been trying hard not to let the Sam thing dampen her reactions to everyone else. "I'm going to have to stop mentioning my favorites, or I'm going to have to go shopping again."

Sam pushed away from the table with a loud scrape of his chair and put his mug—the coffee barely touched—next to the sink. "I'm heading out." He avoided looking at Caroline.

Damn. She hadn't meant to bring up a sore reminder—but the fact was that her very presence seemed to set him off.

"Sit down, son," Astor said. "We still have to call your mom."

"Go on, then." Sam didn't return to the table, instead leaning a hip against the counter. Further away from her, of course.

"Good news," Anna said nearly right off. "Carter should be coming home in about a week and a half. He'll miss the party, but that's probably just as well."

Everyone expressed their relief, then Anna continued, "Thing is, I haven't been able to secure appropriate care. We'd get visiting services—someone to change dressings every couple of days, a physical therapist three times a week for an hour. It's not enough, and none of us have the know-how."

Astor frowned, Ruby leaned into the table, and Sam said, "Whatever it costs, Mom, we'll—"

"I'm right there with you, honey, but it seems live-in nurses are in high demand around here. There aren't many, and the good ones are spoken for. Caroline?"

"Yes?" Caroline said. "I'm here." It was like being called out in class. She had no idea of the question.

"Ruby tells me you have a good friend who is a physical therapist?"

"Yes." Caroline cut a glance to Ruby, who was nodding. "Neve." She and Ruby had chatted a lot over the last weeks, and Caroline had told Ruby about Neve and Bella, how they met when Neve was an ER nurse, that she'd become a physical therapist after Bella had come along, hoping for less stress and steadier hours for her kid.

"You think she would like a vacation to Big Sky Country? Free room and board and travel expenses, excellent pay, and a real special experience for her little girl?"

"And all the cookies she can eat," Will added.

Quite the sell job. Caroline smiled. "I can certainly ask her." Seemed crazy that they could just take off, but Neve *was* dissatisfied with the practice she worked for, and Bella was young enough for school to not really be an issue.

"I'd like to speak with her tomorrow, if at all possible," Anna said.

"I'll call her tonight." God, Caroline would love to share this amazing place with Neve and Bella. Already her head was spinning with ideas.

"One more thing, Caroline," Anna said.

Caroline raised her eyebrow at Ruby, who shrugged with a mischievous smile.

"I'd like you to photograph the party this weekend."

The blood drained from Caroline's head. She gripped the edge of the table.

Anna said, "We really need some great shots for our website, so it's perfect that you're here."

The silence stretched.

"Caroline?"

She forced herself to draw breath. "Okay." Her voice sounded tinny and her stomach rolled. "Of course."

But she didn't know how she'd ever manage it.

21

____

Some days later, Sam dragged a gorgeous but reluctant young palomino by the bridle toward the doors of the horse trailer. Will prodded the stubborn horse near the hindquarter by hollering and slapping its rump.

Occasionally they sold horses or colts, depending on the customer or on the offer. In this case, a wealthy guest who'd visited last month had taken a liking to the beast.

Given Palo's foul temperament and the fact that enchanted Mr. Moneybags hadn't allowed them enough time to accustom the horse to loading, Sam had known this send-off would be difficult. Sure enough, Palo had begun to spook the minute Sam strapped on the first protective knee boot.

Sam valued Will's help, however, his dad and Sissy were occupied elsewhere, and they needed additional hands. He was forced to make do.

Ruby had pinch-hit all over the ranch, of course, but Sam knew that she was most comfortable inside the lodge creating and maintaining the upscale vacation business.

He'd placed her opposite Will, to urge the horse on from the other side, but the diminutive housekeeper sort of danced around, probably no more annoying to the animal as a fly.

Caroline—a total rookie—stood at the trailer's bumper, in order to swing the interior gates shut the second the horse's rump cleared the ramp. He hoped he could count on her in a high-pressure situation. She had worked hard every day and had even asked for additional responsibilities, but he could tell by her stiff movements and reserved manner that she was still strung tight. She'd also taken to disappearing purposely during any free pockets of time, obviously steering clear of Sam—which was fine by him.

Today, however, she seemed distracted, run-down, and even more reticent than had become the norm. During the time he and Will had tried to coax and bribe Palo, she'd stood idly by, staring at nothing and occasionally checking her cell phone. Once it was obvious Palo would require force, Sam had snapped at her.

"Put that thing away."

She'd jumped and slid her phone into her back pocket. He didn't care what or whom she had on her agenda. She'd need her hands free once the beast finally moved, and he needed her full attention.

Suddenly, the horse snorted and reared, his hooves circling the air in front of Sam, who stepped deftly aside. Palo was headed toward a complete frenzy.

"Ruby, go get the broom." He spoke evenly for Palo's sake. "The one with the stiff bristles from just inside the door."

"Good idea," Will said.

Sam concentrated on the horse, speaking to him gently

in a low voice, in order to calm the animal as well as distract him. He still pranced and pulled, but he wasn't quite as frantic.

Ruby returned, broom in hand.

"Stand off to the side in case he kicks," Sam instructed her, "and jab the bristled end, swift and hard, right under his tail."

Her eyes widened and she looked to Will.

"It won't hurt him, honey," Will said. "You'll only startle him into action. Just like Sam said, okay? Pretend he's me if you want."

Ruby rolled her eyes at her husband before nodding at Sam.

He spoke to the horse in soothing tones for a few more moments.

"Everybody ready?" he asked softly, and saw Ruby tighten her grip on the broom.

As soon as he gave the signal, Ruby poked Palo hard. The horse jerked and then shot forward, hooves clattering wildly on the metal ramp.

Caroline rushed forward and pushed the gate closed right on time—but just before it latched, her cell phone rang.

The horse kicked out his hind legs and a crack sounded —hooves against metal. The door flew open. Caroline went down. Sam slammed one gate shut; Will lunged for the other.

Sam saw Caroline roll from her rump to her side and curl up her legs—and his heart stopped beating. Fear doused him like a bucket of ice, though he was covered in sweat.

He secured the gates as fast as possible, then rushed to

Caroline. Almost frantically, he checked her face and head, expecting to see blood.

No gash. His own blood started to pound again.

"You okay?" he asked, as he pulled her into a sitting position. He ached to gather her into his chest, but he couldn't—he had to make sure she was all right. She nodded, just barely. Her eyes were wide and frozen, but she didn't speak.

"Caro?"

Sam smoothed her hair back from her forehead, still searching. No bruise, not a mark on her, yet her teeth were clenched with pain and her face had drained of color.

"I'm okay."

Briiiing.

Sam snapped.

He pulled her all the way to her feet, ripped up her jacket, and yanked the phone out of her back pocket. He hauled back and sent it sailing through the air, before he grabbed Caroline's chin and forced her to face him.

"I don't ever want to see that thing on the job again," he said, barely controlling his anger. A small thud registered in his subconscious as the cell phone hit the soft earth. "You could have been killed." The terrifying thought made his grip on her chin tighten.

Her lip wobbled. "I'm sorry. I was expecting a call."

Briiiing, came the distant sound. Sam wanted to smash something, preferably that phone.

"You shouldn't be expecting anything but orders from me." He knew he sounded like a complete tyrant, a total asshole, but he didn't care.

Her eyes flared, and she tried to extract herself from his grasp. "It was an accident."

"Which wouldn't have happened if you'd been paying attention. If you're too uncomfortable around me to focus so that we all stay in one piece, then it's not an accident—it's negligence." Sam was breathing too hard, speaking too loudly—and he dropped his hand in disgust. "*No* distractions. Get it together or leave."

Eyes wide, she stepped back—as if she feared his blunt anger. He shut it all out and spun toward the trailer. Ruby and Will stood stock-still and gaped at him. As he motioned for Will to take the other side of the ramp, Sam heard Caroline sob and hastily turn away. Her booted footfalls were uneven as she sped into a run.

He and Will heaved and secured the ramp to the trailer.

"Time to go," Sam told Will.

Will turned to kiss his wife and cupped her cheek in his hand. "She's tough. She'll be all right." Ruby's mouth tightened further, and she shook her head, even as her eyes cut to Caroline's retreating form.

Sam ground his teeth, and both men headed for the truck. Will had offered to do the drive, allowing Sam to remain at the ranch. Suddenly he wished he was the one who could escape.

Sam said, "Stop to give him water frequently."

Will climbed up. He opened his mouth, then shut it, with a look of resignation. Sam pushed the driver's door shut.

The horse still whinnied and stamped his feet. Sam hoped the buyer, or at least that man's trainer, knew what he was in for.

Sam laid his hand on the corrugated wall, silently wishing the horse a good life. "Bye, Palo."

He raised a hand to Will and then stood in the

billowing dust, watching until the truck bumped around the curve and over the hill. Hopefully the ride would lull Palo within minutes.

When Sam turned around, Ruby stood with her hands planted on her hips and her eyes full of accusations. In no mood for further confrontation, Sam made to walk past her, but she stopped him cold.

"You *ass*."

Sam's jaw nearly fell off. Ruby never swore, let alone at someone.

"What would you have had me do?"

"Give the poor woman a break."

"She deserves every ounce of what she got."

"She most certainly does not. Caroline is in pain—"

"She brought that on herself," Sam growled.

Ruby's eyes shot daggers. "I don't know what occurred in town last week, but enough is enough. What happened today has absolutely nothing to do with you."

"The hell it doesn't."

"You insensitive, selfish, conceited lout. Would you open your eyes?" Ruby flung her hand toward Caroline's cabin.

She shook her head and stalked off toward the field, then spun around and marched right back to Sam. She didn't stop until she was right under his nose, glaring directly up at him.

"Today is the second anniversary of her husband's death. She lost him in a terrible accident."

Sam's stomach dropped and he squeezed his eyes shut, until he realized Ruby hadn't budged.

"She's still grieving, still haunted, and still very much

unsettled." She looked him right in the eye and said, "Not one of those emotions has *anything* to do with you."

Ruby stalked off, but Sam stood rooted to the dirt drive for a long time, just listening to the incessant ringing of Caro's phone. Four rings, a pause—voicemail and redial, probably—then four more rings. Over and over and over again.

Finally, he moved off the driveway and through the grass. The noise became louder with each step he took.

Sam stood over the phone, wondering exactly how he'd ended up like this. He didn't normally take his anger out on his staff or argue with his family. He didn't throw things, or manhandle women, or—goddammit—sleep with them.

He picked up the phone, which showed a picture of a grinning woman with the name Neve.

The nurse and physical therapist friend. He swiped a finger and accepted the call. "Hello."

A sharp intake of breath before Neve asked, "Where's Caroline?"

He looked toward the woods. "She's taking a walk."

"Is she all right?"

Guilt wormed up his throat. "She will be."

"What happened?"

Her voice brooked no arguments. Still, a real answer was next to impossible to give her. He snaked his hand around the back of his neck and dug into the tense muscle there. "Nothing." Nothing and something.

"Sam, why are you answering her phone?"

That caught his attention. "You know me?"

"Did she tell you about today?"

Ruby had told him. He hadn't been speaking to Caroline at all. "I know about it."

"Good. Help her. She's been…" Her voice was less sure now. "She's had an awful time of it. I mean really bad."

Nearly every word out of this woman's mouth made him feel guiltier. Sam blew out a ragged breath.

"Listen," Neve said, "she's been so much better since she arrived there. I knew today would be hard, but…" Again, Caroline's friend seemed hard-pressed for words. "Tell her to call me," she said. "And Sam, don't let her backslide. No matter what you have to do—don't let her go there."

22

———

Caroline limped from the cramp in her right butt cheek where she'd landed on the edge of her phone. Still, she moved as fast as she could along her favorite trail, well into the woods, with tears streaming down her cheeks. She stumbled as she scrambled over a fallen log and then gave up, sinking to her knees in the damp earth. She panted and sobbed, giving in to it but good, until she was spent.

Then she eased her lower back against the rough bark, tucked her legs into her chest, and rested her cheek on the wet knees of her jeans.

She didn't move for some time, so long that a tiny rabbit ventured out from his hiding place to scurry under the base of a tall pine. Caroline marveled as she watched it. With that gorgeous, mottled coloring and its extra-small size, it had to be a pygmy rabbit. In Montana, they only occupied the southwest of the state, though she'd read that they roamed all over Idaho, Utah, Nevada, and Washington.

A pine cone fell to the ground. The small animal darted away.

Caroline wiped her face and nose on her sleeve, then grimaced as she shifted her bottom. She was certain she had a wicked deep-muscle bruise on her tush from landing just so on the damn phone.

Normally, she wouldn't even have been carrying the cell around the ranch, but she'd known Neve would call to check on her. Not only had she been anxious to speak with her friend, she also knew that if Neve couldn't reach her today that she'd be terribly concerned.

So much for good intentions. Likely Neve was now worried sick. Last year's anniversary had been brutal. And knowing Neve, that phone would ring every two minutes until someone finally went out to the meadow and turned it off. Hopefully that person wouldn't be Sam, or the device would end up smashed to bits.

Caroline sighed. She couldn't blame him for being angry or for flying off the handle.

She'd jumped sky high herself when the ringer went off, so it was no surprise that Palo, who was already scared silly, had freaked out. Man, she'd been lucky to have had her hands up, saving her face when he kicked that door open, but the force had still sent her reeling.

Luck didn't matter, though. The point was that she'd endangered people she cared about. *Again.*

Caroline shivered and hugged her legs.

She wasn't sure she could live with herself if she hurt anyone else. She'd thought things couldn't get any worse.

Caroline squeezed her eyes shut to stave off the memories.

Maybe Sam was right. Maybe she should go. All day long, she'd been struggling with that very question.

She'd held on so tightly to Kevin through most of the past two years…but once she'd arrived here on the ranch, his face, the sound of his voice, the exact color of his eyes —all the details she'd loved—had begun to fade faster. She supposed that was natural as time went on and grief began to ebb, but she wondered nonetheless… If she returned to the condo, to her photographs of him and to his personal items, could she hold on a little longer?

Did she want to?

And Neve was right: Caroline had chosen to forget some of the bad times—fights and frustrations—and built up the good ones.

She'd expected to be with him always, raise a family together, grow old side by side. Once he died, she'd fully expected to pine for him forever. She'd been so afraid to let go, and yet—she shuddered—the process was well underway despite her tight grip.

Tears threatened again, but she squeezed them back. "I tried to hold on to you," she whispered to Kevin. "God, did I try. But I can't. Turns out it doesn't work that way."

She drew a shaky breath. "I'll always love you. Always."

That, she knew without a doubt. She'd also, she was sure, carry the guilt she felt about his death to her own grave.

"I'm sorry for what happened. So sorry." Her voice wobbled. "If I could go back… But I can't. There's nothing to do now but go forward."

Because somehow, almost accidentally, she'd begun living again. There was nothing to be done about that now.

During her many solitary walks, she'd delighted in watching fawns bound behind their parents, but she'd also recognized the fragility of life in baby birds, lying still as could be in a grave of leaves, far below where their mothers sang in the branches. She'd been reminded that the cycle of life and death spun always, aided by time. There was no stopping either one.

She rubbed her forehead on her knee and sighed. Returning to Miami now would be futile. She couldn't go backward emotionally—she was where she was now—and yet she didn't feel quite strong enough yet to return and not be walloped by her surroundings.

Furthermore, she loved Black Hills Ranch and the Black family, and she wanted to remain, at least for a while. Even with all the angst and regret surrounding the situation with Sam, she couldn't imagine a place she'd be happier.

And therein lay more of the anxiety that had tied her up in knots today. What to do about Sam?

Her husband hadn't been gone that long, and here she'd gone and slept with a man. Maybe she should feel guilty about that, too, but she didn't. She *couldn't*, because he wasn't just some random man—he was *Sam*.

Caroline traced her finger slowly through the damp dirt.

She'd found such joy in making love with him. She'd discovered true pleasure in touching his body and had reveled in the passion that had swept through her own. She'd felt rooted and so alive.

But she'd been crazy to think she could use him to heal. In fact, that had been the farthest thing from her mind the night they'd spent together. No, her attraction to Sam hadn't been self-serving at all…

Instead, it was about being close to him, simply because…

She smoothed dirt over the drawings she'd made with the palm of her hand. The truth was that she'd derived just as much pleasure from Sam's laughter as his lovemaking, just as much warmth from his eyes as his touch. And she'd felt the same way listening to his worries about Carter across the table or watching him soothe a troubled horse as she did lying naked and entwined in the glow of the wood stove in that cabin.

How she felt about Sam had nothing to do with Kevin, and shouldn't—Neve was right about that, too—and nothing to do with her emotional recovery.

True, making love with him had only caused her to want him more fiercely, but she was able to remove bodily desire from the equation, at least out here when she was alone. The plain fact was that she didn't want just sex. Her heart spoke loud and clear. She cared about Sam, wanted to spend time with him, yearned to know him better.

Was she ready for a full-fledged relationship?

She snorted. It didn't matter.

She'd hurt him deeply, and he was stubborn and proud. He didn't want anything more to do with her—sexually or emotionally. Period. Full stop.

And honestly? She didn't deserve another good man. It was her fault that Kevin was dead. And now she'd treated Sam terribly. She was better off alone—or at least Sam was better off without her.

Caroline stood, a little shaky, wiping her hands off on her pants and then brushing off her seat. She swiped a sleeve over her face, then shoved her hair off her sticky cheeks.

She couldn't bear to face returning to Miami just yet. But she'd damn well pay attention to her job when she was on the clock. She'd stomp on any desires her stupid heart longed for. She'd give Sam as much space as she could manage.

But unless he forced her, she wouldn't leave the ranch anytime soon.

23

S am sat on the front porch of his cabin with his feet propped on the railing, his Adirondack-style rocker tilted back. Sissy still slept in the main house, as did his brother, Owen, whenever he returned home. Even Will and Ruby had a small suite of rooms there. But Sam and Carter had cajoled his parents into giving them the bachelors' cabins way back when their first priority had been the women guests. Bigger than the other cabins and rectangular rather than square, the shape allowed him to have space for a large desk, a filing cabinet, and a row of bookshelves. He had all he really needed, and he appreciated the solitude.

Normally in the evenings, he worked or read, but tonight he was unable to focus. He found himself instead looking across the clearing to Caro's cottage. He could see her form on her own porch, illuminated softly from behind by the light she'd left on inside.

She sat on the steps, her back propped against a support beam and her head tilted up. The night was dark and crisp, the stars crystal clear against a near-black backdrop. Guests were always astounded at the sight, as well they should be. Sam no longer took the Big Sky for granted—he'd missed it when he went to college—but he knew where he belonged.

Caroline had barely moved in all the time he'd been watching. Then, suddenly, she swiped her face with the back of her sleeve and went inside for a few moments. When she returned, she carried something in her hand…a blanket and a box of tissues.

Sam's gut wrenched at the hard evidence of her tears, even though he wasn't surprised. This was the kind of anniversary a person dreaded. Plus, he'd been hard on her today.

Hell, he'd been a bona fide jerk since she'd first driven up the hill.

But there was something more going on, too—because she'd looked as terrified as an animal caught in a trap when his mom tasked her with photographing the party.

What had she been through? What exactly had happened? She hadn't seemed willing to talk about the details that one night they spent together at Tiller's cabin, and he hadn't pried. In truth, after his immense relief that she wasn't presently married, he hadn't much cared. Call him selfish, but he simply hadn't wanted another man to intrude on his own private time with Caro.

Caro.

Had her husband used that nickname? Sam hoped not. He thought of the name as his own. He wanted her to be only his—

Sam bolted upright, causing his chair to thud heavily against the plank flooring. Caroline turned her head abruptly toward the noise, but she couldn't see him, he was sure. He had no lights on inside the cabin, and even the moonlight would leave him in shadow under the porch roof.

Whoa. He hadn't realized he'd gotten so…attached. How was that even possible in such a short time? He'd only known her for, what? Under three weeks now. She was a constant presence, of course, but they hadn't spent that much time together one on one. Of course, the private time they had spent together had been damn near earth-shattering.

There was more, though. He got a rush at her sudden smile; he got a kick out of her quick wit; he felt jazzed when she was near…

He grimaced. He also felt like shit because she was hurting. And damn, but he felt like a whole wheelbarrow full of it, because he was to blame for some of her hurt.

Sam shook his head and slumped back in his chair. He'd been kicking himself all day. He'd intended to apologize, but Caro had practically run out of the kitchen—that animal sprung from its trap.

He didn't feel he could go over there now. She was upset, and he had no idea what to say.

Sam laughed, a derisive bark. Who was he kidding?

He didn't want to go over there because the tear tracks on her cheeks would tug at his heart, her magnetic eyes would wrap their magic around his mind, and one movement from her irresistible body would ignite demands of his own. In no time flat, he'd be doing his best to distract her—laying her on the rough wood of the porch, baring her body to the chilly night air, and ravishing her completely. It wouldn't even matter to him that they were here, on Black family land.

Sam sat, jaw clenched tight, feet planted like cement, hands squeezing the arms of the angled chair, until he was able to tamp down the image and his physical response.

Neve's words came back to him. *Don't let her backslide, no matter what you have to do…*

And Ruby had driven her point home with a sledgehammer. *Give her a break. The woman is in pain—it's got nothing to do with you.*

Maybe not. Caroline's past was her own, and she'd need to deal with it in her own way. But it was time he separated his own past experiences from the present. Wrapped up in his own anger and wounds, he'd missed important clues. Even worse, he'd been insensitive, insulting, and purposely malicious.

No wonder Ruby and Will had been so stunned.

"Shit."

Sam stood and grabbed his boots from outside the door. He bent to pull them on and then stood to look across the clearing.

Caroline had not meant to endanger anyone today, he knew. A large portion of the blame fell to him. He should have told her to turn the dang phone off, to return it to the cabin, to hit mute, anything, but he'd only snapped, *Put it away*—which in that situation meant her pocket. He'd still been incensed that she'd deceived him in order to get him in bed. He himself was guilty of being distracted—by her presence. And yeah, he'd overreacted. Damn phones were a trigger for him after what happened to Carter—and he'd been utterly terrified when he thought she'd been hurt.

He was the one who'd not been doing his job well, not paying enough attention, and not using his brain.

He stepped off the porch and into the night—feeling far more anticipation than he should and promising himself he'd leave his libido out of it.

Plain and simple, he couldn't afford to want her—and he sure as hell couldn't have her. But it was time to quit being a downright asshole, mind his manners, and show the woman the kindness she deserved.

Halfway there, he saw her wrap an arm around her stomach and bend into her lap.

He quickened his stride. She didn't appear to have heard him yet—but he heard her sobs.

"Caroline?"

She bolted upright and swiped at her face.

"It's me."

She pulled out a few tissues, then stood, turning her back on him, the lap blanket tumbling down the steps.

He crossed the remaining few yards and stood below her as she blew her nose and cleaned her face. "You all right?"

She huffed a tortured laugh, and the sound ripped at him.

He was up the steps before he knew what happened. "C'mere." He turned her gently by the shoulders and pulled her into his chest.

She stiffened for just a moment, and then a small sob escaped and she relaxed into him. Shoulders shaking, she cried.

Sam rubbed long strokes up and down her back over her big fleece, resting his chin on her soft hair, wanting to curl around her and keep her safe from pain.

Finally, she pulled back and, with a clogged nose, mumbled, "I need more tissues."

He bent for the box and handed it to her. Strange—he felt both full and empty now.

"Sit with me?" He sank to the step, turned so his back was against the post. She still looked a little wary, but she took one more tissue to her eyes then sat.

Too far. He leaned forward and pulled her toward him. With swollen eyes and a pink nose, she looked into his face, searching.

"I'm sorry," he said, "for all you're going through." She ducked her head, and he tilted it back up. "I'm sorry, too, about today. With Palo. I was way outta line."

Her lip twitched up even as she shook her head.

"The fault lies squarely with me," he said. "You didn't deserve that."

She sighed. "It was my fault, too, but thank you for that."

"Do you want to talk?" He found he didn't want to leave her. "About your husband?"

She bit her lip. "No."

"Okay." He shifted, making to get up, but her hand landed softly on his knee, halting him.

She met his gaze. "Will you stay?" She dropped that hand. "Just a little longer?"

Sam's heart gave a solid thump in his chest, and he pulled her between his legs and into his chest once more. He pulled his thick flannel around her as best he could, and she laid her cheek against his chest.

Sam rested his arms loosely around Caroline, stroking gently over her hip with his thumb. They couldn't have this for long—so he tried to soak it up. She felt so right in his arms, so perfect.

As badly as it had ended, he couldn't be sorry for the night at the cabin. Not knowing now how raw she was. With a little distance and more information, he could now consider that maybe she'd gotten carried away when she locked those keys in the car. That she'd probably been feeling lonely and needy or was grasping for… Well, who knew what—he was no psychologist. But if his gut could talk, it would swear up and down that Caroline wasn't normally the type to lie or play games or even proposition men.

They sat looking out at the night sky and the sea of stars for a long while. He fought the urge to press his lips to her hair, to tilt her chin up and taste the salt on her eyelashes, cheeks, and lips. There was only so much a man in his position could give.

He hoped she found some comfort in his arms. He hoped she was finding what she came here for. Some peace, perhaps.

She had chosen not to confide in him—fair enough—so he didn't ask about her reaction to the photography request. Instead, he said, "Do you still want to learn to ride?"

24

The next morning, Caroline set the grooming tools back on the shelf and dusted her hands off against her jeans. The horses only needed a light grooming in the morning, and she'd become fairly speedy now that she had some experience. Although she'd already given them clean hay and oats, Caroline grabbed the fresh, leafy carrots she'd brought and walked back down the aisle to the occupied stalls, as she did each day. Sweetness made her laugh, and Sally Girl made her giggle when she nuzzled and blew in her ear.

Caroline had no idea what prompted Sam to offer to spend some time teaching her to ride, but apparently today was the day. She'd assumed after their huge fight that she'd eventually need to rope someone else into teaching her. She tried hard not to take more from last night's comforting or the offer—likely it was simply part of his apology.

Caroline reached for the flannel shirt she'd hung on a hook earlier. It was far warmer in the barn than outside.

She slid her arms into the sleeves, grabbed her brimmed hat from the peg, and slapped it on her head. She didn't want another burned nose—it happened despite the chill in the air, she'd learned—and it helped her hair stay out of her face, too.

She moved to pet one more horse hanging its nose over the stall. "You had yours already, big guy." She turned to go, but jumped when she nearly ran into Sam.

Caroline tried to catch her breath and slow her hyped-up heartbeat. "You startled me."

"Didn't mean to," Sam said. "Ready?"

She grinned as excitement bubbled. A new adventure on a sunny day. A little time spent with a handsome cowboy—straight out of a movie with that square, stubbled jaw and big black hat. And a chance to actually get on one of these gorgeous animals. Hell yes, she was ready.

"Sweetness should suit for today," Sam said. "She doesn't fluster easily, so we often give her to beginners."

Caroline skipped down the aisle to the spotted horse's stall. "Hi, girl, I have good news! You and me, we're going to take a ride."

"Don't get too attached." Sam chuckled. "It's likely I'll switch you up, once we discover what kind of rider you are."

She strolled back toward him.

"If you're a passive rider, you and Sweetness won't accomplish much." Sam paused. "Although I doubt you'll be a passive rider."

Her cheeks positively burned. Whether he referenced her personality or the time she'd ridden him so shamelessly, she could only guess.

Sam cleared his throat. "We'll start with saddling."

Caroline imagined saddling the horse would be far easier than figuring out Sam.

Soon she sat in the saddle, attempting to concentrate on her hands and the placement of the reins between her fingers. The initial rush of sitting six feet above ground on a living thing that shifted and moved of its own volition, yet would follow her commands, had waned given the drudgery of technical details. She and Sweetness, who was indeed aptly named, had been round and round the paddock. The horse didn't seem to mind the repetition; neither did Caroline, really. She had already learned first-hand that Sam's rote but intense method of instruction was quite effective in the end.

"Keep your boot heel down," Sam instructed her. "Good, now don't forget to sit up straight. Nope, not stiff, just sit solid. Sit tall." Sam frowned as he watched her walk the horse, then he shook his head. "Stop. Try to visualize that there's an imaginary pole that runs from your head, on through your shoulders, your tailbone, and your heels." He traced the line with his index finger, brushing lightly against her at each contact point.

Caroline suppressed a shiver but was powerless against the warmth that invaded her body. She envisioned that pole and sat tall.

He smiled. "Much better. Hold that while we walk."

She gave Sweetness a squeeze.

"Too much force, and your signal was too prolonged. The contact between your knees and the horse should be minimal," Sam said while he moved alongside horse and rider. "Think of it as a secret whisper from you to the horse."

Caroline blew hair out of her face and stopped the

horse.

"Don't yank on the reins," Sam said.

"I barely pulled on them at all." She huffed in frustration.

"To you, that's how it feels. The horses feel like they're being manhandled," Sam explained, and winked. "Now, there will be times when you do have to use more force to stop a horse, but even then, only use as many pounds of pressure as it takes, never more."

They practiced a little longer before Sam said, "Don't get frustrated. You're really doing well."

"Could have fooled me."

"There's a lot to keep track of." He shrugged. "But it's important that you learn the correct way right out of the gate."

Just then, Caroline spotted Ruby outside the fence.

"Ruby, I'm riding!" She spread her hands to show her friend.

Ruby grinned and waved. "What do you think?"

Caroline slid her gaze to Sam. "Well, it's not quite as exciting as I would have thought, but I suspect I just have a lot to learn."

Sam inclined his head in acknowledgement.

"Don't we all," Ruby said. She pointed to a square basket at her feet. "Thought you two might be getting hungry." She eyeballed Sam and said, "Make sure you give Caroline a break. You've been at it over an hour already. There's a picnic blanket inside."

As Ruby walked away, Caroline thought she heard Sam snort. But when he turned to her, he was all business. "Now, just the slightest nudge to give Sweetness the signal to walk. She's well trained, so she'll get it."

She nudged, and Sweetness, responding without hesitation, dipped a shoulder as her leg lifted. Caroline smiled at Sam, and he nodded.

"Excellent," he said.

To sit a horse properly, Caroline learned, she had to concentrate on every inch of her body at once. A nearly impossible feat. Oh, she paid attention to her body, all right. Every time Sam smiled at her, she had to fight not to grin in triumph. Every time he physically fixed her hands or the position of her legs, heat rushed to her belly. She was making too much out of this, she knew—but it felt so good. So much better than the tense avoidance they'd had going on.

"Caro," Sam said, interrupting her thoughts, "your hands are clenched, and your legs are lax again."

Dutifully, she righted her appendages and tried to focus on Sweetness, but that malleable horse held not an ounce of the allure that troublesome Sam Black did. Caroline's concentration lapsed almost immediately.

Every time Sam called her Caro, her mind jumped to the intimacy and passion they'd shared at the cabin. She doubted he had any idea what his use of the nickname did to her, because he'd touched her only impersonally, and although he'd alternated between encouraging and tough, he'd kept the conversation limited to saddling, mounting, posture, and safety.

She found herself constantly turning over Sam's motivations. Did he wish to return to a working relationship without all the animosity of the last two weeks? Was a lesson—and a break from work to boot—more apology for flying off the handle? Perhaps he decided he'd better teach her as much as possible about horses so that she wouldn't cause any more dangerous situations. Heck, maybe he couldn't care less if she got her head bashed in, but he needed her to ride to help to exercise the horses.

She hadn't been able to figure out Sam even once since the day she'd arrived, so she should just—

"Caro—you're all off again. Get down." Sam's command was gruff, and his arms were crossed tightly over his chest, muscles bulging through his formfitting thermal.

Caroline blew out a breath, then she hoisted her right leg over the rump of the horse and gracelessly slid off the saddle. The ground was further away than she expected, and she stumbled when she landed, but Sam steadied her with a hand on her elbow. Embarrassment surged, but since that had become par for the course around this man, she lifted her chin and pretended she had executed a perfect-ten dismount.

"We'll work on that another time. Scoot." Sam shooed her off to the side, and with brisk, gentle motions, he unsaddled Sweetness.

He settled the worn leather seat over the rail of the fence and gave the old horse a quick rubdown. So much for the lesson, she thought, annoyed at herself—and him, too.

Sam dug in a saddlebag that had been draped around the fence post and came up with a couple of bright red apples. Sweetness nuzzled him as a thank you, and he murmured to her, stroking her neck all the while.

Finally, he gave the animal a gentle slap on the rump to send her off and turned to Caroline.

"That's it?" Of course, she knew she'd need more instruction, but she didn't want the time with Sam to end.

Disappointment swirled, but she joked, "I didn't even graduate to leaving the paddock?"

He winked. "I didn't turn you off horses forever with all my nagging?"

"No, I loved it. I want more. I want to go somewhere, though." She waved her hand at the gorgeous stretch of mountains beyond the ranch.

"That's a good sign." He squatted down and began poking in the basket Ruby had brought.

"Oh, I forgot," Caroline said. She dug in her back pocket and unfolded the ticket Rita had given her. "I have a ticket for a free trail ride."

He chuckled and reached out. "Where'd you get that?"

The second he grasped the paper, a tiny shock—a little frisson of energy—rushed from her fingertips up her arm. Sam flinched ever so slightly and frowned. She was positive he'd felt it too.

So odd. This paper had shocked her when Rita gave it to her, and now when she handed it to Sam. But it'd been a perfectly normal piece of cardstock when she'd dug it out of the depths of her purse this morning. She wasn't even sure why she had, except his offer of a lesson had reminded her about it.

"Ruby's sister, Rita, gave it to me." Ruby had mentioned to Will and Sam during one of Caroline's first dinners on the ranch that Rita and Reenie had sent her.

"You met her in True Springs, right?" He cocked his head. "You drink the water?"

She laughed. "How do you know about the water?"

"Been there."

"No way."

"Way. One of Rita's sons got married there, but at the

last minute, Will threw his back out and couldn't manage the travel, so Ruby chose me to take his place."

She laughed. "You must have loved that."

"You'd be surprised. I dress up nice."

She just bet he did, and warmth stole into her cheeks.

Bert Hoffman's words came to her unbidden. *Sometimes you have to live life before life leads you to love.*

She and Sam wouldn't end up there. He'd made that clear, and she was… Well, she'd had Kevin. And she wasn't staying. At some point soon she had to return to her job, her condo, her other life… Still, she had to know. "Did you drink the water?"

"Kind of hard not to."

Sam's feet were planted wide, his hands on his hips. He cocked his head and seemed to consider the dog-eared ticket in his big, rough hands. Then he folded it and stuck it in his back pocket before he put his fingers to his mouth and a shrill whistle erupted.

Caroline jumped and stepped back, only to bump into the rails of the fence. Slowly she realized the ground was pounding with…the force of a galloping horse?

She spun around and gasped. An enormous black beast —Bedlam—slid to a halt, dust and grass billowing around his forelegs, his bulging eyes and bared teeth looming over the fence above her. Caroline scrambled backward, her boots trampling Sam's.

"Whoa," he said, and set his hands on her waist, steadying her. "It's only Bedlam."

Bedlam tossed his gleaming mane and snuffed a greeting. There was no "only" about this horse.

"You—you," Caroline stammered to Sam. "And him!"

She stabbed her finger in the air, well out of the reach of the stallion's teeth.

Sam grinned.

"It's not funny. You scared me half to death."

"Didn't you hear him coming? I keep telling you—you have to pay attention at all times. This is not a kiddie zoo."

He reached for the saddlebag as Caroline glared at his broad back. The gall of this man. She still felt a hefty measure of guilt over the Palo incident—she hardly needed a reminder.

He stood and rubbed his knuckles over Bedlam's cheek. The huge horse snuffed with pleasure. Well, of course-she'd experienced it herself: Sam's hands were magic.

He looked over his shoulder at her. "Want to extend the lesson?"

"Sure."

Sam bent down and began transferring Tupperware from the picnic basket to his worn saddlebag then swung it over his shoulder.

Curiosity—and hunger—made her move toward him. What was he up to?

Another recital of rules and regulations? A bareback seminar? A confront-your-fears scenario that would place her nose to nose with Bedlam? She crossed her arms over her chest and rocked back on her heels.

Sam looked every inch the rugged cowboy, standing at ease beside the black beast, worn leather draping his shoulder, his sexy hat shadowing his face, except where crystal-blue eyes burned bright.

He offered Caroline a hand, presumably to climb the fence and mount Bedlam. "Come on."

She narrowed her eyes. "Why?"

"I'm going to honor that trail ride ticket."

Bedlam was not a Sweetness, not even close. He was huge. Fear constricted her chest. "Oh, no, I am not getting on that thing."

"Sure you are." Sam reached for her hand.

Caroline backed up, but only by a few steps—wanting to go, wanting to stay.

"I don't know how to ride a horse like that," she said. "I've only had one lesson, five minutes ago, no less. You weren't impressed, remember? And he's enormous. *Monstrous*. He looks wild, and—and he's got no saddle!"

Sam only smiled, enjoying this. The jerk.

"I'm riding with you," he said.

Caroline's jaw dropped. If he'd wanted to sit her on his lap, all he'd had to do was ask. Or was he too proud for that? She narrowed her eyes. Maybe, just maybe, this was an acceptable teaching method, but given that his anger with her had only recently dissipated, she was shocked that he'd be willing to put them in such an intimate position. She shook her head—she never could figure him out.

"Listen," Sam said, pushing the brim of his hat up to look at her. "You wanted to learn. We don't have a lot of time before the snows come. Riding together is going to be the most effective and efficient way to teach you."

Caroline regarded him warily.

He sighed. "Do you really want to run four hundred rings around this pen? Because you know, Caro, I am a very patient man."

He had her there. Caroline tilted her face heavenward —in supplication for safety. From which she'd need more protection—the man or the horse—she couldn't guess.

25

Caroline gripped the beast's mane in her fists and clamped her legs as tight as possible around its middle. She feared that without a saddle, she'd slide right off the two-story animal.

"When you relax," Sam said, "we'll continue the lesson." His deep voice sent a shiver from her neck to her toes.

She could envision Bedlam turning his head on a whim and snapping off her kneecap for a nice, crunchy snack. "I'll never relax on this thing."

"Mmm, but you will."

Oh, man—Caroline hadn't realized what she'd implied. At Sam's intonation, her body came alive and there was suddenly room in her consciousness for other things. Namely, full-blown awareness of Sam's lower body smack up against her backside, creating delicious pressure with every step of the horse. How could she have not noticed?

Fear must be a powerful, powerful thing.

Caroline squeezed her eyes shut, concentrating on the slight friction of Sam's chest sliding against her upper back. In her mind's eye, she let herself envision them together naked, moving like this on a bed instead. Instantly her body heat soared, and her eyes popped open. It was crazy intense how badly she wanted him.

Did he feel the same attraction and longing? He'd apologized and shown her comfort last night. He'd made good on the promise to teach her to ride when they could easily have gone on avoiding one another for ages. Had he just decided to show kindness? Or did he have an end game? Was it possible he'd changed his mind?

Under the guise of getting more comfortable, she wiggled her bottom and pressed herself full against Sam—an experiment. She heard his intake of breath, felt his leg muscles bunch.

She smiled, feeling rather wicked, and shifted once more. "How do you get comfortable up here?"

"You just do," Sam said, sounding a little choked. "Sit still." His legs squeezed hers as if to keep her from moving.

Caroline was gratified that he wasn't immune to her, but figured she should cool it. Although the messages from Sam's body came through loud and clear, he apparently wasn't ready to renew their sexual relationship.

If she was going to get through this ride without throwing herself at him—and she wasn't keen on repeating rejection—then she needed to find a way to block him out. Him and her fear of Bedlam both, because she really did want to learn to ride.

Caroline tried to count the shafts of sunlight beaming down to the ground through holes in the foliage. She tried to make a mental list of the plants that she didn't recognize so that she could look them up later. She tried to imprint the stunning landscape on her mind's eye to keep. She even tried to get scared about where Bedlam was placing his hooves: on a slippery rock formation, in a hole…

But nothing worked.

The press of Sam's body against her was too insistent to be ignored. Finally, she just gave in—to the feel of him, the heat of him, the scent of him. She reveled in his warm breath on her neck, imagining them lying together again in front of the fire, his lips in her hair, his thumb stroking the underside of her breast…

As she fell deeper into fantasy—a memory she couldn't repeat—her body relaxed.

———

Sam felt the change in Caroline. She leaned more fully against his chest as they moved languidly as one on top of Bedlam, but he was in no hurry. He breathed in her wild-flower scent—sweet like honey and as refreshing as the mountain air. It made no sense, but he'd missed her.

Just like last night, he had an incredible urge to rest his chin on her head, to tuck her into him for safekeeping. No matter that Bedlam wouldn't harm her; her fear of the horse had brought out feelings of protectiveness in him. What in the hell was he supposed to do with that? On the other hand, the sparks in her eyes and her sassy mouth had made him want her again. And he knew, all too well, what to do with *that*.

He'd ached to pull her to him and kiss her until she was dizzy—just to start. It had taken everything he had to stand lazily at the fence. Just as it was taking all his self-control now not to nuzzle her neck and run his hands down her jeans-clad thighs.

Sam's fantasy morphed from tender to X-rated, until he shook himself. There was no point in thinking about how she'd feel, how she'd move, how she would—

No. He'd said—and meant—only one night. But goddammit, how was he to know that spending one night with Caro would increase his desire for her tenfold?

"Okay, Caro—" He had to stop and clear his throat. "As we come into this flat stretch ahead, squeeze just slightly with your knees so that Bedlam will pick up the pace a bit."

Bedlam skittered sideways, not sure of the message Caroline was sending. Sam was pressed so closely to her that he had felt her mixed signal too.

"Focus your attention on my legs." Sam felt her stiffen. "Relax and feel how I move." He gave a slight nudge with his knees, which in turn pressed hers against the horse. Without the slightest hesitation, the horse began to trot. "See? Now, stay loose here," he told her, and leaned forward to trace Caroline's thigh.

He gritted his teeth. What the hell was wrong with him that he couldn't control this insane and constant urge to touch her? Wasn't practically sitting her on his lap enough?

"Try to separate your knees from the rest of your leg." Sam squeezed her knee. "Signal only briefly to the horse with the lightest contact possible. Now try again."

"Better.

"Keep your seat; sit up straight.

"Relax.

"Yes, good."

Sam was impressed—Caroline had needed only a handful of corrections. He shut up and let her take charge, trying not to recall how she'd ridden him with such natural instinct as well.

Caroline sat up in the saddle. "There's steam coming from behind those rocks." She craned her neck around to look at him. "You have a hot spring on your land?"

"Yes."

"And no one told me this when my muscles were screaming in pain?"

He chuckled. "I'll have to add it to the training manual."

"Page one." She smiled. "How hot is it? Can we go in?"

Sam swallowed hard at that *we*. She'd said it innocently, but the thought of the two of them naked and wet… "Lunch first."

"I'm starved anyway." Caroline grinned and nearly bounced on the horse. Between the picnic and the prospect of a hot soak, she was as excited as he'd ever seen her. In fact, she seemed so light at heart that Sam had to promise himself, for the thousandth time that day, not to touch her no matter what happened.

This time, however, he promised it for her sake, not his own. The lesson and now this ride were a peace offering only, nothing more. He meant to ease her burden, not mislead her into thinking there could be anything more between them.

Sam handed Caroline the thin blanket to spread out, and he unpacked lunch. He'd managed to stuff everything Ruby had prepared into the saddlebags. It wouldn't matter that the food was mushed or upended; he was hungry. Caroline headed for the spring, but as she approached, the wind shifted. She wrinkled her nose and changed direction.

They sat twenty feet from the pool, facing it, with a large slab of rock for a backrest, and dug into the picnic fare. He'd set his hat on the ground beside him, no different than if he'd been sitting at the family table, so she did the same.

"How does Will do it?" She licked her lips. "They are just chicken fingers, but somehow, with the sauce and this breading—wow."

"Tell me about it," Sam agreed. "I'm so spoiled eating Will's cooking that anytime I go off the ranch, nothing tastes right. I usually end up ordering burgers and fries because at least I know how bad they'll be."

Caroline groaned. "Don't mention burgers and fries. I hope I never see either ever again."

Sam laughed at her pained expression. "Why's that?"

"I didn't come straight here from Miami. Let me tell you, there is nothing but hamburgers on America's highways."

"Sure there is," Sam said. "Fish sandwiches, chicken sandwiches, chicken nuggets, white salad in plastic cups, and occasionally mushy fruit in plastic cups."

Caro laughed. "You know your fast food."

"You don't opt for fried food usually?" Sam had an overpowering urge to keep her talking. They'd been as intimate as two people could be, and yet he really knew very little about her.

"Not usually. And I guess I was in a burger-ordering phase." Caroline paused. "Oh, what the hell, I was not myself. Probably full-on depressed. I didn't care what I ate. I didn't really want to eat. I just knew I had to have some sort of fuel for my body if I was going to operate a vehicle at sixty-five-plus miles per hour."

"Kevin?" Sam asked, hating that he couldn't seem to forget her husband's name.

"Yeah."

Caroline looked over the spread of food Sam had laid out. She obviously didn't want to continue that conversation. Streaks of gold shone throughout the soft mass of her hair. Sam's hands itched to slide through it as he had done at the cabin. Her skin had a healthy glow too, and even though she'd been on an emotional rollercoaster the last few days, she still seemed lighter than when she'd first arrived on the ranch. His home was working its magic on her, like it did on almost everyone who visited.

"Even the combination of cheeses and crackers is so yummy," Caroline mumbled around a bite. "Seriously, how did Will learn all this flavor stuff?"

"He was a chef at the Ritz-Carlton in Boston."

"Ooh, schmancy. How'd he end up here?"

"Well, Ruby worked there too. She was some high-profile event planner or something. She organized a singles vacation out here with a bunch of folks from work."

"So they fell in love on vacation and stayed?" she asked.

"Actually, they fought like wildcats when they were here, but eventually ended up together. They honeymooned here, then continued to come for vacation for years. Finally decided they wanted a different way of life, ditched their high-stress careers, and moved out here for good. Will says he was born in the wrong region of the country."

"Wait a minute. He was raised in Boston?"

Sam smiled; he knew where she was going. "The accent? A put-on. According to Will, no one comes out west to hear Boston."

"Wow," Caroline said. "He's good. I haven't even heard him slip—not once."

"He and Ruby have embraced this life and the ranch in full. Can't imagine the place without them." He shrugged. "They're family now."

"I know what you mean. It's the same with my friend Neve and her daughter Bella."

"She must be the one I spoke to yesterday," Sam said.

"You talked with Neve?"

Sam tensed. "Your phone wouldn't stop ringing, so I answered it."

"I assumed Ruby had left it on my porch." She narrowed her eyes. "Neve didn't mention you'd had a conversation."

"I wouldn't call it a conversation, really." His mouth twisted—somewhere between a grimace and a smile.

Caroline laughed.

"So, is she considering coming out?"

"She was this close to booking tickets when I spoke with her last." She reached for another piece of cheese. "You know, it's actually Neve's fault that you're saddled with me now."

"Why's that?"

"Basically, she kicked me out of my own home." She shook her head. "It sounds harsh, but she knew I needed to get out of there. She was right."

"So you were in a sorry state, well after Kevin's passing."

"I didn't actually have a sense of time. I can see now that I was emotionally paralyzed. Frozen." She frowned and dropped the cheese into her napkin. "Unable to face anything. Just…afraid to move forward."

"Why?"

"I don't know, really." Caroline ducked her head, seemingly concentrating on folding the napkin just so around the cheese.

Sam reached out and tipped up her chin with his fingers, forcing her to meet his eyes. "You do know. You can tell me. I won't judge you."

"It's not that, it's… I can barely face it myself."

"That awful?" What had happened to her husband? To her? What would make her run so far from her old life?

Caroline set the napkins down and tucked her hands in her armpits. She took a deep breath. "I killed him."

26

____

Caroline—a murderer? Sam forced himself not to react. Deceit she'd handled like a pro—but he couldn't imagine she was capable of bodily harm. He decided to go for humor—bad humor. "You planned out the perfect murder, laced his beer with cyanide or something?"

"No!" It was halfhearted and fleeting, but she did crack a tiny smile. "It was an accident, but still, it's my fault he's dead."

"Tell me what happened."

Caro pulled her knees up and stared toward the steam drifting from the spring. "We were driving on the highway. In the Everglades. It had just started pouring. Out of nowhere, I yelled—and told him to stop." She glanced at him briefly then away again. "I saw a Florida panther—a rarity because it's endangered—up in the trees. I wanted to photograph it. That's what I do, or did. He lost control of the car. We spun, flew off the highway, flipped. I can't stand that..." Her voice cracked, "It was me. He was a cop. If he was going to die, it should have been on the job, saving someone or stopping a crime. It shouldn't have happened that way."

Caroline twisted her napkin round and round her fist. She wouldn't look at Sam.

"There's more?" he asked.

"I was unconscious, but later when I woke…there was…a piece of metal that had shoved through the soft top and plowed through his head. Through his eye. And I can't, I can't—"

Caroline was struggling to breathe. Sam pulled her onto his lap, and she buried her face into her napkin and his chest. Muffled, she said, "He was so handsome. But that's the picture I can't seem to get out of my mind."

Then she sobbed, her chest heaving as she clung to his shirt. He sat cross-legged with her all tucked up inside his limbs. He stroked her back, rocked a little, and crooned to her as if she were a small child.

Eventually she was spent. Sam held her a while longer and then said, "Did you talk to anyone about all this?"

Caroline shook her head into his shoulder.

"Not even Neve?"

Another shake of the head and sniffle.

"You should have. She would have told you it wasn't your fault."

"But it was my fault."

"I don't know. Officers are trained to assess threats in a split second and to handle vehicles at high speeds," he said. "There's almost no way he should have lost control over the car. Maybe something malfunctioned in the steering column because of a recent pothole you'd hit. Maybe he saw something you didn't see and tried to avoid it. Maybe a truck had spilled some gasoline and, coupled with the sudden rain, you would have hydroplaned anyway. I could probably come up with another fifty possibilities, but my point is: you can't take all the blame on your own shoulders." He rubbed his hand up and down her arm.

"And he knew you well, right? Surely, it wasn't the first time you suddenly yelled for him to stop." Sam pushed the strands of hair sticking to her wet cheeks out of her face and handed her his own unsullied napkin.

"Thank you," Caroline whispered.

"As for the other, well, there's nothing I can say to that except I'm sorry you had to see that." Sam stroked her back. "If Neve's your best friend, why didn't you tell her everything?"

She let out a shaky sigh. "Because she knew Kevin well, and loved him too. Because I couldn't stand for her to hate me."

"You ought to tell her sometime."

"I might have to." She blew out another breath. "She can't understand why I won't shoot anymore."

"Are we back to murder again?"

Caro shoved a hand against his chest, and a tentative, wobbly smile graced her lips. Putting it there gave him an oddly satisfying sense of pleasure.

"Shoot photos. I was on staff at a newspaper. After the accident, I took an indefinite leave of absence. I haven't been able to touch my camera." She grimaced. "Neve and everyone else thought getting back to work, back to something I had loved, would help. She even stashed my equipment in the trunk of my car before I left."

Sam chuckled. "She *is* pushy."

"She is." She sniffed, then her mouth turned up at the corners a bit. "Heart's in the right place, though."

Sam smiled too, curling his hand tighter around her hip. She held her gaze, and he found he was holding his breath. Their lips were only inches apart, and he sensed she was about to lean in. He wanted her to. He downright ached for just a taste, even though—

"I should get up." She uncurled her legs.

Deflection from the sexual tension, but necessary. "You should use your camera."

Caroline stood, swiped at her cheeks, pushed her hair out of her face, and then offered a hand to Sam. He nearly laughed. Although she wasn't as thin as when she'd arrived, she was still likely to topple if he gave her his full weight. He took her hand anyway—for another chance to touch her.

She said, "Well, I told your mother I'd document the party, so I need to find a way to be okay with it fast."

He squeezed her hand before dropping it. "Would it make it easier if I was with you the first time?"

She tilted her head side to side, considering. "I think I'd rather be alone, but thanks." She rubbed a hand over her other arm. "It's probably just as well Anna roped me into this. I'll have to go back to the newspaper soon."

Sam's lungs felt crunched, like he couldn't draw a full breath. Go? When? How long could she be away from her career and her home? Indefinite must not mean infinite.

Hell, it wasn't any of his business. Not even as her employer, because he'd never meant to hire her anyway, and she'd only bargained for a temporary spot.

He released her and asked, "You've had your fill?"

"Of the food?" she asked, an eyebrow raised.

"Yes," he answered as flatly as possible. Would the heavy-duty sexual tension that constantly zinged between them ever ease?

"Yes, but I'm not sure I could ever get enough of..." Her eyes dropped to his lips.

If she spoke the words aloud, Sam would lose it. He'd never been so turned on than when she'd become so verbal at the cabin. She was already nearly irresistible; telling him in no uncertain terms what she wanted, in her sexy voice, would send him over the edge.

"...this place." Her eyes sparkled with mischief.

Sam sagged with relief and no small measure of disappointment.

She turned a full, slow circle and said softly, "It's so beautiful. Every bit."

"Damn straight." Sam felt that way every day. And not just here. In the mountains, in the meadows, in the barn, in the lodge. Every board, every blade of grass, every nicker of a horse... To be part of this ranch was all that had ever mattered to him.

They worked together repacking the saddlebag. As Caroline folded the blanket, she asked, "So, are we going in?"

"You are," Sam said.

"Why just me?" she asked.

"Because."

Caroline's eyes narrowed. "So, I'm supposed to shed my clothes and hop in, while you sit out here like a voyeur?"

"I won't watch," he said, although he would love to see her naked again—this time with water glistening over every inch of her luscious body.

Caroline didn't speak, but her mind must have veered in the same naughty direction as his own, because her eyes and posture had changed. She was looking him over, blatantly assessing the goods.

Uh-oh, this was bad. This meant she was going to—

"I could use a back massage," Caroline said, inviting him to oh so much more.

"Caro, this"—he gestured to the land, to Bedlam, to Caroline herself—"is my life's work." He couldn't explain further than that.

"You're sure?" Caroline asked, beginning to unbutton her shirt, her eyes trained on his face, willing him to say yes, though he saw doubt there.

He burned hotter for Caroline Murphy than any woman he'd ever met. Here she was, offering herself to him, both vulnerable and sexy.

Sam was unable to move, his eyes following her slender hands. She wasn't opening her shirt to skin; she had on a thick, long underwear shirt. Where was that sheer stuff he'd found so sexy? It didn't matter. She was undressing for him, and he was dying. Dying to keep watching, dying to push that shirt off her shoulders and kiss the daylights out of her. Dying inside, because he really couldn't.

He'd made an exception for one night because they'd been off ranch property, because he didn't think anyone would find out, because he'd wanted her that badly, because he was crazy...

Totally crazy for her.

But even though they were completely alone up here, this was his family's land. The last time he'd had a woman on their property, disaster had struck—so yeah, he understood Caroline's guilt about the accident that stole her husband from her all too well. He'd promised himself: never again. It didn't matter if no one ever knew but him. *He* would know that he'd broken his own vow. He still—after all these years—felt remorse. He'd lost precious pride over the years because of the ridiculous stud rumor—which should have ended the same night as the fire.

At this point, however, his reputation was as pock-marked as a lava rock, his heart about as hard as one. He refused to sully his honor as well.

Caroline peeled her overshirt off her shoulders. She crossed her arms in front of her to grasp the hem of her long underwear top. She held his eyes and raised that eyebrow in invitation…

For him to make a move.

Or for him to shut this down.

But he was frozen in place—so torn between what he needed—a solitary, focused life—and what he desired—this amazing, challenging woman.

Caroline's face fell. She tucked her chin into her chest, then she bent and picked up her discarded overshirt. She crumpled it and clasped it over her chest with both hands.

When she raised her eyes, she looked pained. "I'm sorry, I…"

The challenge, the sensuality, and even the spark had vanished. Sam felt heavy too. He didn't like that blank look in her gaze.

"Aren't you going to look away or take a walk or something?" She focused on the view beyond him.

Sam reached out—still aching for a connection with her despite himself—but dropped his hand. "Caro," he said softly.

She looked at him then, a bit of hope resurfacing on her face. Sam had an insane urge to make this woman smile, at any cost to himself.

"Is this"—he waved his hand between them—"what you really want? Would it make you that happy, us being together again?"

Her eyes came to life instantaneously and her hands dropped to her side, one clenched around her shirt. "Yes, but…"

Sam waited, his breath held. She scuffed her boot on the ground, then seemed to rally herself. When her beautiful brown eyes locked with his, he felt he could see clear through to her soul.

"Only if it's what you want, too."

To Sam, those words were magic. They couldn't change what was, but still, an enormous sense of relief and peace flooded his mind, while his heart overflowed with warmth. He smiled then, the genuine article, like he hadn't since they'd laughed together in the cabin.

Caroline smiled back, tentatively at first, and then she beamed, bright as could be. He'd never seen anything more breathtaking.

"Thank you for that." He took her free hand. "I do want you. I just can't do a relationship—not serious or casual or any of this in between. It's not you. I just have my reasons."

She searched his face and then pulled loose. She crossed one arm over her middle, the other over her chest. Protecting herself. "You weren't kidding when you said only one night, were you?" Her smile was halfhearted and gave away her hurt.

She pressed her lips together, then shook out her shirt,

yanked the arms right side out, and struggled to get both arms in.

"You can still take that soak."

"Let's just go."

"Caroline—"

"I'll come back another time." She shoved into her shirt.

Sam put his hands on his hips, ready to argue, wanting to give her more, hating that he'd hurt her, no matter how necessary.

"It's okay, Sam, really." She grabbed the blanket and her hat, leaving the saddlebag for him, and turned toward Bedlam. "You never promised me anything more than the one night—and we both know you wouldn't have even gone for that if I hadn't done what I did." She paused when she reached the horse, looking over her shoulder at him. "You didn't let me say it before. But I am sorry."

She smoothed a hand down Bedlam's neck, then half turned again to meet his eye. She gave a tight smile and a firm nod. "I shouldn't have pushed you. Not then and not now. It won't happen again."

27

That evening, under the cover of a black night with few stars, Caroline snuck from the cabins, past the main house, and well past the barn to where her car was parked. She kept to the grass and avoided the gravel. She didn't want to announce what she was up to—she didn't want company.

She hadn't driven since that shopping excursion. There'd been no reason to. Everything she needed these days was here on the ranch. The animals and land and straightforward work filled her in a way she never would have expected. And so quickly, the Jenkses and the Blacks had become her people. Even Neve and Bella would be here come Saturday.

Sam, though… He was more than one of her tribe and yet not hers at all. She needed him in a whole different way. After that complete humiliation this afternoon and the tense ride back, she'd kept to herself the rest of the day.

She worried that she'd shoved Sam into the hole that was Kevin's—latching on to him as some sort of substitute lifeline. But no—she still felt Kevin's loss, still loved him. And yet her heart had made a new place somehow for another man. Something she'd never have dreamed possible.

It scared her how much she liked Sam, how badly she wanted him, how hurt she felt that he didn't want her—or at least not enough to win over whatever demons he carried.

Sam's rejection had shredded her. And yet…he'd given her so much. The night they were together. A place where she belonged on this beautiful, healing land. A shoulder to cry on—quite literally—twice now. A sounding board. And today…a true gift in the form of alternate theories.

"*Oh.*" She gasped and jumped when she passed the driver's-side door and the locks clicked, sensing the key in her pocket. She shook her head and put her hand to her racing heart. She was too primed about this. She stood in front of the trunk and took a big breath.

It's not a snake, just camera equipment.

She popped the hatchback, then cringed when the light spotlighted her. She reached in and tugged the beach towel off the two camera bags she'd shoved in the back corner.

Another deep breath because her chest felt tight and her pulse was too fast. Excited? Uneasy? Both?

She gritted her teeth, then reached for the bags. Quickly, with movements remembered from thousands of times before, she threw them just so over her shoulder. She carefully closed the trunk with a soft thud and subsequent click. She didn't lock the car, wanting to avoid the loud beep and flashing headlights.

And then, like a thief, she smuggled the emotionally loaded goods back to her cabin.

Caroline set the bags on the bed and stripped out of her coat and boots, taking the time to steady herself. Then she crossed her arms over her chest and turned to face this piece of her past.

She'd thought long and hard today about what Sam had said. Guilt hadn't miraculously vanished, but it helped to think that there may have been more at play, that the blame didn't rest squarely on her shoulders.

She'd forced herself to think of even more possibilities than Sam had come up with. What if that accident Kevin had had a few months prior had thrown off the balance of the steering despite the repairs? What if the repair shop said they'd fixed everything but hadn't? What if the extra-hot summer had wasted the tires faster than normal and they should have had them replaced?

Because if any one of those things had happened, then…

She smoothed her hand over the bag as she unzipped it, suddenly worried her equipment would be ruined. Normally she'd never have left it in the trunk of a car, subject to the constant temperature changes.

She checked the power, the particular click of the expensive machine turning on feeling surprisingly comfortable.

She'd expected for this exercise to feel like a mine-field. So far, it was okay.

The memory card, though… She'd barely touched the laptop she brought, but she could use it now to upload the data. Except she didn't want to see all she'd shot on the trip through the Everglades with Kevin.

No, she definitely didn't.

She flipped open the panel and popped the thin

card out.

She let out a long, slow breath and tucked it in its own little case and then into a compartment in her bag.

She opened a fresh memory card and pushed it into the camera. The Black Hills Ranch deserved its own.

She'd start over.

Caroline put the camera to her eye and scanned the cozy little cabin. She shot artistically: the pattern in the blanket, the beauty in the grain of the wood, the angle of her hat atop the bedpost.

She lowered the camera and dropped her chin to her chest, emotion overwhelming her.

She'd built up a whole mess of fear and guilt and loss around her photography. But Neve's orders had made her consider things. Anna's request had created the necessity to try. Sam's support had helped her clear a hurdle.

Okay, she might never again shoot from a moving car. But she knew now she could capture the Blacks' party, an alligator who'd blocked traffic on a downtown Miami street, a suspect being taken into custody…

She half sobbed, half laughed. The relief that washed over her was enormous. A huge missing piece of herself—not to mention her livelihood—had been restored.

"Oh, God."

She held the camera to her chest, pressing the hard edges into her breast.

Gently, she packed the camera back into its bag. Then she picked up her cell phone. There was still something she had to make right.

It was after one a.m. back east, but Neve answered right away. "Everything okay?"

Caroline released a long breath. "Almost."

28

———

As far as Sam was concerned, the days leading up to the season-ending bash were even more chaotic than usual. Sam's mother kept calling with instructions, his dad refused to be ordered about by anyone but his wife, and, of course, Carter normally would have helped Sam with the heavy lifting.

Sam had lobbied to scrap the event this year and bring a party to Carter instead. But his mom wouldn't hear of it. Far as she was concerned, tradition, thanking the seasonal staff, and connecting with the neighbors were all important. And, well, the clincher was that she didn't believe Carter would take being swarmed very well right now.

Sam found himself worrying more and more about Carter. His body was healing, but something deep down was broken. He'd be home soon, likely early next week, and Sam hoped like hell once Carter was where he belonged that he'd begin to feel more like his old self.

Speaking of healing, Caroline seemed to be enjoying herself. Sam couldn't help it, but he'd kept his eye on her all evening. She drew him in, but he also knew she'd been dreading using that camera—and he wanted to be there if she needed support.

She must have been introduced to fifty new people by now, and she greeted each warmly. He loved seeing her laugh and smile and have a good time. Because with him, she no longer did. They'd put animosity behind them and seemed to have finally reached an understanding. Only that meant that she chose aloof and polite: not warm, not cold, just walking the line—the line he'd asked for—with plenty of distance in between. It fit wrong on him, like a saddle that chafed.

He changed out the beer keg to a bunch of good-natured ribbing. The tightness in his shoulders eased—last year, two of the guys had gotten skunked, ended up in a fistfight, and one nearly sent the other into the bonfire. Tonight, everyone seemed to be behaving. Whenever extra people were on the ranch—guests, neighbors, anyone—he was on high alert.

When Sam extracted himself from a circle of men, Will appeared at his side. "You take time to eat yet?"

Part chef, part mother hen. "Hell yes. Getting ready for round two."

"Good. You let me know if there's something getting low."

"Everybody on this spread knows to let you know." Sam didn't see Caroline, and scanned the various clusters of revelers.

Will cocked his head. "Your little lady took her new charge to the bathroom."

"She's not my little lady."

"Daresay you're the only one thinking that."

"Jenks—"

"Ask her to dance."

"Whatever you're cooking up, just can it."

Dead keg handle gripped in one fist, Sam stalked off toward the back lot, shaking his head. Now he couldn't get the idea of Caroline swaying in his arms out of his head.

Dammit. The last thing he needed was a bunch of matchmakers making things tougher. Like he didn't have enough to contend with.

Tromping back to the party, he spotted Bella busting out of the kitchen door, Caroline hot on her heels.

Unfortunately, with party preparations in full swing, Neve and Bella hadn't really been given a proper welcome. Ruby had gotten them settled, and Caroline had given them a tour. By all accounts, the little girl had practically vibrated with joy at the horses, the tractor, the hay loft, the log cabins. He grinned. There was so much more to show the kid.

Bella had been attached at the hip to Caroline since she'd picked them up at the airport around lunchtime. Now the duo was talking with Kim Reese, the next-door neighbor. Kim caught his eye and waved him over.

He nodded a greeting to them all and gave her a kiss on the cheek. "Did you bring that gooey chocolate pie I'm so crazy about?"

"You know I did. There's one on the dessert table and another in the kitchen just for you. Promise me you'll freeze a big slice for Carter?"

"I'll be sure to do that." It felt wrong that neither Carter nor his mom were here, and yet the outpouring of concern from all the neighbors and hands was heartening.

Bella's eyes were like saucers, and she tugged excitedly on Caroline's hand until she bent down so that Bella could whisper in her ear.

"His name is Sam, and he's nice." Caroline winked up at Sam, but told the girl, "Ask him."

"Mr. Sam," Bella said. "Can I have some too? Chocolate everything is my favorite."

"Of course," he said, squatting down to look the little girl in the eye. "Pie is meant to be shared—even pie that has my name on it."

Bella bounced excitedly on her toes, and Sam rose. His mother was going to adore this kid. Shame she wasn't here.

"Well, look at that, Kim. You got me a pie *and* a kitchen date. I owe you double now."

"I'm gonna cash in right now, then," Kim said.

"Shoot."

"Well, we've got a new litter of kittens in the barn."

Bella gasped, and all the adults laughed.

"As many kids as I have," Kim said, "we *still* need more hands to give those wriggling little fluff balls enough attention. You think you could spare Miss Bella here sometime tomorrow?"

"Mommy says I'll have to do my part," Bella piped up. "But I don't have my own job here yet. I can definitely come help your kittens."

"Perfect," Kim said. "Tomorrow, then." She took her leave.

Neve was talking with Astor nearby, and Bella darted away to tell her the news, leaving Sam and Caroline alone for the first time since that loaded conversation at the hot springs. He knew she'd been purposely giving him space. He also knew he shouldn't miss her like he did.

Caroline grinned at him. "So that's the one, huh?"

"One what?"

She waggled her eyebrows.

"Ah, yes." He laughed. His virginity. "That's the one."

She grinned, then looked at her boots, and he just knew she was thinking of how to extract herself.

He said, "Neve and Bella seem to be enjoying themselves."

"You all certainly know how to make guests feel at home. Add in a party, pie, horses, and kittens?" She grinned and shrugged.

"How 'bout you?" He held her eyes.

"It's fantastic." She looked around. "I can see why Anna pushed to keep the tradition. People must look forward to this all year."

"They do. And there's always enough gossip to sustain them for a good while afterwards, too."

She smiled but didn't look at him. He waited her out, then looked pointedly at the camera she held in one hand, despite the strap around her neck. "And that?"

"It's actually…really good."

He smiled with relief. "Glad to hear." Even though she'd seemed to be okay from a distance, she often hovered at the edges of the action. He'd worried she was holding herself back, maybe struggling to embrace the task fully. Maybe, though, it was simply how she worked a job. Like herding cattle, a body needed to be on the outside.

She made to go, then paused and turned back. She laid her hand on his chest—just a press. "Thank you, Sam." And then her warmth was gone.

29

———

The next few days were fuller than usual. Besides setting things back to rights after the bash, they'd been sharing the delights of the ranch with Neve and Bella.

Will made sure they all gathered for Bella to roast marshmallows and gorge on s'mores—her first, given her Miami upbringing. Ruby made sure to outfit the child with genuine cowboy boots and a warm coat from the costume gallery, and Sam made a mental note: if they were still here when the pond froze, skating was a must. Astor had led them on a gentle trail ride out to the hot springs, where he'd left them with a picnic and towels and returned in a couple hours to lead them back home. Sam had stuck miked helmets on their heads, packed them into the RZRs, and guided them up the mountain trails to see the prettiest view there ever was.

Caroline snapped pictures of it all.

Now, midweek and midafternoon, they hovered close to the main house, anxiously awaiting Carter and Anna's arrival.

Finally, Sam heard the SUV coming up the hill and called to the others.

"'Bout time," Will said, joining him on the porch.

"Damn straight."

The SUV pulled to a stop and Sam's mom got out, smiling and waving. They all raced down the steps hooting and hollering.

Man, but his mother was a sight for sore eyes, even though she looked tired and stressed. This place just wasn't quite right without her—and neither was his father.

She rounded the car, hugging them each in turn on the way, and Sam realized Carter was in the back seat. Of course he was. He couldn't bend his leg.

"Sam, lend me a hand. The rest of you, give us some space." Anna opened the car door.

Sam bent down to greet his friend. "Welcome home, my brother."

Carter's face was covered in bandages—less then when Sam had visited the hospital, but still he was half hidden. The other half looked like a storm cloud about to let loose.

"I told her to drive right up to my cabin," Carter said.

"Come on, man. Everybody's been dying to see you."

"The last thing I need is an audience." But Carter shoved the crutch out the door and let Sam grasp his arm. Sam cringed inside. Carter had lost a lot of weight, and he looked as pasty as bread dough.

Sam took his friend's weight, careful not to jostle his leg or help too much. Sissy—despite their mother's orders —was right there and got the crutch upright and under Carter, who hopped for balance, grimacing the whole while. She kissed his good cheek, then said, "Good to see you're no uglier than ever."

"Good to see nothing changed while I was gone," Carter said. "You still haven't learned an ounce of manners."

That broke the ice some, and everybody surged forward to welcome him home, except for Caroline and Bella, who sat on the top step of the porch.

Neve stood at the edge of the pack, until Anna waved her forward. "Carter, this is Neve, the nurse who'll be assisting you."

"Welcome home, Carter," Neve said.

He glanced at her then flinched away.

To Anna, he said through gritted teeth, "I told you a million times—"

"And I told *you* a million times." Anna's tone brooked no argument.

Carter had grown up in Anna's home and adored her maybe even more than her own children did. He simply turned away from Neve.

The two women exchanged a glance, and Neve gave the slightest inclination of her head. Sam realized she and Anna must have discussed far more than bandages and dosages.

Carter adjusted his crutch and lurched in the direction of his cabin. Sam stayed by his side.

"Neve," Anna said, "let me show you everything the hospital sent. Sissy, grab our bags, please. Astor, go open Carter's door and roll up the runner. We can't have the crutch snagging on the carpet."

Carter grunted with every step.

"Looks mighty comfortable," Sam said.

"It's a real blast." Another grunt. "Gonna take me ten years just to cross the damn field."

"I could just pick you up."

"Over my dead body."

"Yeah," Sam said, "about that."

Carter didn't even send him a sideways glance.

"You gone and died on me? Jesus, usually you're all over a pretty woman," Sam said. "You should be playing the ooh-nurse-I-need-your-soft-touch card."

"Shut the fuck up, man."

"You shut the fuck up. We flew the woman all the way from Miami to be at your beck and call."

"Fly her on back. I don't want her."

"You need her."

Carter's visible eye flashed with heat and then turned flat. "Like hell I do. This"—he flicked his free hand toward his face—"can't be fixed."

By now they'd reached the cabin. Astor had already ascended the porch and gone inside.

Anna and Neve came up behind them.

Carter yanked his arm from Sam's grasp and lurched over to the banner hanging from the rails of the porch. *Welcome home,* it read. Every single person at the bash had taken time to sign it, and the kids had drawn little pictures of hearts and horses and Band-Aids in all the free spots.

Carter reached out—nearly toppling himself—yanked it down, and tossed it to the ground. "This isn't a goddamn celebration."

"All right," Neve said, waving Sam and Anna off. "You've had your tantrum. Inside you go."

Carter scowled at her. She just stared him down.

Sam turned with leaden steps. Anna had tears in her eyes, and Sam squeezed her hand.

He snuck a glance over his shoulder and saw Neve

pointing to the step railing and taking Carter's crutch from him. "Angle yourself so your foot doesn't bump the step."

"They taught me how already."

"Seems you forgot already."

Sam smiled at his mom. "Caroline said Neve won't take any crap."

Anna smiled back. "God brought us Caroline to bring us Neve."

He huffed. "Or Rita sent her." Rita and some of True Springs' legendary water, if one put any stock in that ridiculousness. He didn't.

Anna shook her head. "There's far more at play here than you know."

Oh, he and his aching needs knew. All too well. Only he wondered what exactly his mother thought was at play.

30

───────

Will had enlisted Bella's help in the kitchen ahead of dinner, so Caroline took the time to retreat to her cabin. She'd already uploaded the photos from the end-of-season party to her computer. She had even sent a whole slew to Neve.

Proof.

And although Neve's crazy quest was officially complete, of course she didn't drop it. Neve had asked all the tough questions. *Was it okay? How do you feel? Can you work again?* Caroline smiled. Neve was annoying as all get out, but Caroline was lucky to have her friend in her corner.

Now she scrolled through deleting the ones not worth keeping and organizing the rest for Anna to use as she pleased. An amazing candid of Sam popped up.

She leaned back in her chair, tucking her hands between her thighs. Throughout the party, she'd snuck shots of him—laughing with the men, ribbing Sissy, clapping his hand on Astor's shoulder, and standing in the shadows watching like a hawk—for what, she couldn't tell.

When she'd first met him, he'd seemed so serious, so harsh and angry. But she'd come to learn he was a giver. Taking care of everything and everyone. Running the show and giving orders, but also always lending a hand and offering support. Motivating, comforting, steady.

Everyone relied on him. Certainly, he'd been the rock she'd needed.

Not to mention incredibly sexy: his rough hands, his strong build, his rugged good looks. His smile could melt her, the concern in his beautiful blue eyes made her feel cared for, and his embrace made her feel like all was right with the world. And talk about a skilled lover. She'd only had one night—but oh, what a night.

Desire, need, regret, pleasure, warmth, longing—all of it swirled together in her chest, palpable in her body, crashing hard against what she knew logically. She couldn't have him. He didn't want her, or wouldn't let himself want her. And she'd promised to stop pushing. She drew a shaky breath into her too-tight lungs.

Holding yourself apart only hurt this bad when you were in love.

Her hand flew up to cover her mouth as if to keep the thought from taking shape, but no—it already existed.

Damn. She got up to pace the small space. She'd fallen in love, in a few weeks? What were the chances?

That was crazy insane and should have been impossible. Two years since she'd lost Kevin. Not that long—and yet in many ways, it felt like forever ago.

What was the point of finding love again—against all odds—and opening herself up to it, if she couldn't have it?

And Bella being here was a huge wake-up call. Caroline didn't want just love—she wanted it all. Love, a husband, a baby, or more, a whole family of her own— what she'd always wanted. But Kevin was gone. And Sam didn't want her.

Such a cruel joke on the universe's part.

Her cell phone buzzed again. She'd been ignoring it. She knew who it was, knew what he wanted.

She'd only just begun to use her camera again—and yet it was as if popping off the lens cap had opened her very own Pandora's box.

She picked up her cell phone and stared at the display.

She'd been happy in Montana—in the cocoon of the Black Hills Ranch. She'd learned to live again in this amazing place with this incredible family. She had every- thing she needed, everything that mattered, and, most of all, everyone she needed.

Except Sam, really.

The phone was still vibrating. This time, she answered.

———

Normally, Caroline would have joined Will and Ruby in the kitchen ahead of dinner to help out and chat. Tonight, she waited to cross the field until she heard the dinner bell.

Soft light glowed in one of Carter's windows. So far, he'd chosen to take meals in his cabin. Anna had told him she would allow him one more day to sulk. After that, she'd have him hauled physically to the main house if need be.

Everyone else was already in the kitchen, pulling out chairs or transferring dishes to the table.

"Hi, Aunt Caroline." Bella hopped off a stool, wearing a too-big apron patterned with horseshoes.

"Hi, Bug."

Neve took one look at Caroline's face. "Oh, no. What is it?"

All eyes swung toward Caroline. So much for waiting until dessert.

Caroline took a deep breath. "My editor called."

"That rat," Neve said. "We just got here."

"Well, all he knows is that I had a whole two years' leave, one of the team moved out of state, and my counterpart just broke his leg. He needs me back."

"What about freelancers?"

"It's time," Caroline said, her voice gentle. For her own sake or theirs?

She smiled sadly as she looked at all these people she loved. Disappointment from Ruby; a comical scowl from Will. "Well, hell's bells," he said.

Sissy frowned. Anna stepped forward and wrapped Caroline in a hug. "I'm only just getting to know you, and yet it feels like you belong here."

Astor laid one hand on his wife's shoulder and patted Caroline's with the other.

Tears pricked Caroline's eyes. "Thank you."

Despite herself, she glanced at Sam, who was stone-faced.

"When?" Ruby asked.

"As soon as possible. I'd like to enjoy tomorrow, so early the morning after."

Bella tucked a hand in Caroline's front jeans pocket. "What's going on?"

Caroline bent and scooped her up. "I have to leave. My job needs me back."

"Don't you have a job here?"

"Yes. I mean my job at home in Miami." Except Miami seemed like the farthest thing from home right about now.

"But I still miss you from before." Bella pouted, little eyebrows inverting.

That nearly broke her, so Caroline laid her forehead against Bella's for a second to gather herself.

Finally, she straightened with a big grin. "You know what I'm going to do? Vacation here! The first chance I get."

She tickled the little girl's belly, and thankfully, the squealing giggle that erupted put everyone back in motion.

———

That night, Caroline had been getting organized to leave when a knock sounded on her cabin door. It was Sam. She knew it. She'd felt his gaze on her all through dinner, pushing her, pulling her, gauging her, calling her.

She shoved her hair back off her face, hoped like hell her eyes weren't too puffy and her nose wasn't too red, and swung open the door.

Damn, but he looked good. A lined Carhartt jacket made his wide shoulders look even broader, his jet-black hair shone in the moonlight, and his blue eyes focused on nothing but her.

"Shall I come out, or do you want to come in?"

He looked down at her thick socks and thermal long underwear bottoms—which she often wore to bed. Her big sweatshirt covered her rear, but then, he'd seen her in her birthday suit. Nothing about this getup was showy. Just warm.

He stepped inside and shut the door. "You okay?"

"Sure," she said, her smile as stiff as it had been during dinner. "Why not?"

He rubbed the back of his neck. "You don't seem happy."

She blew out a long breath. "Well, we don't all get to just choose happy."

A pained look crossed his face. "You should get to." He reached out, almost but not quite cupping her face. Instead, he stroked a thumb along her cheek.

She wanted to turn into that hand, burrow into him, step inside his jacket…but she just shook her head. "No. Not me." She gave him a sad smile. "It's fine, really. It's past time I got on with my real life."

"This isn't real?" He almost looked wounded.

She wanted to snort or maybe shove him. But she didn't have much fight in her tonight. "You know what I mean. My job. My contract. My condo."

"You have a place here, you know." Sam was solemn, that crystal-blue gaze pulling at her.

She cocked her head. "Do I?" His rejections were still fresh in her mind, cutting her deep.

"You have friends here—they've all adopted you like you are family. You love the horses, your hikes. It's been… Well, look at you." He swept a hand up, encompassing her knees, all the way to her face, whatever that meant. "It's been really good for you here. And now even Neve and Bella are here."

Neve and Bella were here temporarily. As for the

rest… Caroline stared at him for a long moment. "What about you, Sam? I don't have a place with you, do I?"

Like blocking the sun by pulling down the blinds —*whoosh*—all the warmth disappeared from his expression. Could he even explain it if she pushed him? Whatever it was that always held him back?

Caroline shook her head. "It hurts to leave." That, she could admit. "But I'll be okay. I feel strong now. I can shoot pictures again and earn a living. Be out in the world." She gave him a gentle smile. "Thanks for all of that."

It did hurt to leave, but it also hurt—so damn much— to love him. Inside, she positively yearned for him—a word, a glance, a touch. But although he looked distressed, he didn't move toward her. He didn't even speak.

The rest—these people, this land, this life—was incredible, but if she couldn't have Sam, then she couldn't possibly stay.

It was that simple.

She turned away. Her suitcase was on the bed already, all the Florida weather clothing beside it. She picked up a stack and tucked it into a corner of the suitcase. She needed to borrow a bag or something for all the bulky clothes she'd gained while she was here. Actually, she'd give them to Ruby for her costume gallery. Someone should enjoy them. Caroline wouldn't need this cold-weather stuff again, no matter what she'd told Bella. It would be too painful, too surreal, to ever come back here.

"You should go," she said over her shoulder.

Nothing in response, only the thud of his boots and the slide and snick of the door. Sam…letting himself out and closing himself off.

31

While Caroline would have loved to take a horse up the mountain on her last day on the ranch, she was content with a truck. She hadn't had many more chances to build confidence riding.

She hadn't had her camera the day Sam led them up the mountain in the open razors—spelled RZR, it turned out. Today, she wanted to capture the view, including the ranch far below. Not just as a selling point for the Black Hills website, but for herself. To keep and cherish.

At the last minute, she ended up with a seven-year-old companion. Neve had her hands full with Carter, and everyone else had chores and obligations. It was just as well. Caroline didn't really want to have to converse, and Bella would keep her from getting maudlin.

They left right after lunch. The route was different— the truck couldn't handle the rocky terrain that the RZRs bumped right over—but it was still rugged enough to leave Bella wide-eyed. Caroline appreciated the beauty.

"Fairies live here," Bella announced at one point where the tree cover was thick and mist hovered across the trail.

"You think so? How come?"

She had brought along a plastic horse with a long blond tail and mane, and pointed with it now. "See those magic sparkles?"

The sun slanted down through the trees here and there, and Caroline admitted that the landscape looked other-worldly. "You believe in magic?"

Bella gave her a look. *Duh, of course, doesn't everybody?*

"Believing does run in your family."

Bella tilted her head, considering.

Caroline said, "Your Grandpa Bert definitely believes."

"I know," Bella said matter-of-factly. "Next time, I'll send him a fairy with sparkly wings and green hair and pink eyes swimming in magic water. Fairies love to swim."

Caroline smiled. She didn't know if fairies loved to swim, but yep, even grown men, like Bella's grandfather, believed that True Spring's legendary spring water held magical properties that would lead you to your true love. *Hah.* She'd consumed that water in Bert's very own kitchen—and him, the grandson of the supposed legend makers. Furthermore, Sam, too, had had the town water pass his lips. Fat lot of good any of it had done her.

"I made some for Carter. But his fairy matches his horse. Sissy told me what colors. And she flies. I don't know if he likes swimming, but it's good to fly when you can't walk."

"He must have loved that." Highly unlikely that Carter

believed in magic, especially right now. Still, maybe Bella could charm some bitterness out of him.

Bella stroked her horse's tail. Caroline smiled. The girl had certainly been a bright spot for her. She was so thankful to be able to love this kid. She and Kevin had planned on children. She still wanted a family of her own. But given that Kevin wasn't coming back, and Sam wasn't hers to keep and build a future with, Bella might well be the only child in Caroline's life. She simply couldn't imagine falling in love a third time. There was always adoption, she supposed, but she needed to look to her immediate future first.

They bumped further up the trail, snaking back and forth through the trees. At times she worried she'd lost her way, that Sissy and Astor had neglected to mention an important instruction. But there really weren't any forks in the road or choices to make. She just climbed steadily in a roundabout fashion, and—finally—they reached the spot they were meant to go to.

They hopped down onto frozen ground, their breath frosting in the air, and she was glad Astor had insisted they bring winter coats. She popped a knit cap on Bella's head and then her own.

Bella's eyes were as round as saucers as she pointed. "Is that snow?"

Caroline laughed. The clearing they stood in obviously received afternoon sun, but deep in the shade where there were gaps in the tree cover, yep, snow. Even she was enchanted. "Come see."

They lifted scoops with their hands and tossed it in the air. Bella gasped. "It's cold!"

"Of course, silly."

Caroline packed a little snowball and threw it at a tree trunk, where it stuck, and her charge grinned.

"You could make a tiny snowman. I'm going to get my camera, okay?"

Caroline shot Bella playing first, joy on her face and pink in her cheeks, then, sure that the little girl was both occupied and safe, she turned to the landscape.

She sometimes lost track of time when she shot pictures, but when her hands became stiff with cold, she pulled out her cell phone and checked the time. Past two thirty. They had a little time before they had to head back, but it grew dark fairly early, and no way did she want to navigate the trek down the mountain in the dark.

She spread a blanket and got out the thermos of hot chocolate, baggie of marshmallows, and big sourdough pretzels Will had sent along. "Snack time!"

She and Bella took some selfies with the view behind them, and then each with a big, gooey marshmallow clamped between their lips.

Caroline's heart was full to bursting. She hated to leave everyone and was dreading returning home alone. But inside, right this minute? She was so full of love and gratitude for all she had found here.

Conscious of the hour, she had them packed and back in the truck by three fifteen. It would be dark by the time they got home, but she wasn't worried about the regular roads once they reached the bottom of the mountain. She adjusted the heat.

"It'll be warm soon," she told Bella, whose nose was pink.

Although there was clearing enough for a great view, there wasn't much room to maneuver a big vehicle. She Kturned cautiously. This monster was about four times the size of her little Honda.

Facing downhill, she pulled forward, and the truck dipped hard to the left. She hadn't seen it, deep in the shadow as it was, but the front passenger-side tire seemed to have dipped into a sizable hole or crevice.

She pushed the gas pedal, only managing to rock-spin the tires. Again, more gas. She tried reverse. No dice.

She just kept herself from swearing aloud.

"Aunt Caroline?"

"Let me see what we're dealing with." She jumped out and made her way around the vehicle, hoping like mad it wouldn't be too bad.

Her hopes died instantly. Holy cow. That was a big hole. Deep and oblong. The RZR could have managed it— or maybe she could have even lifted the RZR—but the truck, canted like it was?

She tried not to panic, tried to think. If she was stuck in sand, she'd let the air out of the tires. But this was an entirely different situation. She racked her brain. Would it make any difference if she could shove a log in there somehow?

She pulled her cell from her coat pocket. Sam would know what to do. So would Astor, Sissy—hell, even Ruby probably knew better than Caroline.

Oh, God. No signal. She walked around the clearing with the phone held high spinning this way and that. Not one single bar.

She took a deep breath. "Okay."

She looked around, chose a log, and shoved it in that big hole. But she could see it wouldn't work. The other three wheels kept the truck upright—that wheel sat in the air of the hole.

She found sturdy sticks and stabbed at the dirt, trying to push it into the hole so the log could be raised, then shook her head at seeing the futility there. She and Bella both gathered rocks—but the trouble was that anything big enough she couldn't pry loose from the land, and anything small enough wasn't effective.

They'd worked so long that the light was already waning.

Shit, shit, shit.

"Okay, Bug." Caroline controlled her voice and expression for Bella's sake. "I think we did all we can do. We're going to have a sleepover in the truck while we wait for them to come get us."

They had water and a blanket—two, actually. And she'd checked the tank—plenty of gas. She could run the heat off and on to warm them up if it got too cold. In the truck they'd be safe from animals. Other than a couple of pretzels, which she'd feed Bella for dinner, the food was gone. The rest of the hot cocoa was sealed in the thermos. Bears might come investigate, but she thought they'd be safe.

"I have to go to the bathroom," Bella said with a worried expression on her face.

"Good idea." Because no way were they getting out of that truck in the night and stirring up the wildlife if they didn't have to.

Turned out, squatting outdoors was another first for Bella, which made for some funny moments, despite Caroline's concern about this situation.

When they weren't back by dinner, and they couldn't

be reached, Sam would come. She just didn't know how long it would take, or if he'd decide it wasn't safe to come in the dark.

A few hours later, when they'd exhausted fairy stories and Bella grew drowsy, Caroline also gave up checking her phone to see if they'd miraculously gotten service. She wasn't truly worried, even as the hours stretched on. If they were stuck here all night, Sam and the others would come. Worst case, in the morning, they'd take the water bottles and start walking.

Bella was tucked up into a ball beside her, head on her lap, covered in a blanket. Caroline's feet were cold even in her boots. Her coat was zipped and she wore both her hat and hood, just as she'd made Bella do. But her nose and cheeks were still chilled, as were her hands. She was hungry, and by morning, she knew she and Bella both would likely be ravenous.

Granted, no one had thought it would be a dangerous excursion, or they would never have let her and Bella go alone.

What she did worry over, however, was her culpability in this. She kept thinking of Neve, probably beside herself with concern for Bella. They wouldn't be here alone, at all, if it wasn't for Caroline wanting to photograph, to use her camera, creating a dangerous situation because of that inherent need she had.

Her heart lurched sickeningly. *Kevin.*

As an inner-city Miami cop, he'd been in danger more times than she cared to consider. Drug busts, shootouts, robberies, violent crowd control… He'd even regularly accompanied the coast guard on smuggling busts of both immigrants and contraband.

Caroline had seen her share of dangerous situations, too. In fact, that was how she and Kevin had met. She was always rushing into the middle of things to get shots of the action for the newspaper. The *Herald* wanted gory, down-to-the-minute breaking news. Full color, larger-than-life photos smack in the middle of the front page. Caroline was picked for the action, the murders, the shootouts—anything at all that was dicey—because of her nerve. Kevin was present at the scene more often than not. They had joked over bad situations and even dead bodies, bonding through a need to detach from the harsh realities they each faced daily. He'd never shunned her because she'd been a member of the press, just admired her for her dedication and skill with a camera. And one day, he'd asked her out for a drink. When she'd accepted, he took her to the local precinct hangout, signaling his long-term intentions loud and clear.

Funny that she had met both Neve and Kevin on the job. The two most important people in her life, until now. But neither she nor Kevin had been working when she lost him.

They'd been aiming for some peace and quiet at a small cabin in the Everglades. They'd wanted someplace close that would only feel like it was worlds away. Caroline loved wildlife and animals in general. She'd always dreamed that someday she could sell a piece to *National Geographic*, but she'd gotten caught up in the thrill of the city long ago. That trip she'd brought her camera just for fun, hoping to capture some wildlife in its natural habitat, to dabble and play. Never in her worst nightmares could she have dreamed the outcome.

Caroline had had her eyes half-closed in the passenger

seat that day, cozy and content. Dusk had begun, and so had a steady rain. She had nearly been asleep when she saw that panther ready to pounce. Her zoom lens would capture every detail—the color in his eyes, each stiff whisker, the whiteness of his teeth, the muscle at play beneath his fur, and whatever prey he'd seen below. Being that Florida panthers were endangered, it was a photo opportunity like no other, and Caroline had shrieked with excitement. Yelled, abruptly and loudly, at Kevin.

"Stop!"

Then the odd feeling of sliding, the shocking force of the spin, the thunderous noise of rolling…then pain, shock, horror, disbelief.

She remembered it too well, and her heart rate jumped while panic stole her breath.

It was pitch black now, both inside and outside the truck, but Caroline shut her eyes anyway. She put her hand to Bella's cheek—needed to check on her, despite the heavy weight of Bella's warm head in her lap. Her skin was cool, but Caroline could feel the warmth emanating up from the little girl's neck under her jacket.

Caroline forced her lungs to expand, breathing in and out, adding to the humidity of all their exhales in this enclosed space.

They weren't hurt. They were together. They were safe.

It was okay. Everything was okay.

What would Sam say right now?

She hadn't poised Bella on a precipice for a photo; she hadn't dragged them into a lion's den for the shot of a lifetime; she hadn't left Bella alone to creep up on bear cubs with her camera to her face…

No. Getting stuck on the top of this mountain was just a thing. It wasn't caused by her camera or poor judgment. Originally, she hadn't even planned to take Bella. And numerous adults, including the child's own mother, had thought it was a fine idea.

Accidents happened. Accidents that sometimes had nothing to do with her need to shoot.

Caroline shut her eyes again, this time with a hefty wash of relief. She wasn't culpable for the current debacle. Now, if only they could get off this mountain unscathed.

32

———

When Caroline and Bella didn't show up on time for dinner, Sam was concerned. When they hadn't shown up by the time the meal was through, he was worried. But they'd also eaten in a hurry, the mood serious.

Everyone was careful not to speak aloud the possible calamities—they didn't want to worry Neve any more than necessary. Instead, they discussed how long they'd give it before taking action.

Sam pushed for going after them now.

"Give it a little more time," Astor said. "I bet they just lost track of time and will be rolling in any minute."

But Sam had that acid creeping up his throat. He did not feel good about this. He felt his mother's eyes on him; he saw Sissy check the clock; he saw Will squeeze Ruby's hand; he sensed Neve's growing worry.

The minute plates were cleared, he escaped outside and tried to draw full breaths. He hated when he didn't have control. He despised feeling helpless.

He paced the front porch, listening for an engine. When he was about out of his skin, he climbed into the hayloft with binoculars, hoping to see the wink of headlights weaving through the trees.

But it was pitch black. Exactly as dark and ominous as he was feeling.

If something had happened to Bella, Caroline would have found a way to handle it, to get her in the truck and back. But they could have crashed. Or something could have happened to Caroline. She could have choked on something, broken her leg in a fall, gotten a snakebite and be near death… And little Bella. Kid was way too young and way too green to be in charge.

Sam kicked at a bale of hay, swearing, mentally kicking himself. He'd wanted to go with them up the mountain to show her the best overlooks. He would have enjoyed sharing the beauty of the land with her. Who was he fooling? He'd ached to be in her presence a little longer before she left.

But he'd begged off. He was too conscious of how much he thought about her. He'd spent years paying for one distraction, one mistake born of poor judgment. He'd made promises and had held himself to the highest standards ever since.

Distraction caused accidents. And he didn't ever want to be the one responsible for harm to people or animals again. He needed to be constantly focused and clearheaded. Always anticipating, always on guard, ready to handle any situation with swift, effective action.

And yet because he'd held himself back, saying he'd had chores, Caroline and Bella might well now be in real danger.

If he'd been there, would he have been able to ward off whatever trouble they'd found? Protect her and Bella? Get them down the mountain to safety?

He thought about the swift fear that had surged when Palo knocked Caroline over. That was nothing compared to the terror building inside him now.

He looked down from the loft, spotting Carter's cabin. He'd been trying not to think about it...but bears. Goddamned grizzlies. Or, if provoked, even American black bears.

Shit.

Enough was enough. Caroline had said they'd be back by dinner. She'd known the going would be tough in the dark. She wasn't irresponsible. She mothered Bella—with a side of fun aunt—just as well as Neve.

If they were able, they'd have been home already.

Home.

It wasn't hers. It was his. She'd only been here a short time, and yet—it was crazy—it felt more like home to him now, with her here, than it had in years.

Except she was leaving tomorrow. Her life was elsewhere.

His heart pumped hard, his throat burned, and his neck muscles ached something fierce with the need to act.

Screw this. He wasn't waiting another single second. He jumped down from the loft and ran back to the house.

"Let's go," he said as he burst into the kitchen. "Two vehicles. Dad and Sissy together. Neve, you're with me."

Bella would want her mother. Sam wanted her emergency medical training.

———

Caroline heard the rumble first. A vehicle. No—make that more than one. Coming fast.

She sat up straight and powered up the truck, flipping the lights on.

It could only be Sam and the Blacks—nobody else would be crazy enough to career up these roads in the dead of night—and yet fear still skittered under her skin. She'd spent hours worrying, primed for all kinds of disasters—she wouldn't be able to relax until she saw their faces.

She opened the door and slid out, attempting not to wake Bella, but the child sat up.

"It's okay, Bug."

"What's that noise?"

"Trucks. They're here to get us."

Bella rubbed her eyes.

"Stay warm in there." Caroline shut the door and looked down the hill. She could see headlights flickering in and out—so much tree cover—but steadily nearing.

The noise became a roar. And then, finally, two sets of headlights rounded the last bend.

The first pulled right up to them, skidding to a stop. A passenger door swung open, and Neve hit the ground running. Caroline's shoulders dropped in relief.

"Are either of you hurt?" Neve asked.

"No. We're both fine." Tears sprang to Caroline's eyes —both empathy for a mother's worry and pure relief. "She's in the truck."

Neve veered around her, and Caroline saw the second truck come to a halt a bit further downhill.

Sam—his expression pained—rushed forward and

grabbed hold of Caroline's upper arms. "You're really okay? Both of you?"

"Yes."

"Thank God."

He pulled her close, and she pressed her cheek into his chest. She gulped his unique, masculine scent—all heat and strength and solidness. "You came."

"Of course." His arms tightened around her. "What happened? I'm sorry. Jesus, I should have been here."

She shook her head. "You can't be everywhere at once."

He pulled back and looked down at her. "I'm responsible for your safety, for Bella, and—"

"Stop." She put a finger to his lips. "You're not." He looked absolutely tortured. She shrugged and smiled. "This was just a thing."

He tilted her chin up with his thumb. There was so much emotion in his eyes that she was sure he was going to kiss her.

But right then, Astor spoke. "Sure am happy to see you ladies in one piece." Caroline kept her eyes trained on Sam's face, but heard Sissy teasing Bella, "See? This would never have happened on a horse."

Sam flinched, dropped her arms, and stepped back. And that was it. He was lost to her once more.

33

When Sam hit the kitchen for coffee early the next morning, Caroline was already saying her good-byes. She'd wanted an early start and hadn't changed her plan any despite the previous evening's scare. He didn't like it, but what could he say?

She gave hugs all around—his the briefest. And she didn't speak to him directly. But what had he expected?

Will passed her a bag of food and treats and a thermos of coffee.

"Thank you," she said. Then she somberly looked at each of them in turn. "Thank you all. For everything." Her voice cracked, but just when he'd expected her to cry or break, she laughed lightly. "Especially for the daring rescue. At least I'm heading off with a real adventure under my belt."

Acid hovered at the back of his throat, burning like never before. He'd been terrified last night that he'd lose her.

Now he really was.

She set Will's bounty on the counter and scooped up a sleepy Bella—hugging her hard and twisting side to side so the girl's pajama-clad legs swung out. "You are the best partner in crime. I'll miss you."

Then, before Sam had uttered a word, Caroline was in her tiny car, pulling away, the light just creeping up.

Gone.

He'd lost her. He'd let her go. No—he'd practically pushed her off the property. But what choice did he have? She had another life. And he wasn't selfish enough to keep her here when he could offer her nothing.

The rest of the day dragged on, every task unappealing, every minute a struggle not to think, not to feel.

When the dinner bell rang just after dark, Sam paused in the barn. He hung his head and rubbed his tight neck and shoulder. He had zero appetite and dreaded entering the kitchen.

But he couldn't beg off tonight. His mom had held to her promise; Sam had seen his dad and Neve escorting Carter ever so slowly from his cabin to the main house.

Everybody was already seated when Sam arrived. He clapped a hand on Carter's good shoulder, washed his hands at the sink, and then took his seat.

Astor quickly thanked the Lord for his bounty and ended by asking Him to watch over Caroline during her travels.

Sam clenched his jaw.

"Blessings done, grab some grub," Will said with a wink at Bella.

Dishes were passed and conversation commenced, even if things felt a little forced. Despite Will's good-looking spread, Sam had to force the food past his tight throat.

Neither Carter nor Sam spoke unless forced to directly answer a question, until Carter pinned Sam with his one good eye. "What are you so miserable for?"

"I'm right as rain. You just forgot what I look like."

"Bullshit."

"Carter," Anna said, and Sam was glad the focus was off him. Didn't matter to his mother that all her children were well into adulthood. She didn't allow cussing at the table. Though Sissy was usually the one getting scolded.

"Sorry." Carter looked around. "What did I miss?"

No one spoke. Bella looked solemnly at Sam. "Do you miss Aunt Caroline like I do?"

With the nail hit so squarely on the head, Sam froze, but Sissy snorted. "He misses her an awful lot more than that."

Sam forced himself to act casual. "You're so off the mark. And mind your own business."

"I don't think we will." Anna sat back in her chair and crossed her arms. "It's plain as day you're in love with the woman."

"Mom—" But there was nothing he could say that didn't involve cussing a blue streak. Sam shoved his chair back and bolted.

Why he went to the living room instead of escaping to his cabin, he didn't know. Habit, he supposed. Big family discussions always took place in the great room around the fire, everyone together—and sure enough, they were right on his heels: Mom, Dad, and Sissy. Owen, of course, hadn't been home in ages. Will, Ruby, and Bella would hang back in the kitchen for this one.

Troublemaker Carter was likely stuck at the damn table until Neve helped him. *If* she helped him. If she made him mobilize himself, he'd miss the whole thing, because Sam didn't plan on being here long.

His mother didn't waste any time. "It's obvious you two have something special."

Sissy smirked. "Yeah, they can't keep their eyes off each other."

Both Sam and Astor shot Sissy a warning glare.

"It's more than that," Anna said softly to Sam.

"It's not." He shook his head.

"Don't you know how rare it is to find what you and Caroline seem to have?"

Sam felt like a cornered animal—his family the predators—and paced in front of the fireplace. Heat from every direction. "It doesn't matter. She has a life somewhere else."

"Everyone who falls in love has a life somewhere else." His mom's gentle tone just made him want to yell. "She very well might have been willing to create a new one here with you."

Astor said, "Even I can see she loves you."

Love. She didn't. She couldn't. Sam said through a clenched jaw, "It doesn't matter."

"It matters!" Anna said, her own frustration level obviously peaking. "You didn't even try to make her stay. Did you?"

Sam wanted to scream, but the word was more of a pained grunt. "No."

"Whyever not? How could you just let her go?"

"You don't understand."

"Make me understand, then. Because—"

She'd never stop pushing—he knew it—and he broke. "You can't, Mom! You can't understand because you don't know!"

"What don't I know? Tell me."

"I made myself a promise!" The words spat from him like poison before he could stop them. "You want to know the reason we lost the barn? Cinnamon and Smokey and Rudolph?" He looked only at Anna. He'd seen Carter hobble in and lean heavily against the doorframe, but he couldn't, simply couldn't, face anyone else. "It wasn't because I didn't secure the lantern and the cat knocked it over! It was me. I forgot about it altogether—left it blazing near the hay—because I was screwing some girl behind the barn! I didn't even know her name!"

There was a full pause—breaths held, memories surfacing, pieces coming together.

"Oh, Sam." Anna's voice was soft—mother to child, acknowledging his hurt, absorbing his pain, absolving his guilt.

He held out a hand as if to ward her off. "So I promised myself: no women, no distractions. None. Never again."

"We suspected there was more to that night," Anna said, exchanging a look with Astor.

Sissy said, "Wait—you've been celibate? For, like, over a decade? Resident stud to complete monk?"

"You are such an asshole," he told her. His mother didn't even scold him.

"Only here," Carter said.

Sam was grateful not to have had to say it himself.

His dad said, "You were young. Mistakes happen."

"This wasn't a mistake," Sam said. "It was stupidity. Negligence. Carelessness."

"But you're an adult now," his mom said.

He snorted. "I was an adult then, too. Twenty-three, Mom."

"But surely it's different now."

"It's not different." How in the hell to make them understand how important this was? "Women are distractions. Distractions are dangerous. And if my heart's involved—it's even worse." And that was it. Caroline was the *worst* distraction of all, because his heart *was* involved. His lungs felt like a vise. "This place, our family, everyone's safety—that's what's important. I won't compromise that. That's all there is to it."

Sam stalked out of the room and left through the front door.

He was already halfway to his cabin when he heard his mom call through the dark, "Samuel Black, I'm not finished with you."

Dammit. He could have ignored anyone else. Kept on walking. Acted deaf or been rude. But not his mother. He stopped in his tracks and turned, arms crossed over his chest.

She hadn't grabbed a coat and wrapped her arms around herself. He was too worked up to be cold.

"Accidents do happen—sometimes, yes, from being young and careless, but sometimes just because they do," she said.

It was an echo of what Caroline had said about getting stuck on the mountain: *This was just a thing.* He'd known what she meant. It was an accident. Nothing anyone could control. But that didn't mean he had to like it. And he certainly wasn't willing to make light of it.

"I can tell you've paid plenty and done your time torturing yourself. It's time to let that part of the past go." She stepped closer and looked up at him earnestly. "Sometimes it's even okay to let important promises go. Even the honorable ones. Life changes. The ones we love make us better—better people, better at what we do."

He gritted his teeth. Nobody understood that this was everything to him. Ever since that night, his sole focus was protecting everything and everyone he held dear. He couldn't do that if he was torn in two all the time.

A frustrated growl of emotion was the only sound he seemed to be able to make.

Her blue eyes, so like his own, narrowed. "I'd also like to point out that last night, you left the barn door open."

Delayed fear skittered up his spine. Coyote, cougar, bear—any manner of beast could have wreaked destruction on the horses.

"And," she said, "your father found the truck running today long after you'd returned from checking the property line."

Dear God, they had a child on the ranch right now. Bella could have—

"You are perhaps more distracted by not being with Caroline than being with her." Anna looked pointedly at him with one eyebrow raised. "Think hard on that."

34

———————

Caroline pulled her car in to her building's garage after three days on the road. Early October and it was a beautiful, sunny, seventy-two degrees in Miami.

Her butt was numb, and her left leg tingled. Yet she turned the car off, and just sat, leaning back against the headrest. She should be leaping out of this metal box, skipping up to her condo, jumping for joy to be home after all this time. After all, she hadn't wanted to leave her condo in the first place, had she?

But everything had changed while she'd been gone. Everything and nothing.

Finally, she shook her head. She unplugged her phone and texted Neve.

Arrived safe.

Before she'd even unclipped her seatbelt, a message came back: *That's it?*

Neve always had something to say, but she did make Caroline smile. *Miss you all already. Kiss Bella for me.*

Caroline dumped the phone in her purse, stuck her

sunglasses on top of her head, and shoved the trash from her last meal in its greasy bag then got out. She grabbed only her camera totes from the trunk, figuring she could come back later for all the rest.

Near the elevator, she ditched the stinky bag in the trash can. She pushed the button and smiled sadly, thinking back. Sam's silly joke about there being plenty of options other than burgers on American's highways, and that inane conversation leading to a more serious one. One he must have sensed she desperately needed. One that had helped her find her way past some of her guilt and back to her camera, her career.

She already missed the Blacks and the Jenkses, the big house, the beautiful Montana landscape, the horses, her cozy little cabin, Neve and Bella…

All of it was a terrible ache.

Then there was *Sam*. Oh, Sam. He was a fierce longing, a gaping hole.

It was nuts, she knew, to fall so hard and fast for a man she'd known such a short time…especially after all she'd been through. Though who knew? Maybe that was exactly why.

She pressed the back of a fist to her sternum. She hurt. She hurt so damn much.

The elevator doors slid open. She hesitated, then reluctantly forced herself inside. She'd only been in one elevator since she'd left Miami, and that was inside Moe's Department Store in Hopewell, Montana, where she'd first kissed Sam.

That pain in her chest flared. She squeezed her eyes shut and breathed deep.

This hurt was completely different than how she'd felt

when Neve kicked her out of here over six weeks ago—though it felt like a lifetime. Then she'd been dead inside. So used to distress that she could barely feel, think, or function.

Now, she *felt*. She felt so damn much. She'd learned to live again—in a big, full way—only to end up with another heart-wrenching loss.

Caroline bit her lip as she watched the numbers tick upward on the elevator's display. She'd cried enough. It would take time, but she would create a new life for herself. A good one. A fulfilling one. Maybe alone with her work and her friendships. Maybe with a new someone —someday—who had room in their life for her.

But she wouldn't allow herself to wallow in depression like she had after Kevin died. That simply wasn't an option.

She arrived on her floor. A trendy young couple waited politely for the elevator. The man held the door open; the woman barely smiled in greeting. Caroline nodded and exited, no words exchanged.

She'd found it unsettling when she got back on the highway. So many strangers everywhere. And now, even here, at her home.

How fast a place like the Black Hills Ranch got under your skin.

She walked slowly, fishing in her purse for her keys, putting off the inevitable. But it shouldn't be too bad. Neve had told her that Noreen had come back to clean and organize. Likely the place didn't look anything like Caroline's anymore.

One last hurdle—cracking open the door again to what had been her and Kevin's life together.

She took a deep breath and put her key to the deadbolt.

The first thing Caroline realized was that someone had left the lights on, the second that there was noise.

Then a figure bust into her foyer, making her yelp.

"Noreen! You scared me half to death!" Caroline managed to set down her camera bags before Noreen rushed her.

The woman was not as tall as Caroline but thicker and soft, with arms like a vise. She wrapped Caroline up and rocked her side to side—and despite feeling smothered, Caroline soaked it up. She'd lost her own parents so long ago. Noreen was a lot to handle, but Caroline loved her.

Noreen straight-armed Caroline to look her up and down. "Oh, thank God, Neve was right. You look so good. I'm glad you are eating again, because I filled your pantry and your refrigerator."

She launched into a list of what she'd bought, then a noise sounded from the living room.

Noreen stopped talking and turned her head to bark at whoever it was. "Stay right there."

"Noreen?" Caroline was shocked. Had Noreen started dating? Did she have a man in tow?

Noreen raised her chin and leveled a look at Caroline. "I will be watching carefully. If you aren't thrilled about this, I'll take care of it. No questions asked. Set your purse down."

What in the world? Caroline did as she was told.

Noreen parked herself, arms akimbo, where the foyer opened to the living room, then told Caroline, "Come."

Noreen was prone to drama and overreacting—hell, that was Neve's ace in the hole when she'd forced Caroline out. But now? Caroline had no idea what was going on.

She slid around Noreen, turning toward the sitting area and—

She blinked rapidly, not believing her eyes. There—bathed in sunshine from the big window-was the handsomest cowboy she'd ever seen, in worn jeans and a navy flannel button-down with the sleeves rolled up and…flip-flops?

Her heart leapt. "Sam?" She stepped forward, then halted. He was smiling and yet looked so uncomfortable. Maybe… "What happened? Who's hurt?" A million terrible thoughts crowded her mind at once.

"Everyone's fine. Promise."

Relief flooded her.

He stepped forward and grabbed her hands, bending at the knees slightly to level their eyes. "I came for you. I should never have let you leave."

Tears sprang to her eyes.

But he wasn't finished. "You do have a place with me." He drew her hands to his chest over his heart. "It's right here."

Caroline threw herself against him. He wrapped his arms around her, and he lifted her off the ground and spun her around. He set her back down and took her face in his hands. "I'm so sorry."

She came up on tiptoes and pressed her lips to his. He returned the kiss, but kept it sweet, throwing her off. She looked up at him, eyes searching, and he dipped his mouth to her ear. "We still have an audience."

Her eyes snapped open wide. *Noreen.* Caroline kept one hand on Sam's chest and turned.

Noreen was smiling broadly, her hands laced together in front of her generous bosom.

"Noreen," Caroline said, "I love you. You know I do. But could you leave now?"

Noreen grinned but didn't move an inch.

Caroline said, "I promise to call you soon and tell you all about Bella's adventures in Montana."

"I'll be holding you to that." Noreen looked at Sam. "Sam."

"Ma'am." He raised a hand and tipped his head, just as if he was wearing his Stetson.

Noreen couldn't help herself, apparently. She rushed forward, rubbed both their arms with an expression of glee, and then kissed Caroline on the cheek. *Then* she left.

Neither Caroline nor Sam moved until the heavy door clicked shut.

"She must have read you the riot act," Caroline said.

Sam whistled. "You have no idea."

"How did you beat me here?"

"I flew. Neve gave me your key."

"And Noreen happened to be here when you arrived?"

He grimaced. "I was already here when Noreen arrived. We're very lucky you aren't bailing me out of jail right about now."

Caroline laughed. "Oh my God. I can only imagine."

But Sam was looking at her solemnly. "We need to talk."

———

Sam suggested Caroline freshen up, but he was on pins and needles as he waited, pacing the living room. She'd been happy to see him. Clearly, or Noreen Hoffman would never have left him alone with Caroline.

But did that happiness extend to forgiving him once she understood what had kept him from her? His family had, and he thought they hadn't even been that surprised.

Most of the promises he'd made himself still held. The ranch, his people, the animals and the land—they'd have to come first a lot of the time. He'd done a lot of thinking both before he left and during the travel here. He'd have to set boundaries—on himself. To protect and safeguard where he could, where it made a difference—but to let go of things that might simply be out of his control.

He expected Caroline would be able to help with that. Because she got it. She had similar demons. And just like he'd helped her see Kevin's accident more clearly, she'd immediately stopped him when he tried to take responsibility for her being stuck on the mountain. In this, he thought they'd balance each other out.

His biggest worry, now that he was here in her world— where she'd lived with Kevin—did that change anything for her?

Caroline returned. She looked a mite nervous too.

"Do you want to sit?" he asked.

She shook her head and approached, stopping right in front of him. "Kiss me. A real kiss this time."

She smiled up at him, looking surer of herself. He smiled back. This was a language they spoke easily. He took her face in his hands and slanted his mouth over hers.

She'd brushed her teeth and tasted like mint and salvation. Her hands slid up his back, and he dipped his into her hair. It wasn't near enough, and he slid his hands down her back and over her ass, pulling her flush against him.

Things got hot and heavy lightning fast. She tugged him toward the bedroom.

"You don't want to talk?"

"After," she said.

She went straight to the bed, then turned toward him. She pulled out of her light sweatshirt to reveal a formfitting tank top underneath. Miami clothes again.

He'd always wanted her, since that first moment he saw her tiptoeing around pine branches in that ridiculously skimpy outfit, but lust roared now.

Still, he had to be sure.

"It's okay?" He gestured halfheartedly to the bed—the one she'd shared with her husband. "Here?"

"Yes. Even here." Caroline's smile was gentle. "A part of me will always love Kevin; a part of me will even always belong just to him. But he's my past."

Her smile grew bright and wide, and she reached out to Sam. "You're my future."

EPILOGUE

One week later

Neve escaped out onto the porch of Carter's cabin. She'd come close to beaning Carter over the head with the nearest hard object this time. Insufferable man, rotten patient. She blew out a hard breath. He didn't want her there, and he definitely didn't want her to forget it. She got it. But caring for him—and yes, pushing him—was her whole job description right now.

She huffed out a breath, her exhale visible in the crisp mountain air. She'd give them both a few minutes and then go back inside.

She tucked her hands in her pockets and burrowed down into her fleece. She'd given up her scrubs after two days here, being the wind whipped right through them. Good thing Caroline had told her exactly what she and Bella would need, and yay for online ordering. This place was soooo cold—though it was also stunning, she admitted as she looked out over the Black family's land.

Sissy had Bella seated before her on a horse—again. The horse-crazy girl was already riding around the paddock by herself, but Bella liked to go fast, and thank God nobody would let her do that alone.

Neve waved as they streaked past, headed for wide-open spaces. Just over two weeks in Montana, and she was pretty sure that her Miami-raised kid was just plain ruined for city life. Neve shouldn't be surprised. Bella had absolutely adored Rand's family farm in True Springs. Every visit more than the last. But here, in the wilds of Montana, she was really in her element. Neve shook her head. She'd cross that bridge when it came time to return to Miami.

Neve stretched her arms over her head, her zippered fleece riding up, and tilted her face to the sun. A warm feeling tingled not on her face, but at the nape of her neck.

Carter was watching her again. She'd left the door open on purpose, hoping the fresh air would be good for his overall outlook.

They'd been in awfully close quarters. Not just in the cozy confines of his cabin, but in what she'd needed to do for him. At times, she had to stand between his legs, her breasts at his eye level. She'd needed to lean over his face to change bandages, so close that she could see all the multicolored flecks that made his hazel eyes. She'd bent to get something she'd dropped or he'd dropped—her rear on fully display.

And Carter Cross wanted her—badly. The evidence of his need was clear. Sweatpants and pajama bottoms hid nothing. And Neve could now vouch that he hadn't suffered any injuries *there*.

He was fighting the attraction hard. Probably as hard as he'd fought that bear—though she didn't know any details of the attack.

She finished her stretching and made sure her fleece re-covered her bum.

Much as she hated to admit it, she was feeling it too. Carter was a handsome man: ruggedly sexy, and virile in every way. His wounds didn't faze her in the least.

She supposed she should count herself lucky that he was as crabby as all get out—because if he ever turned on the charm, she'd be stealing his ice packs for her own overheated libido.

Her phone buzzed in her pocket. Neve checked the display and was thrilled to see Caroline's picture.

"I am so glad you called. Tell Sam he's got to leave you alone for five minutes and talk to this stubborn friend of his."

"Carter's giving you trouble, huh?"

"Nothing I can't handle. He just doesn't know it yet." She hoped he could hear her right now.

Caroline laughed. "Almost wish I was there to see it."

"How'd your editor take the news?"

Caroline snorted. "He had a few choice words to say, but nothing I can't handle."

Neve laughed at hearing her own words. "I bet. When are you two lovebirds leaving the nest?" More like rabbits, Neve thought with a smirk, but good for them.

"Showings on the condo start Thursday, so as soon as possible. Sam will fly so he can get back. He worries about the ranch and all the work he's not doing. Besides, his legs are an awfully tight fit in my car."

Caroline sounded happy—truly happy. She'd officially

retired from the *Herald*, hired movers, listed her condo with a realtor, and had agreed to live on the ranch. They planned to throw a big—though low-key—wedding bash next spring. Neve could not have been more thrilled for her friend.

"I have to warn you," Neve said. "There's regular conversation over dinner about all the photography work these folks are planning on setting you up with. Pretty sure Ruby and Anna have been circling things in the want ads, too."

Caroline laughed. "I'm not too worried about it. I've talked to the paper in Billings, and they might have some work for me occasionally. And apparently, the sheriff that covers Hopewell may need some help photographing the rare crime."

"Like what?"

"Sam says someone took old Mr. Tiller's tractor for a joyride recently and overturned it."

"Ooh, you've hit the big time now." Neve frowned. "You really don't think you'll miss the action of Miami? Your job?"

"I don't," Caroline said. "I want to work on a compilation of ranch-esque pieces, maybe for a book. I'll help on the ranch just as I was. And if the odd job comes through —crime or no crime—great."

"It's good to hear you happy again," Neve said, leaning a hip against the porch railing.

"It's good to be happy. And I'll be even happier when I get back. Sam wants to know what's going on there."

"Status quo. Carter is miserable, and Will seems to think pie will sweeten his mood." Then she remembered.

"Late-breaking news, though: Ruby's sister Rita has scheduled a visit."

"Perfect. I need to give that woman a big hug. She was the one who pointed me toward the ranch."

"Ruby is hoping you can give her some advice. Says Rita's wandering a bit. Still trying to figure out what to do with herself after losing her husband."

"I doubt I have any decent advice. But," Caroline said, "you know I did meet her in True Springs."

Neve heard the speculation in Caroline's voice loud and clear. "Is that so?"

"Yep. She's been there at least twice. Sam met her during her son's wedding. And she was there again when I met her."

"Well, we don't have to worry about Rita, then." Neve chuckled.

"Even if she's already had her love?"

"Look who's talking," Neve said. "Did you learn nothing? What did Bert tell you?"

Caroline laughed. "Sometimes you have to live life before life leads you to love."

"Exactly. Bert Hoffman is a wise man. And if you found love again, then Rita can too."

But it wasn't Rita that Neve was thinking of when she stepped back over Carter's threshold and caught his eye.

Such longing, such heat, such despair—and then he became an impenetrable slab of cranky male again.

He was going to be just fine. His body was going to heal. He was just trapped right now—stuck in this cabin, stuck in a wounded body, and, most of all, stuck in his head.

Oh, she knew how to fix that—but making him feel

like a man again would mean she'd feel like a woman again. That way lay trouble.

Crossing that line was about as unprofessional as it got. Although she was willing to bet that Anna Black would personally turn down the sheets if she thought it would help her Carter.

As for Neve… Out here in the middle of nowhere, in this cozy cabin, so far removed from her real life, with this wounded but still commanding cowboy only she knew how to heal?

Hell, it was like every woman's fantasy—and, Neve realized as her whole body tightened in anticipation, she was hardly immune.

———

Thank you for reading *Starting Over Together*!

Neve's story is coming… Rita's story is coming…
Meanwhile, did you know you can read all about the Legend of True Springs? Bert's tale isn't the half of it. Join his ancestors, Miles and Adele, in their very own historical novella and experience the love that created the magic!

Read the ebook *Making Forever with You* now!

———

Love That Lasts series:

Faking It Together (#1)
Second Chance Love Affair (#2)

Dreaming of Forever with You (#3)
Starting Over Together (#4)
and
Making Forever with You (Prequel
—*co-authored with Savannah Kade!*)

———

Have you already read the whole *Love That Lasts* series?
Then, check out JB's romantic suspense books! Start with
the *Unlikely* series, book #1: *Unhinged*.

Tori Radnor is determined to overcome the past and forge
a new beginning with her start-up venture. Her new
contract makes it all possible, until her successful (and too
sexy) partner suddenly reneges. An undercover police
investigation means Aiden Miller's hands are tied. But he's
far less worried about letting enticing Tori down than
keeping her and her teenage son safe from an increasingly
dangerous situation. When undeniable attraction and
unthinkable fears collide, Tori and Aiden must act fast
before it all becomes *unhinged*.

Read *Unhinged* and the *Unlikely* series now!

THANKS AND MORE

I'm so thrilled you found *Starting Over Together*! Would you kindly share your enjoyment of the story by leaving a brief review on Goodreads, BookBub, or your retailer? Reviews and word of mouth (*please do tell a friend!*) are still the best way for readers to find books they'll love. So grateful for each and every review—thank you!

I love to hear from readers, and these days there are so many ways for us to connect! On my website (www. jbschroederauthor.com), you can subscribe to my newsletter to have news delivered right to your email inbox or visit the Finding JB page to reach me via my social media links—choose what works for you. If you prefer *only* new release alerts, however, simply follow me on BookBub or Amazon.

ACKNOWLEDGMENTS

The *Love That Lasts* series would not be possible without out Savannah Kade and Eli Collier. Thank you both from the bottom of my heart for keeping me sane and moving forward, and more than anything for your friendship.

Savannah Kade also gets a huge shout out for talking me off the ledge with this manuscript. Did you know I cut a good 35,000 words from this baby? Ouch! But Savvy saved the day by reading fast, seeing what I couldn't, and hitting the perfect balance between tough, practical, and supportive.

Montana fact-checker, Shauna Tindall Gummere: thank you for reading and subsequently putting my mind at ease! Any mistakes—Montana or otherwise—rest squarely on my shoulders.

To an amazing team of editors, Trenda Lundin, Arran McNicol, and Jen Coleman: you make it easy to put my trust in you. Thank you for your speed, dedication, insights, and eagle eyes.

To my review crew: huge thanks for your willingness

to help and your kind words. I am so lucky to have readers like you!

And last but never least, dear readers, thank you for each and every purchase and review, along with your ongoing interest and support. It gives me such joy and motivation to know that you love my books!

ABOUT THE AUTHOR

JB SCHROEDER, a graduate of Penn State University's creative writing program, writes both contemporary romance and romantic suspense—in other words: *romance to make your heart race*. She adores stories about everyday people embracing new beginnings—especially when the characters need a little help from true love.

www.jbschroederauthor.com